The Lady on the Train

*More Humorous Paddy Pest Yarns
for Children over Thirty*

Gerry Burke

iUniverse, Inc.
Bloomington

The Lady on the Train
More Humorous Paddy Pest Yarns for Children over Thirty

iUniverse books may be ordered through booksellers or by contacting:

iUniverse
1663 Liberty Drive
Bloomington, IN 47403
www.iuniverse.com
1-800-Authors (1-800-288-4677)

ISBN: 978-1-4697-4691-3 (sc)
ISBN: 978-1-4697-4693-7 (hc)
ISBN: 978-1-4697-4692-0 (e)

Printed in the United States of America

iUniverse rev. date: 05/08/2012

EXPLANATORY NOTES

The likes of Stormy Weathers, Nadia Nikoff, Otto Straussburger and Gregoria Killanova are all fictitious figments of the author's imagination and bear no resemblance to anyone past or present.

Mr Pest's so-called special arrangements with international intelligence organizations cannot be substantiated by fact. However, these people are renowned for their apathy in the face of public scrutiny.

Some of my friends have been reticent in purchasing my heart-warming stories, so I have included them in this book in an effort to stimulate sales. I hope that they are not traumatized with the revelation of crimes committed in their names. They are not really bad people.

* * *

ACKNOWLEDGMENTS

Editing Services: Kylie Moreland

Pictorial content courtesy of various
Thinkstock / *Fotolia* collections

I thank the many dear friends who have provided
shelter and hospitality during my journeys
of research and intelligence gathering.

INTRODUCTION

I have been writing short stories for some time, but crime has never been my area of expertise. Then along came Paddy Pest.

Paddy is an Australian crime fighter with a dubious Irish background. He has an engaging personality, and displays a degree of confidence that is quite overwhelming. His enthusiasm for finding trouble is only exceeded by his incompetence. Fortunately, his pal and sometime sidekick, Stormy Weathers, is usually available to rescue him from his ill-advised forays into foolish and reckless situations.

Because Mr Pest likes to tell his own stories, I have been pushed into the background; I don't mind. I just sit back and marvel at his almost unbelievable energy, and yes, I am a little jealous of his remarkable success with the ladies. *The Lady on the Train* is a modest suburban story that is supplemented by other tales of international intrigue and adventure.

Paddy would like you to think that there is a terror plot on every page, but this is not so. There is murder, mayhem and general chaos, but the man does have his soft side: babes, broads and bimbos appear with constant regularity. Quite frankly, I don't know where this will all end. Crime has never been my area of expertise.

Gerry Burke

Paddy Pest

Contents

PADDY PEST'S SWISS ROLE

The Swiss police are clever, and the Italian police are the Italian police. However, a slippery, hard-nosed Aussie journeyman was able to outsmart them both. I had disappeared into the Pennine Alps, and was slowly picking myself down the north face of the Matterhorn, one of the most treacherous climbing mountains in the world. I was sure that my pursuers would have alerted the air-wing, but I was confident that they would not spot me in my goose-lined, snow-colored sealskin cover-all. I was more worried that I might run into some animal activists. They have been out to get me ever since I barbecued that small puppy in Bratislava. When you are hungry, you've got to look after number one.

Baron Mularczyk's luxury home on the banks of Lake Como is sometimes unoccupied. He is an international commodity dealer, and the man travels quite a bit. Mularczyk is unmarried, and his personal history is camouflaged by a distinct lack of detail. This kind of thing irks British Intelligence immeasurably, and they contacted me with instructions to break into his safe, and deliver the contents to them. I think that it was generally accepted that if I were to find any hard currency, it would go straight into my Ladbrokes betting account.

When the bean counters in Vauxhall tried to equate Mularczyk's income with his wealth, they came up with a strong smell of borscht. Could he be a long-term sleeper on a mission from Moscow? I wasn't that fussed. Who wants to save the world, these days? I was happy to take my sling, and get home to some sun, surf and a decent beverage. Whoever invented this Glühwein stuff must have had shit for brains.

The job was a doddle, but one can stay too long at the fair. I thought that I would fix myself a little snack, and catch up with the evening news on the English-speaking television channel. I had dismantled the security system, but some clever clogs had put a trip-wire in the remote control. The bells and whistles that went off were ear shattering. I made a hasty retreat with sandwich in hand. The documents from the safe were small in number, but they were so hot, they were burning a hole in my pocket.

After three days trudging through the snow in the Swiss Alps, one longs for a hot bath, and a cold beer. If I was James Bond, I would have been whisked away in one of Q's contraptions, but the man in question was now doing zeds in a small cemetery in Sussex. On arrival at Zermatt, I was keen for a sauna and spa in one of that town's up-market resorts, but I didn't have Bond's credit card with me. One of the youth hostels was a viable alternative, but there was an age restriction. I no longer looked twenty. In the end, I claimed to be their maintenance guy, and that gave me access to both the male and female steam rooms.

I didn't tell management the joke about the naked nun who invited the blind maintenance man into the bathroom. He then asked which blind needed maintenance. The people in these parts didn't have a sense of humor, so I maintained my disguise, and enjoyed some relaxing downtime with a buxom blonde from Bulgaria. When I reappeared on the streets, I was refreshed, and ready for action.

Although I had given the police the slip, I knew that I would be under observation. Almost every intelligence agency is represented in places like this. A hardship posting with an allowance can often be more desirable than a steady income. It would not be so easy to get my information back to my MI6 masters. What I needed was a mule. An anonymous somebody who could ferry the documents to London in a discreet way would be ideal. I thought of my blonde friend from Bulgaria, but I knew that she would be diverted too easily. I cabled headquarters, and they decided on affirmative action. A female courier would arrive within twenty-four hours.

I was reading the local newspaper in the hotel lobby when Penelope Farthing checked in. Penny Farthing may sound cheap, but this English rose was a classic beauty, and dressed to kill. Perhaps her attire was a little too conspicuous for the job in hand, but I wasn't complaining. The plan was for me to transcribe the most important parts of the stolen documents onto Penelope's back in invisible ink. I guess that when she returned home, they would put her in an oven or under an Ultra-Light or something like that.

Of course, I had to make contact first, and I was more than happy to go with one of my most successful covers: the Swedish massage therapist.

I had forgotten that the Brits were weighed down with conformity, and so I accepted their tiresome code exchange as our introductory salutation. I gave the lass time to reach her room, and picked up the house phone.

"Love birds kiss at midnight" I hissed into the phone.

"Only if they are married" was the whimsical reply.

I could tell by the jocular manner of her response that this bird was ripe for the plucking — only it would not be that easy. Any high level of perspiration would affect the quality of the message. After the invisible ink had been applied, there was to be no skiing, no sauna, and definitely no sex. This whole scenario was the kind of thing that M's secretary would come up with. I can't remember her name, but she always had an unhealthy interest in my sex life.

I knocked on the door to Miss Penny Farthing's suite, and was invited in.

"Hello Paddy, it's nice to meet you. Did you bring the writing utensils with you?"

"I certainly did, Penny, but I need a few more items that you can acquire from room service."

The smoked salmon, Beluga caviar and champagne arrived within minutes, and we helped ourselves. The small pitcher of lemon juice remained untouched. It was the ink for my back scratcher.

I have never been one for long sentences, but that night I got very cheeky. Penny's rear just seemed to go on forever, and I nearly got writer's cramp. I wonder what Shakespeare would have made of all this. It would have been a great thrill with a quill. It was a long night, but in the end I transcribed all the relevant information. If the girl from MI6 didn't have a hot bod before, she would have one now. There was a chilling conspiracy in the wind, and I had to get her back to base, fast.

Penelope was now a marked woman, and would be the target for every dastardly desperado that had been drafted from the depths of depravity to destroy her, and her delectable diaphragm. These are the types of fiends that are recruited by big-time villains, who call the shots from their axis of evil. It wouldn't have been healthy for Penny to be seen with me, so I instructed the lady to get out of Zermatt with haste. I then slipped into the early morning mist.

The truth about Baron Mularczyk was that he was not who he said he was. No wonder his palatial mansion was empty for half of the year. A little dye in the hair, a pencil mustache and horn-rimmed glasses converted him into Otto Straussburger, the most senior physicist at the Wusskamp nuclear facility in Nuremberg, Germany. I think that the Muscovites spent too much time at the war trials. They were able to pick up all the best scientists, and now the free world might once again be squashed beneath the footprint of the Russian bear — but not if this pesky little Aussie journeyman had anything to do with it.

You may think that I have acquired an increased degree of patriotism since I last waxed lyrical, and I have to say that a beautiful woman can do that to you. The morning news had just announced that Otto Straussburger had been elected as the chair of an important nuclear armament committee at the United Nations. We already knew that he would be one of the passengers on Richard Branson's first commercial flight into space. It was due to depart from southern parts of America very shortly. I didn't like where this was going.

Bunson Frauschmarkel was our man in Zermatt. I was disappointed to see that his place was in a bit of disrepair since my last visit. Still, he was the guy to get me out of town with the least amount of trouble.

"Good to see you again, Bunson. Can you get me out of Zermatt within the next eight hours? There are people who are trying to eradicate the Pest."

"There's not much left, I'm afraid, Paddy. This classic dog sled is a remnant from the good old days. It has front and rear missile launchers, snow-melting equipment and twenty-four hour flea protection. I can get you a dozen dogs in an hour."

"That sounds fine. You had better throw in a box of hand-grenades, ear-muffs for two and a cuddle blanket. You never know who I might meet along the way."

True to his promise, I was on my way within the hour, but my departure was not unnoticed. On the third floor of the building that housed the Ukraine Workers Union, a curtain slipped back into place, and a thirty second telephone call was initiated. The game was on.

The Visp Valley is as beautiful as any that you could see, but I was not a tourist, and my escape route was limited. There are no cars in Zermatt, and the train ride out of there is easy to monitor. The sled trail is also predictable, and I knew that they would be waiting for me in Täsch. The machine gun post that they had set up was two miles out of town. Fortunately, the huskies had their radar working. King Wenceslas, the lead dog, swerved onto a side trail, just as the hail of bullets reverberated through the forest. I could hear the acceleration of snowmobiles and the chatter of desperate men. I hoped that the missile launcher hadn't gone rusty on me.

Bunson's startlingly attractive daughter, Mauricette, was waiting for me at the train terminal with a first class ticket to Zurich in hand. I made the platform with seconds to spare, and returned the unused hand grenades. What a shame I didn't get a chance with the cuddle blanket.

The train to Zurich

It is easy to provide surveillance on a train. Your movements are restricted, and there is nowhere to hide. Most of the bad guys have one of their operatives permanently employed as a porter, waiter or ticket inspector. In that way, they can steal your luggage, poison your food or spray Sarin gas into your compartment. Yours truly can usually pick them a mile off. In this case, it was the comfort officer.

Ms Schnicklfart was far too young to be a competent comfort officer. You need years of experience for this kind of assured service, and she was just a slip of a girl. Nevertheless, I would not be underestimating her. She did have some qualifications. The top three buttons of her blouse were undone, and she really did look very comfortable. My antagonists were shrewd people, and they had been well briefed. They knew that I had a bit of a weakness for the ladies.

"Mr Pest, 'ello. I am Anita Schnicklfart, and I see to your comfort in this first class compartment. We 'ave complimentary hot beverages available. Also superior reading material! The train vill stop at Visp and Bern, and we vill arrive at Zurich at approximately ten o'clock. Is there anything more I can do for you?"

I don't need to tell you what thoughts were passing through my mind, but the presence of another person in the compartment stymied that kind of thinking. A portly parson was slumped up against the window of the carriage, quietly snoring into his double chin. It was hard to believe that this sweet young thing was a cold-blooded murderer, but if I didn't entertain this possibility I could end up as a cold-blooded corpse.

The parson alighted at Visp, and two passengers replaced him. They finished their trip in Bern, and this left me alone in the compartment for the final leg of the journey. With little Ms Schnicklfart patrolling the corridor, I didn't want to nod off, so I opened the window for a blast of cold air. I also helped myself to a small nip of whisky from my hip flask. That worked a treat, so I took a few more nips. Eventually, I nodded off.

There is a knack to being a light sleeper. I can sleep through a brass band recital, and yet awake at the sound of a pin drop. I had just heard the lock click on the compartment door, and my eye-lid slowly lifted in anticipation of a cautious entrance from the comfort officer. Nothing could have been more predictable. The door was hardly ajar, and she squeezed through the opening like Catwoman. I wondered why she was wearing a gas-mask.

I must admit that I was stunned when the she-devil hit me over the head with a fire extinguisher, but only for a while. When she started removing her Swiss Rail tunic, I wondered if this was some kind of sexual foreplay to arouse my interest. In actuality, she was reaching for the small Sarin gas canister that was hidden in her bra. Bloody hell! Train travel is not supposed to be this dangerous.

I had never kicked a woman in the groin area before, and it is not something that I would have done unless my life was in danger. She doubled over, and I snatched the gas-mask off her face before the pellets could explode. Her screams of agony confirmed everything that they say about this lethal dose of death. With one hand, I held the mask to my face, and with the other, I bundled the would-be assassin out of the window, and into the path of the eight-thirty bullet from Zurich. I looked at my watch: it was time for dinner.

The dining car was nearly full, and I had to share a table with a spoilt brat and his mother. I slipped the lad a few coins, and asked him to fetch my glasses from my compartment. If he came back, I would know that the gas had dissipated. If he didn't return, I had his mother's complete attention. She was a good looking woman.

The five minute arrival warning was announced as we completed our cheese and crackers. The lady turned out to be a real charmer, and I would have liked to take our relationship further. However, she needed to go looking for her son, and I had a plane to catch. Nuremberg here I come.

* * *

They didn't encourage visitors at the Wusskamp nuclear plant. It would not be easy to approach Straussburger, and I didn't even know if he was in town. The wall at the outer perimeter of the facility was adorned with razor wire, but this was no impediment to a slink merchant like me. The guards outside the main building were something else again. They were all strapping young lads, and appeared to possess all the enthusiasm of youth. In fact, their cheeks were positively glowing — an occupational hazard, I guess. I looked around for a down-pipe. My rat-up-a-rope climbing technique had served me well in the past, and although the whisky had slowed me down a touch, I was still slippery and supple. I saw an effluent discharge pipe, and timed the gap between the security patrols. I had five minutes to scamper up the pipe and onto the second-floor landing. I did it with seconds to spare. Unfortunately, my hip-flask became dislodged, and dropped to the ground with a clang and a clatter. Whisky a Go Go!

"Achtung: Sie suchten nach." cried the young man who had just turned the corner of the building. His buddy came running behind.

"Give us a break, Nigel. You went to Cambridge. Why can't you speak English?"

"Hello! Is anybody there?"

Up on the second floor, I nearly fell off my perch. Two more university graduates who can't find work in their chosen profession! What possessed them to come to Germany? On reflection, they did come from Cambridge, so they could be spies. If they sampled the whisky, they might recognize the Scottish product but, fortunately, the flask had bounced into the nearby undergrowth. It would not be found until morning.

Hanging from my bootstraps, I had located an air-conditioning vent, and immediately crawled into the small space. I managed to move forward using my elbows and toes. It was slow work, and they had the reverse-cycle going. It must have been about ninety degrees Fahrenheit. Eventually, I fell through an inlet grill, and landed on top of a couple who were having sex on a table. I think that it might have been the staff room. The staff had certainly been produced.

The man was knocked out, and the woman, who was naked beneath her open white coat, was suitably shocked. I apologized for the coitus interruptus, kissed her on the cheek, and slid through the door. I didn't expect that the alarm would be raised as I figured that she wasn't supposed to be doing what she was doing.

The walkways and walls were all shiny white, and the whole place had an antiseptic feel about it. An eerie silence belied the fact that the facility was probably fully operational. I heard voices approaching so I ducked through the nearest door. The room was empty, but it still had secrets to surrender. There was a large glass window that stretched across one side of the room, and I concluded that this place was a viewing or meeting area. There was a small bar, a sink and a refrigerator, which contained any number of German sausages, some salad, sauerkraut and a half-eaten pizza. The contents of the freezer compartment didn't look edible at all. I saw half-a-dozen test tubes that contained frozen liquids of various colors.

Through the panoramic window, I gazed down on a busy scene. It looked like an aircraft hangar. It might have been, except that the three units that were being worked on by a dozen busy bees were not planes but rockets. No wonder they had rocket salad in the fridge.

The glassed-off area beyond the hardware looked a bit spooky. Men and women were walking around in biological protection suits, and the traditional nuclear radiation symbol was plastered everywhere. There was a sign-writer perched at the front of one of the rockets. I always carry my miniature binoculars with me in case I happen upon a race meeting. I retrieved them, and focused on the inscription.

It read: *From Russia with Love.*

I was thinking about departing the room when a deliberate movement from one of the floor workers attracted my attention. He was carrying a clipboard, and may have been some kind of foreman. His destination was soon obvious. On one side of the expansive concreted area was a mezzanine floor landing. I had not noticed it before, but I now saw a man in a white coat; he was sitting in the shadows. The fellow was flanked by two alert Doberman Pinschers. Once again, I lifted the binoculars, and immediately confirmed what I had already suspected; Otto Straussburger was in town.

Given that I had never met Baron Mularczyk, it should have been difficult to make the comparison, but it wasn't. Rip off Otto's mustache and horn-rimmed glasses, and he was identical to Mularczyk's last-seen photograph. It was a bit like Clark Kent and Superman — Lois Lane must have been one dumb chick.

From my perch in the panorama room, I couldn't lip-read, so I didn't know what was being said. Nevertheless, the foreman was getting an ear-full, and he didn't appear to be enjoying the verbal exchange. I could see that Straussburger had one lazy eye, but the other one was working overtime. It bored through the poor man with the clipboard like a laser through ice cream. If looks could kill, the fellow would be dead meat. That would certainly be good news for the Doberman dogs.

I had seen enough, and thought it a good idea to retreat in the same unobtrusive manner in which I had arrived. During my time in the staff room, I had managed to lift Romeo's security pass, and all I needed was a white coat to confuse the most vigilant door patrol. I found one hanging in a toilet cubicle in the men's lavatory. The owner was caught with his pants down, and could offer no resistance as I coshed him over the head.

Paddy, the scientist

I slipped into the night, and headed for the Wax Bar at the American Hotel. This place is a hang-out for black-ops people, news-hungry journalists and lonely women. I combed my hair, and ordered a Stinger. One of the lonely women approached me. She was a most attractive barfly.

Brandy was the kind of dame that every wife and mother hopes will never cross paths with her husband. She was tall and statuesque. Her false eyelashes automatically flittered with practiced skill, but beneath those hooded lids, her ever alert peepers circled the bar area for prospective punters. These long sweeps of the room were so subtle that few people would have noticed, but they were as regular as clockwork. As she came closer, I saw a face that had seen a lot of good times: and bad.

Her long platinum blond hair was a credit to Mr Clairol and his bottled magic. Nevertheless, her locks were unruly, and she pushed them off her face with great regularity. There was an increased irregularity in my heartbeat, and I now knew how my old man used to feel when Veronica Lake graced the silver screen.

"Hello there. Is this seat taken?" she purred. I gulped.

The lady was wearing a low-cut red dress that left little to the imagination. When I say low-cut, her décolleté was slashed to her stomach, and her modesty was preserved by virtue of a wide gold belt that circled her slender waist. Her firm young puppies were bouncing around and trying to get out. They wanted to play.

She could see that I was giving her the once over.

"Do you like Brandy?" she asked, knowing full well that there wouldn't be a negative reply. I looked at my Stinger, and then at her.

"I certainly do, Brandy. My name is Patrick Pesticide. People call me Paddy."

"Then so shall I. Would you like to buy me a drink, Paddy?"

Can a dog bark? In fact, I bought her two drinks, and before long it had been established that I had a room in the hotel, and that she would love to see the wall hangings. I sent the bar lackey up in advance with a bottle of champagne. I was sure that MI6 would not object to the fact that it wasn't British.

My room was on the 6th floor, and the elevator was empty. In a jovial mood, we entered the small space, and I pressed the button. An almighty snapping noise rang out from above, and the lift started to plummet downwards. The lass screamed, and in an automatic reaction, I jumped in the air and wrapped my legs around her waist (this is what I had been planning, anyway). There were only two levels to the lower basement, but the impact was severe. The poor girl had both her legs crushed, but I was alright. Before staggering out of the shambles, I quickly checked her purse. My intuition had been right on the ball. I discovered a flattering photo of me with the hotel address scrawled across my grinning countenance. I had been targeted.

Nevertheless, I put through a call to the medicos. She was just a pawn in the game, and obviously her employers felt that she was expendable.

I quickly slipped out of the hotel, and hailed a cab. Frau Nipplemeyer would be my salvation. She was the bureau's man in Nuremberg. If you forget the fact that she is a lecherous, cross-dressing tart, you have a very efficient secret agent. Liesel took me to a safe house, and immediately contacted London. We chewed the fat while waiting for a reply.

"You are very handsome man, *meine Liebe*. Vould you like some schnapps to help you relax after your ordeal?"

Does Dolly Parton sleep on her back? Of course I would like some schnapps to help me relax after my ordeal, but I didn't want to get too relaxed. Liesel Nipplemeyer was a person who should be taken in small doses. I was contemplating whether to take her or not when the phone rang. It was London.

Otto Straussburger had just arrived in New Mexico in preparation for Branson's commercial space flight. The word was that his excess baggage request had been approved. The flight manifest indicated that this was for his cigar cylinder. I wondered if they knew how big the cigar was.

"I'm sorry M, but I think that we have to make a pre-emptive strike; hit the Wusskamp facility before they can get those missiles out of there."

He agreed with my assessment regarding the nuclear facility, but was quite disbelieving about my contention that there was going to be a destructive device placed aboard Virgin Galactic's rocket, which would take-off, attached to their White Knight spacecraft. After all, the launch-pad was a long way from Germany, and the craft would be piloted by Sir Richard, himself. Nevertheless, he said that he would discuss the matter with the appropriate minister over lunch at Boodles. Well, there goes four hours.

One could only think about my opponents, and the extent of their ineptitude. They should have executed that elevator drop from the sixth floor, not the first. Their bullets had been astray in Täsch, and their surveillance was slack at the nuclear facility. I wondered if they might mistakenly drop their target bomb on Disneyland instead of the White House.

They were a little more alert at Wusskamp, this time. The Special Forces team pounced, as they do, but a truck had already departed with one of the rockets. Their destination was predictable, but time was on the wing.

As the head of MI6 was breaking bread with the Prime Minister at Boodles, the White Knight countdown had already started. Otto Straussburger had paid a premium price to occupy the co-pilot's seat in the cockpit of the space vehicle, but he was astounded to find that the chief pilot was Charles Manson not Richard Branson. The marketing people and their typos! One could only ask whether it was intentional or not.

Although he was shocked, Straussburger was relieved that he was still within arm's length of the switch that would liberate the cigar cylinder from the external baggage compartment. Unbeknown to both of them, the side-by-side seats were of the ejector variety, and could be regulated from the Spaceport America control center.

The lift-off was beautiful, and Sir Richard, in the control tower, had a smile all over his face. So did Otto. Once they ditched the booster rockets, he could activate his own missile. Destruction could be delivered wherever he wanted.

The thing about early guided missile systems is that, for the most part, they relied on heat-seeking data that was computed into the rocket. However, if you are a top-notch German scientist with hate in your heart, you can do better than that. Otto had perfected a homing device that could be inserted in the smallest of targets. In this case, the target was a diminutive stick-pin that had been attached to a commemorative White Sox baseball cap. The cap had been presented to the President of the United States.

In the few weeks since he had received the cap, the President wore it everywhere. Sometimes, he wore it backwards. The killjoys in the Kremlin were delighted when they saw this, and urged Straussburger to activate his plan as soon as possible. They were very smug when they saw the leader of the free world on the news with his best friend, Slick Gallante. They were heading-off on one of their frequent big-game fishing trips. What they didn't see was that when the President returned, he was without his hat. He had left it on the boat.

A few days later, from outer space, Otto released the instrument of destruction, and it sped off towards Washington and the east coast. The next few lines will be quite distasteful for the Gallante family, and I do apologize for that. Slick was very proud of his boat, and he was one of the first to get a charter if there was one in the offing. He and half-a-dozen Taiwanese tourists were sixty miles off-shore when the rocket hit. Mr Gallante was wearing the President's baseball cap when sea-zero was reached. If this detonation had been closer to shore, there would have been devastation over a wide radius. However, there were few islands and atolls in the vicinity of the blast, and they were uninhabited, so the damage was limited.

I was already on my way to New Mexico, when I heard of this cowardly attack, which had been initiated by a two-faced rogue, who was just a puppet in this current game of contemporary espionage. All free-thinking individuals would regard his actions as intolerable and repugnant: well, perhaps not the taxi driver who picked me up at the Las Cruces International Airport. He was more interested in the bonus that I offered him to get me to the launch pad, quickly.

I burst into the mission control room as Richard Branson was coming to terms with what had happened. A CIA agent was explaining exactly who Otto Straussburger was, and the multi-millionaire was visibly shocked. For me, the picture of Charles Manson and Otto on the monitor was too much to bear. They were grinning with delight, and had broken open the commemorative bottle of vintage champagne; this bit of sparkle was provided in order to celebrate a successful return to earth. It was time for me to call last drinks.

I leaned forward and pressed the ejector button.

A RAT IN THE VAT

I was in Rome to catch up with an old friend, who had turned his back on the hedonistic life, and embraced Jesus. It must have been quite a hug, because a few short years after this life-changing decision, he is firmly entrenched as a mover and shaker at the Vatican. Most people don't get this kind of a promotion unless there is nepotism involved, or you are married to a nun.

You have probably never heard of Monsignor Dominic Lopes. He is a covert presence who moves amongst the shadows in the Vatican. I first met Dominic when he was a field agent for MI6 during their busiest years. He was a cautious man, but very good at his job. In the end, he got sick of it all, and took up holy orders. The transfer to Rome came some years later after he had micro-managed a few difficult situations. There are very few Brits in the Holy See, so his contribution must have been appreciated.

They gave him a small office in the basement, and stuck his name on the door in Italian. Translated, it read *Dom the Pom.*

So, here I was, sitting in this dark and dank excuse for an office when, upstairs, the Pope was handing out sacred accreditations. While Dom was finishing his telephone call, I rolled out a few to see how the monikers might fit on someone who was less pious: St Paddy Pest; Blessed Paddy Pest; the venerable Paddy Pest. The click of the receiver brought me back to reality.

"Paddy, there are dirty deeds afoot, and they have their origins right here in the Vatican. You are one of the few people that I can trust."

"Holy Moses, Dom. Are you sure? Everybody seems so devout."

Dominic Lopes was a shadow of the man that I once knew. He used to be a large, lumbering kind of fellow, but now he was all grit and gristle. His face was drawn, and those bags under his eyes gave up the fact that he indulged in a lot of night-time activity. He confided that it was necessary for him to put on a disguise whenever he ventured out into the streets of Rome, or beyond. He always carried a Glock hand-gun under his cassock. There was conspiracy and intrigue in this religious region, and he wanted me there to see if I could bring it into the open.

"Excuse me, old chap. I'm a bit short. Is there a toilet down here?"

"It is the last door on the right, my friend. Don't mind the cigarette smoke. It's our only refuge."

In truth, there was no urgency to relieve myself, but I did need time to think. What would I be getting myself into? Could Dominic be trusted? After all, I had heard all about this Opus Dei mob, and their fondness for self-flagellation was disturbing. I don't mind a bit of flagellation, but only if my chosen neddy needs a bit of encouragement to get to the line.

I decided to reserve my judgment until I had heard all the gory details. I returned to his office, and sat down in front of the papal sherry that he had placed on his desk for my convenience. It had been a long time between drinks, but he still remembered that I had a liquidity problem. I liked to wet my whistle.

"OK Dominic. What seems to be worrying you? I will do my best to help, just for old time's sake. Of course, if there is a remuneration aspect to your dilemma, I will be even more diligent. Perhaps, some piece of Vatican art-work that they no longer require!"

He smiled.

"Nice attempt at humor, Paddy. No, I'm afraid that this job is dependent on your desire to see the Catholic Church protected from the demons that decry its good name and reputation. I believe that there is also a definite plan to desecrate some of our most cherished landmarks, and the clock is ticking. The task will be fraught with danger, but you don't have to worry. I have a spare St Christopher medal that I can let you have."

Now, who was attempting humor? From my experience, St Chris was very picky about who he protected, although I have experienced a few situations where I should be dead. I had always thanked my Beretta semi-automatic for my continued existence.

The plan was to insert me into Vatican society as a visiting prelate. You are probably surprised that there is such a thing as Vatican society, but the Holy See is so large; it is a city within itself. There is no way that they can keep tabs on everyone. It was a long-shot, but I did enquire whether there would be a ban on sex. Dom's frown said it all.

"You can drink as much as you like, Paddy, but watch out for poisoned altar wine. You will still be able to operate your betting account, but the Vatican will not be responsible for losing wagers. We all bet on horses with religious names, and this has proved quite profitable."

That was it. I was escorted out of the dungeons, and led to the accommodation wing, where I was deposited in comfortable quarters. They treated their visitors quite well. On the side-table was a pile of priest's clothes, shoes and their traditional clerical hat, the Biretta. I now had a Beretta and a Biretta — both made in Italy.

If I haven't made myself clear, I can do that now. The imminent danger did not just threaten to damage the church's reputation and its grandiose places of worship. This was a plot to destroy the Pope, himself. A bullet for Benedict, if the intelligence was correct! If yours truly could prevent this wicked assassination attempt, I would probably be covered in glory, and absolved from all of my past sins. I might even end up as the Honorary Commander of the Swiss Guards.

I had to treat this job as I would any other investigation. You have to try and keep the opposition guessing, while you pad around in an absolute quandary. Where do I start? Who is a potential suspect? Would they really poison the altar wine?

Cardinal Quinlan was my first port of call. He was Australian, and although he had never heard of Fr Pesticide, he provided me with a tour of inspection, and introduced me to some of the other high-ranking officials at the Vatican. They all looked a bit serious, and I hoped that they were not looking forward to my discourse on matters philosophical. I had boned up on the Serie football league, Berlusconi's babes and Sophia Loren. That's about it. Fortunately, they were pretty excited about all of these subjects.

It is always best to keep a low profile when you are in the early stages of an investigation. However, I often fly in the face of conformity, and chose to advertise my tenure in the most obvious manner. I sang *Waltzing Matilda* in the refectory, and followed up with *Tie me Kangaroo Down, Sport*. Here, meal-time is usually a time of quiet reflection and meditation, but I thought that they could all do with a bit of cheering-up. The performance was certainly talked-about, and news of my vocal skills even made it to the big room by the balcony. A message from Pope Benedict arrived the next day. Was I familiar with *Lili Marlene*?

"Fr Pesticide! The pontiff has a sing-along with his house staff, around the squeeze-box, every Thursday. You would be welcome to join them, should you wish. Pizza will be served afterwards, and a personal audience has also been arranged for you."

"Thank you, Father. Please convey to His Holiness that I would be delighted to attend, and will try and bring my best voice with me."

Can you believe it? One day in the palace, and I'm playing sing-a-long with the Big Cheese. If it is that easy, why can't the rogues get equal opportunity? I made a mental note to check out the squeeze-box player. You could hide an arsenal in that particular musical instrument.

Of course, who was to say that an attack on the papal person may not happen before the designated Thursday. The 'morrow was the Ides of March, and Romans with long memories can fill you in on what that's all about. The Pontiff would be saying High Mass at St Peter's Basilica, and I would have his back. The Commander of the Swiss Guard would have his front, and believe me; this Swiss soldier had more front than a rabbit with a gold tooth. I was sure that he was related to Donald Trump.

It was important that I survey the venue for the next day's service. I made my way over to the big church, and found the main entry closed, but I knew that they would be making final arrangements for the 'morrow. I entered through a side entrance, and discovered that these arrangements had already been completed. The place was looking a treat. I don't think I have ever seen so many candles. I really didn't want to beat the gun, but I just had to light a candle for my dear departed pooch, Roger. You know how it is — man's best friend and all that.

I made a thorough search of this gigantic house of worship, and was almost out the door when the first drop of wax from my candle hit a trigger point, and there was an almighty explosion. If I wasn't in the door alcove,

I would be history. In fact, I nearly got decapitated by a flying statue of St Ebenezer, the patron saint of money-lenders. Need I say that chaos reigned? People came running from everywhere to be confronted by carnage. Pews had been turned over, and paintings were strewn around the altar and through the church. Who would have thought that the harbinger of evil would be announced with a single candle wick? In fact, every candle in the whole basilica was a stick of dynamite. Imagine how catastrophic it would have been with a church full of pilgrims.

It looked like Roger had saved the day, from Dog Heaven, but what would tomorrow bring? At least the list of suspects had been reduced to those who had access to the holy temple. This included those in high places as well as the lackeys. Meanwhile, the forensics people would do their stuff, and the Vatican folks would put the church back together again in time for High Mass. I arranged another meeting with Monsignor Dom.

"It was a close call, Dom. Your anxiety was well founded. These are desperate individuals. However, this little hiccup to their plan will give us time. What I need is a list of everyone who might have access to St Peter's after the front doors are closed. Is this a problem?"

"Not in the least, Paddy, but I think that our priority is the safety of the Pontiff. What can we do to protect the Bishop of Rome, tomorrow?"

"A bullet-proof vest would be a start. I would also drug-test the communion bread, and all of the altar wine. Let's put guards on all the entrances, and we should frisk all the priests and nuns. Fake clerical gear is easy to come by."

"Surely, you don't mean a body search?"

"That's exactly what I mean. Of course, it should be someone that they trust. Why don't you do the priests, and I'll do the nuns?"

I don't think that he was totally convinced that I had my finger on the pulse, but I wasn't really that worried. We had stymied their little surprise, and I doubted that the villains were prepared to become martyrs for the cause. They would try again a little later, but it would require more planning. I wondered what other feast days were coming up because I was sure that this had something to do with everything.

The list that I received was quite extensive, and I was quick to do a probity check on everyone. There were a few Opus Dei delegates on the list, but I was happy to disregard them. At the time that the church was being set-up, they were having an Opus day at the picnic grounds at Lake Bracciano, quite a distance out of Rome. This is their once-a-year day, where the secular priests and Opus 1 (the bishop) mix it with the lay people.

I guess they play Tommy Dorsey music, and talk about mortification of the flesh, and other succulent subjects. Anyway, this group has separate headquarters in Rome, and would not spend a lot of time at St Peter's.

One of the most consistent trigger-points for violence is ethnic division. As the Catholic Church is such an international presence, it accumulates a vast array of culture and color within the framework of its structure. People of many races are represented in the Holy See. Such was also the case with my list. I counted nine Italians, two Froggies, three South Americans, two Africans, a Pole, an Austrian and one German. Of course, he was the one that really counted.

I was fascinated by the Austrian. He was the entertainment director: if you could call solemn organ music entertainment. I asked around, and learnt that he was also responsible for all of the music and television distractions that were piped into the pontiff's quarters. He was also the chief censor. This was a whole heap of power, but as he was the Pope's best friend, he sometimes got away with murder: in a manner of speaking.

If you didn't think that the Vatican was a hotbed of innuendo and rumor, you would be wrong. I listened to all the informed gossip, and put two and two together. It came out IV. The number one dude and his mate had fallen out. Evidently, the Pope liked happy music, and was sick of the all the Benedictine dirges that were coming through, courtesy of his friend. He was arranging to have the fellow repatriated back to his home town of Linz.

Now, Linz is quite a nice place, but Fr Shnigglestein would lose all influence, and be forever banished from his Vatican power base. People have killed for less.

The Director of Candles at St Peter's was Fr Bubooloo, one of the Africans. It was his duty to maintain the wall of wax that is necessary to light up this cavernous barn of beatitude. He also had to polish the candelabra and distribute the tapers. Let's give the menial tasks to the black guy.

When I met him, he didn't strike me as being a cold-blooded murderer. Nevertheless, he was holding something back. Guilt can sometimes propel your bodily reactions to unexpected limits. When I asked him if he was on duty last night, his face went a whiter shade of pale. That was quite a feat for someone like him.

"Well, er, ah" he stammered. I knew that I was onto something.

"All right, Father. Let's hear it. You were not here, were you?"

"Well, I was in the early evening, but I had an important assignation. Fr Shnigglestein said that he would cover for me. He is very good with candles."

"Fr Shnigglestein, the Entertainment Director!"

"Yes, that's the one."

The priest from Pretoria had delivered me a slam-dunk. Shnigglestein may have called in some cohorts to spread the dynamite candles around, but there was no doubt in my mind that he was the main man. It was now time to apprehend him. I called Monsignor Dom, and he hooked me up, once again, with the Commander of the Swiss Guards. I must say that it worried me that he was such a show pony. I hoped that he could get the job done.

The Swiss have a reputation for not wanting to offend anyone, so it was difficult to see how this might go down. I had to explain to Axel Volker, the commander, that this Austrian psychopath was mentally deranged, and would do anything to achieve his aims. The Pope was in deep shit. This kind of language got through to him, and snapped him out of his complacent dream world. After all, this was their brief: to protect the Vicar of Christ.

"We're with you, Paddy. Lead the way."

I suppose that if you are not a night person, it may seem ludicrous to be chased by people who appear to be wearing their pajamas. Nevertheless, the Swiss Guard is a potent force, and Fr Shnigglestein would be well aware of their capabilities. He may also have heard us coming because he bolted from the choir loft and raced towards the pontiff's private quarters, brandishing a mean looking double-edged sword. The doorkeeper, Sister Sally, screamed in terror. The Pope looked up from his breviary as Shnigglestein burst into his room.

I didn't know what to do. The mad priest had His Holiness in a head-lock, and had edged him out onto the balcony, with sword in hand. There was an almighty roar from below. The square was full of people, who are always there to try and get a glimpse of the great man. They had no idea what was going on, and probably presumed that the priest was doing an exorcism.

It is rare that I find myself in a state of perplexity. If I tried to unarm the mad monster, the great man could be injured, even killed. If I did nothing, the result could be the same. Perhaps the assailant was also considering his options because, all of a sudden, there was silence on the balcony. Even the crowd below was hushed in anticipation of what might come next.

The next sound I heard was the bark of a small dog.

I then felt the brush of something against my leg, and looked down to see a small Pekinese hurtling towards Shnigglestein with his teeth bared. He sank his ivories into one of the Austrian ankles, and the entertainment officer immediately let out a howl, and dropped his sword. Sensing an opportunity, the Vicar of Christ elbowed him in the stomach, and followed up with a perfectly executed over-throw, which saw the would-be assassin plummet to the pavement below. Was this something he learned when he was with the Hitler Youth?

The one thing that I can say about all this was that it was a great day for the dogs. Firstly, Roger had come to the party in St Peter's, and now Tiny Tim had covered himself with glory.

Now I know what you are all thinking. "Who the hell is Tiny Tim?"

I may not have mentioned that when Fr Shnigglestein arrived in the Pope's quarters, with me on his tail, followed by the Swiss Guard, the vestibule was already full of people. They had been promised an audience with the number one guy, and were waiting in fervent anticipation. One of these people was none other than the famous American television celebrity, Charlotte Tomic, who wondered why her dog, Tiny Tim, kept barking.

Charlotte and Tiny Tim

Well, wonder no more, Charlotte. Your pooch got the job done, and became the toast of all Rome. He will surely receive the appropriate recognition, when the time comes for him to ascend to Dog Heaven. I hope that he looks up Roger. They should get on like a house on fire.

I was feted for my efforts in thwarting this devious plot, but there were to be no military rewards unless I was prepared to take out Swiss citizenship. I did have a Swiss bank account, but I was keeping stum about that.

Of course, it was hard to believe that Shnigglestein could get so riled up over a matter of music. It wasn't as if he had a fifteen year-old daughter or anything like that. Eventually, it came out that the prickly priest had a dormant medical condition that became accentuated when his blood pressure increased. In his youth, he used to fox-trot when everyone else waltzed. In short, he was a nutter, and you can't come up with rational explanations for people like that — so, I didn't try.

Monsignor Dominic saw me off at the airport, and it was good to see that his ruddy complexion had returned. His load was much lighter, and his stocks had risen at the Vatican. It seems that I was about to leave the country without scoring an own goal. That was a bit of a first.

"Thanks for all your help, Paddy. I must say that you looked good in clerical garb. Is there any chance that you might make it permanent?"

I grinned sheepishly. There was a certain lady back home that would have something to say about that. Then my mouth dropped open when I saw the painting that he had brought along as a farewell gift — a rolled-up canvas of a naked man. It was painted in oils, and signed by the artist: a young local painter called Michael Angelo.

"Here's a little something for your troubles. It might be worth something in a few years. You won't sell it before then, will you?"

What could I say? Is the Pope a Catholic?

PEST AND THE JEALOUS NEIGHBOR

In the place where I live, Sam's Fly by Night Club is quite an institution. It is a well-known fact that yours truly warms one of the bar stools when I am in town. However, most of the punters are there to commune with the most popular bar-maid in the business. Stormy Weathers used to be a secret undercover agent. Now, with the advent of certain publicity, she is just an undercover agent. She is too busy to sign autographs, so I oblige for both of us.

We don't always get called-out on the same job, but it can happen. Such was the case when one of our mutual friends became a victim. Willy Murphy was not universally liked, but to murder Murphy in a mountain of molasses was mischievous, to say the least. I suppose that you could say that to shoot and bury him at the same time was economical. Funeral costs are so expensive these days.

The man part-owned a very successful confectionary business, and had acquired it on the back of an aggressive take-over deal that left him with few friends. Sometimes people can get a bit testy about these kinds of things. I knew a New York mobster who had his masseur whacked because he rubbed him the wrong way. Read into that what you will.

There was no body at the murder scene. We only had two eye-witnesses, who declared that he had been shot by a lone gunman, and that the sweet-talking con artist (they called him Willy Wanker) had toppled into the middle of the marinating molasses mucous that was being mulched. We were told that draining the sticky mess was not an option. However, management offered to rebrand this particular batch of candy as *extra crunchy*. You can always rely on advertising people, can't you?

Stormy and I were both aware that the witnesses were holding something back. The fact that both gave conflicting reports of the gunman was suspicious. After all, how can you have a small, tall man with blond, red hair? I wondered if there were two villains. This would certainly mean a mob hit. Perhaps he had been late with his chocolate deliveries.

One of Willy's fellow directors, Malachy McKeon, arrived at the factory in a dither. He was a well-dressed man of average height, and well-groomed to boot. I noticed his buffed finger-nails, and that touch of gray in his hair was probably acceptable to women who might like older men. I was told that he was usually a joke-teller, but not today. He was devastated by his friend's death. Well, he seemed to be. I asked Stormy to profile him, and see if he was in any kind of trouble. The acorn never falls far from the tree, and business partners are the first that should be placed under scrutiny. McKeon's expertise was in healthy confectionary, if that is not a contradiction in terms. He had a Master's Degree in muesli bars, so that put us on an equal footing. My experience was in all-night bars.

A surprise no-show was Murphy's wife, Paulette. I didn't know her that well, but had been invited to their house on a few occasions. Stormy and I departed the murder scene, and drove the few miles to their contemporary home in a rather up-market suburb. She was alone, but already had the cork off a bottle of Veuve Clicquot. It seemed like the news had already filtered through.

"We're sorry for your loss, Mrs Murphy. It looks like Willy was murdered. Do you mind if we ask you a few questions?"

"Sure Paddy. Would you like a glass of champagne? There's a whole cellar full of the stuff."

"I should go easy on the sauce, Paulette. It never helps. Just tell me the facts, as you remember them. Was anything worrying him when he went to work today?"

"Nothing ever worried my husband. He was just so cock-sure and confident. Let's face it. How can you mess-up marzipan and Mint Meltaways? It wasn't murder by chocolate was it?"

"It was murder by molasses. He didn't feel a thing."

"I'm glad of that. He was a bit of a bastard, but he did have his moments."

Weathers and I could see that she was going to make a night of it, so we took our leave, and closed the door behind us. I looked at my watch. Happy

Hour was just about to start at Sam's, and the atmosphere was a little more jovial. We retired to an environment that we were comfortable with.

Stormy and I both had valuable contacts at police headquarters. Favors were often asked for, and occasionally given. Part of this was down to the fact that I had a female snitch, and Stormy's mole was a bloke. One of my mates in marketing is adamant that sex sells. In law enforcement, it depends on who's buying. I gave Sergeant Kat Murtiati a call. She was still purring from our last encounter.

"You're not going to believe this, Paddy; one of the witnesses has looked through the mug shots, and come up with a positive ID. The guy has his hair parted down the middle, and it is blond on one side and red on the other. Can you believe that? He is a tall guy, but his name is Richard Little."

I discounted the description attributed to his cranial features. The fellow had to be wearing a rug. I conjured up a picture of a bald guy called Little Dick, and memories came flooding back. Was it three years ago that Chops Carter imported a young stand-over man from New Zealand to do his dirty work? He had a growing scalp in those days, but a life of crime can be full of anxiety, and hair loss is often the result. It would be reckless to assume that he may have lost his skills with his follicles.

Carter used to frequent Sam's in the old days, but now he had his own joint. There were hot and cold running dames, drugs, and deputations from City Hall. There was always someone wanting to close down this blot on the landscape, and who could blame them? In contrast, Sam's Fly by Night Club was a class establishment. Why else would I give it my custom?

We decided to send Stormy in under cover, and she easily acquired a job as a hat-check girl. It wasn't such hard work because nobody wears hats these days. It didn't take long for Chops to notice that there was a new skirt in his employ.

"G'day babe, you must be the newbie. You look like you've done this kind of thing before. Have you met my PA, Richard Little? We call him Little Dick."

Little was not overly enthusiastic about his nick-name. He flinched, noticeably, and grunted at Stormy. His red and white hair glinted in the strobe lighting, and he looked quite patriotic. Stormy guessed that other members of the staff were a little more respectful, and addressed him as Mr Little. She didn't want to get him offside until it was really necessary.

The hat-check girl made pals with a chick called Dirty Dot, and it wasn't long before she had the low-down on everyone who mattered. All the big deals were made on the first floor. Chops had an office where he could look down on the club activities, and also peek into the cubicles that offered unsupervised lap-dancing. It wasn't that he was a voyeur. He just wanted to keep track of workplace relations.

Certainly, Carter had an over-active libido. By contrast, Richard Little was almost passionless. Stormy flashed her boobs at him a number of times, to no effect. She did say however that he introduced sex into their conversation a number of times. I had to educate her regarding his native tongue.

"Stormy, he's a New Zealander. When they say sex, they mean six."

She looked at me dismissively. I could only laugh.

"Paddy, I've been here two days, and seen nothing out of the ordinary — just drugs, pimps etc. Why is the agency so worried about a simple murder?"

"There's more to it than that. I don't know squat, but something smells fishy in the state of Louisiana."

"That would be your breath, partner. Would you like a Mint Fresh?"

We decided to give it one more night, and I staked out the entrance to Carter's club. It was a mild evening, and I had the top down in my sleek convertible. The front door was clearly visible from my vantage point, and there was no mistaking Willy's former partner.

Malachy McKeon had just arrived, and he was wearing a hat. He would surely recognize Stormy when he appeared inside. While he was chatting up the door-bitches, I quickly texted my partner, and she deputized Dirty Dot to stand in for her, while McKeon passed through.

It was time for me to make an entrance. Did I tell you that I was a master of disguise? Most people have a spare tire in their car boot. I had my box of tricks: mustaches, wigs, fake noses etc. A job like this called for my Prince Charles ears.

"G'day, Paddy. Nice disguise! I really like those Prince Charles ears."

You've got to be good to get past Stormy, and I didn't want to. I expected that McKeon would be heading for Carter's office. This association was a bit out of left field, but it appears that I had presumed too much.

"Chops is not here tonight. He's gone to his wine appreciation class.

"Wine appreciation class! Who told you that?"

"Dirty Dot, of course; she's a mine of information. Evidently, Carter embarrassed his wife when they dined with friends, and he ordered red wine with fish. She insisted that he improve his knowledge."

Bloody hell! Chops Carter under the thumb! I couldn't believe it.

It didn't take long to find out where McKeon's assignation was. He was holed up at a corner table with Little Dick, and they had their heads locked together in fervent discussion.

You had to think that these two dudes were on about something serious. There was some serious flesh on show, and they weren't giving it a glance. I propositioned Dirty Dot, and we moved to an adjoining table. The good thing about the royal ears is that they are twice as efficient as normal ears.

Dirty Dot

What I hadn't picked up on before, and it was now patently obvious; Malachy McKeon was also a New Zealander. Alarm bells started ringing. In recent years, Australia's Pacific neighbors have looked at our nation with malicious intent. Fiji has become grumpy, Indonesia has been offended, and New Zealand has really wanted to spit the dummy. After all, we cheated at cricket.

If there was some kind of action planned against my fair country, I think that it would be covert. After all, I think that the Kiwis only have a limited defense force, and I am being kind here in not quoting numbers.

"Gee Paddy; you don't think that McKeon is putting poison in his chocolates, do you? Willy could have discovered their plot, and been eliminated."

Stormy had a vivid imagination at the best of times, but this was rather fanciful. Nevertheless, I checked on their dispatch records. The clerk was most forthcoming.

"Well, Mr Pest. I can tell you that the Melbourne Cricket Club has a standing order of a confectionary line called *Sticky Wickets*. Complimentary boxes have also been sent to the Wallabies Rugby Team, the Prime Minister and Russell Crowe."

Russell, the turncoat, eh! Perhaps the actor might regret becoming an honorary Australian.

Eventually, Dick and Malachy broke up their tête-à-tête, and the hoodlum disappeared into the night. McKeon remained for a bit in order to socialize with some of the girls, but then he hit the road when he sighted Stormy. She was doing a Mexican hat dance for one of the clients, who had obviously had too much tequila.

"C'mon Stormy; I think that it's time to hand in your resignation. Let's get out of here."

My car was still parked across the road, but it may have been a bridge too far. As we left the club, a dark-colored sedan rounded the corner, and tried to run us down. We bounced off the bitumen, and I let off a few rounds at the departing vehicle. I may have drawn blood, but the car didn't stop. The game was now in the open and the players were well defined.

It was wrong of me to reject the chocolate-poisoning plot that seemingly had been hatched at the Willy Wanker Chocolate Factory. I realized that Stormy was right on the mark, and I should have noticed the conspiracy a little earlier.

"Paddy, did you see the driver? He was covered in tattoos."

"Not only that, Stormy; he was singing *The Maori Farewell*."

I may have mentioned that my classic convertible was still parked, hood down, opposite *The Garter Club*. When people have got it in for you, it is not always advisable to drive a convertible with the roof down. It is easy for bad dudes to lob grenades and other incendiary devices into the vehicle. Once, a man with a fire hose attacked me, and I have also had wet cement poured into my car. My dog, Roger, was asleep on the back seat at the time.

However, this was the first time that I had ever had a venomous snake in my car. When the car door was slammed shut, it slithered out from under the passenger seat, and there it was, contemplating a delightful journey up Stormy's lithe and lovely legs. She was wearing a mind-snapping micro-mini skirt, so it was going to be a long journey.

The black-eyed, yellow-bellied south island viper is one of the deadliest snakes in the whole world, and very rare; in fact, it is so rare that I don't think that anyone had ever seen one, before.

I knew that Stormy would freak out when I told her the bad news, but she had been in this kind of trouble before. Her one-and-a-half back flip out of trouble was a beauty, and this was just what was needed here.

"Stormy, I want you to remain calm, but think of James Bond and that tarantula situation in the Bahamas."

"I think it was the Caribbean, Paddy."

"Whatever! Just go for your back flip when I slam on the brakes, but make sure that you grab something. I don't want you flying out the back of the car."

"Right, Paddy. I'm ready whenever you are."

I had built up some speed when I hit the anchors hard. Stormy went backwards, and the snake went forwards. Before it could recover its equilibrium, I grabbed it by the neck, and hurled it as far as I could.

My rev-head exercise had almost taken me past the famous Café de Wheels, which is parked in the same spot every night/early morning. The viper sailed through the canopy opening, and landed on the hot grill. Sam the Man had the reptile's head off in seconds flat, and tossed the remains into the fryer. Two minutes later, he was spruiking fresh calamari. You've got to like a quick-thinking entrepreneur.

So there you have it. Hands across the water and all that crap! The varmints from the Land of the Long White Cloud were out to get us, and Malachy McKeon, the Scottish Kiwi, may well have been their leader. I may also owe Chops Carter an apology; just because you're bad, doesn't mean that you are not a patriot. I expect that he was ignorant of this whole New Zealand plot.

I used to know someone who knew someone from the Chocolate Lovers Club at Melbourne University. These were the people who could definitely tell us whether Willy's chocolates and candies had been tampered with. We needed someone to do a taste test, and I specified a student who was doing an arts degree. If we lost them, no one would notice.

Juliette Park was someone who looked like she had been eating chocolate all her life. I couldn't believe that she was just twenty. I suspect that her drama opportunities were limited because of her size, but she was a good kid, and up for the challenge. We promised her a posthumous award if the taste test proved fatal. Artistic people will do anything for a go at immortality.

At this time, details of the gratuitous confectionery gifts to our sporting stars and political bigwigs were passed on to the Australian Security Intelligence Organisation (ASIO). No one was worried by the possible political loss, but if our sporting stars were in danger, they would make every effort to foil this shameful plot. I alerted them to the possibility that Malachy McKeon was involved. For this, I received a visit from Kevin Connellan, their chief spy in Melbourne. He was a friendly kind of fellow, and I liked what he was doing with his hair. Other than that, he didn't inspire me with confidence.

"Kevin, what do you know about the Rugby World Cup, The America's Cup, and the ICC Cricket World Cup?"

"They are all boring sporting events."

"No, Kevin. That is not the answer. The answer is that New Zealand will do anything to win these trophies. Until recently, their highest paid sports person has been Tiger Wood's caddy. They have even lobbied for sheep-shearing to become an Olympic sport. They are desperate people, and no one is more desperate than Mr McKeon and his disreputable side-kick. They are prepared to chocolate-poison our best sport stars, and they have already claimed the life of a poor university student, and a chap called Murphy."

"Well, one less Irishman can't be such a bad thing."

You can see why I was less than enthused with the assistance that I was getting from Australia's crack spy network. This guy Connellan was probably Irish himself, but didn't know it. My guess was that he wouldn't know chocolate from shit, so I excused myself, and caught up with Stormy. When we got together, things happened.

"Paddy, I think that the man with the gray hair is on the run. He left the country under cover of darkness, and Richard Little has gone to ground. I have heard that Paulette is now running the factory. I have asked her to dump all her stock and start again."

So, Paulette has stepped up to the plate. Good girl! I went over there to see what I could do, and she had everything under control. The lady even had a new range of confectionery going.

"I wasn't going to let all that booze in Willy's cellar go to waste, Paddy. The kids won't even notice the subtle difference in their tasty treats."

"Let's hope that it isn't habit-forming, Paulette."

"I can't believe that Malachy is responsible for my husband's death. You will get him, Paddy, won't you?"

"I assured her that I would, and mentioned that I had already sent Stormy over to the Shaky Isles."

I thought that my beautiful side-kick would be able to double-up with some language training. I hoped that she didn't return with a tattoo. I knew that I would be vulnerable without my wingman, and although Little Dick was mentally inferior, he would be a handful if we came to blows. I had booked Stormy on the first available flight to Queenstown. My intel had told me that McKeon would be there or in Dunedin.

The further south you travel in New Zealand, the more Scottish everyone becomes. They are the only ones who can survive the cold. By the time you get to the ass-end of the country, Invercargill, you will want a wee dram of something to keep you alive. If you live in Invercargill, you have to be convinced that you are alive.

So, McKeon was bound to have lots of friends on the South Island. Then again, nobody makes friends as quickly as Stormy Weathers. I was confident that she would track him down. Her cover as a croupier at the Queenstown casino was ideal. I just hoped that she wouldn't have too much trouble with the number six.

Meanwhile, the Australian cricket team had arrived at the Melbourne Cricket Ground for their clash with the Kiwis. It was a big game, with the Chappell-Hadlee Trophy up for grabs. I had acquired a pass to the hospitality rooms in order to check out the lunch menu. Cricket is the only game I know that includes meals as part of the sporting encounter. All bars of *Sticky Wicket* confectionery had been removed, and I could see no foodstuff that might be contaminated. The match commenced as scheduled.

By mid-morning, the Australian opening pair had established a sizeable run total. They also seemed to be establishing some kind of rapport with one of the umpires. The man in white seemed to be offering them something at every opportunity. So far, they had refused. I put my binoculars on zoom, and tried to determine what he had in his hand; it looked like chocolate-coated gum.

"Excuse me, Mr Clarke (Michael was the next man in), are you allowed to accept food from the umpires? This is what seems to be going on out there."

"Well, er, ah, I don't know. I don't think so."

Right there and then, a gust of wind blew across the ground, and knocked off the umpire's hat. His hair was parted down the middle, and it was blond on one side and red on the other. Stone the crows. Richard Little was standing in the middle of the Melbourne Cricket Ground with a pocket full of chocolate death, and I believe that one of the batsmen was getting a bit peckish. What could I do?

In cricket, the fastest means of getting from the edge of the oval to the center of the ground is by way of the sponsor's drink trolley, which is mounted on a golf cart. It doesn't go very fast so you don't have to yell out *fore*. However, there is an allocated time for this foray onto the field, and the driver was not prepared to waive convention. I pistol-whipped him, and took over the controls. There would be retribution, but if I never saw another game of cricket, it would be a blessing. I would call Kevin Connellan as a character witness.

I was half way to the pitch when security wised up to what was happening, and so too had the national television audience. I was not too adept at driving a vehicle with a large orange drink bottle on top of it, and my path to the wicket was not straight. In fact, I ran over two of the opposition team members. It would be touch and go as to whether I would reach Little before they reached me. In the end, one of the Kiwi players that I was about to pass, let fly with a Hanamahihi haymaker, and put out my lights. The vehicle ground to a stop within inches of the pitch.

In the confusion that followed, Richard Little escorted himself and his fellow umpire off the ground. He then bolted from the sports complex. Eventually, they found the real umpire tied up in a locker, and I was exonerated. The television audience was led to believe that it was just another ground intrusion, and ASIO's spy man arrived to tell me that the game wasn't as boring as he first thought. What a shame that there were no chocolates left. He deserved one.

If you thought that every single person in New Zealand saw the above-mentioned charade, you would be right. Malachy McKeon was being feted by friends at an isolated property on the shores of Lake Wakatipu, not far from Queenstown. These people were movers and shakers of the highest order, and I don't know how Stormy managed to get a gig on the catering staff, but she did. The word is that they ooohed and ahhhed every time that one of the batsmen looked like accepting the gum. Being an Australian waitress in the midst of such hostility must have been scary stuff, but my girl pulled it off. She had even mastered the language.

"Oh look, the bowler has been hit for sex."

When Stormy contacted me, she said that McKeon was up for a knighthood, should the Kiwis win the World Cup. This was never going to happen; especially if they beat England. His demented plans were probably accentuated by some goading that may well have come from Willy Murphy. Or it may be that the muesli man was just plain nuts. Insanity is more prevalent in cold climates, don't you think?

Stormy on the job

The death toll, so far, had only been two people, and the security services knew enough to be on the look-out for the killer confectionery. However, we really didn't have any solid proof that Richard Little or Malachy McKeon was the culprit. Certainly, those eye-witnesses put Little Dick at the scene of one of the crimes, and McKeon's fingers were stained with chocolate; would this be enough for a fair-minded judicial arbitrator?

The management at Sam's Fly by Night Club was becoming annoyed with Stormy's continued absence, so I recalled her from her overseas posting. Patronage at the club immediately doubled. Unbeknown to me, there was a shadowy presence that lurked outside the premises, and he was very keen to remain in the shadows. On the occasions that he passed the lone street lamp in the vicinity, the casual observer would have noticed his metro-sexual hair style. One side of his head was blond; the other side was red.

Little Dick would hold his sentinel position for two successive nights. On the third night, he came out of the darkness, and I was glad that I was completely oblivious to his plans. You can never enjoy your tipple if you know that someone is trying to kill you.

There have been any number of attempts on my life, and that is why vigilance is one of my personal priorities. When you are off-duty, your defenses are down. However, I am never off-duty. Even with a Martini and a few Pink Ladies under my belt, I could smell trouble as soon as I arrived at the front door of Sam's pleasure palace. Because I was leaving before dawn, I may have caught Little unawares. However, the farewell acknowledgment from the door-man would have alerted him.

"Good-night, Paddy. See you tomorrow."

When I say that the Kiwi hoodlum had a plan, let's not gild the lily. He was going to follow me from the club, and when I had left the warm welcoming lights behind, he was going to shoot me in the back. Do you call that a plan?

I'll give you a plan, and it's the reason that I am still alive, today. The fact is that the Kiwi killer had been spotted outside the club the night before. One of Stormy's transvestite friends had gone to the rest-room on the second floor, and seen Little Dick. The toilet window was directly above his hiding place. By the time Richard Little was moving into place behind my back, ASIO's master spy, Kevin Connellan, was emerging from a tin garbage can, where he had been lying in wait for four hours.

Connellan called Little, and he spun around with his gun blazing, but it was too late. The cool dude from Secret City put five bullets into the mean man's torso. When we inspected the corpse, back at the city morgue, Stormy was at her most observant.

"Can you see that, Paddy? The bullet holes are the same design as the Southern Cross. What a guy."

It is relevant to point out that New Zealand also boasts a depiction of the Southern Cross constellation on their flag, but they choose to only recognize four stars. It was probably a bit extravagant of Connellan to waste Government Issue ammunition like that, but I'm not complaining. He saved my life, and I may invite him to the cricket as a grateful gesture. What do you think?

The demise of the Maori mobster had not only saved the world from another bad hair day, but the Crown would not have to put out for an expensive trial. I was pretty happy with the way that things had gone, but I would not be totally at ease until we had put McKeon away. I suspected that he had also been tickling the kitty at the chocolate factory because Paulette was raking-in profits like they had never seen before. Of course, this could have been down to the alcohol-laced confectionery that she was now selling.

The cricket tour finished without any further drama, and the months slipped by. There was no way that Malachy McKeon would be crossing *the ditch* (Tasman Sea) any time soon. However, the Australian Rugby Union team would be visiting their Kiwi cousins for their yearly confrontation on home soil. It is usually a knock 'em down, drag 'em out kind of affair: a real war of attrition. In fact, the locals insist on performing a war dance before every game. This is called the Haka, and concludes when the players stick their tongues out at the opposition. Now, if that isn't provocation, I don't know what is.

The Wallabies had never had a masseuse like Stormy Weathers before. From what I heard, the boys were just about living in the steam room. I know these things because I became their new skills coach, and I had drafted Kevin Connellan as my assistant. After all, he was a straight shooter.

These new appointments to the touring team were not meant to improve their performance, but to keep the lads out of harm's way. At least, I hoped so. Chocolates may be off the menu, but I was sure that there would be another attempt to discredit one of the most distinguished sporting teams in the world. Admittedly, we could be even more distinguished if we won more games, but victory over the All-Blacks is an aphrodisiac that is all-powerful. Unfortunately, such a result would only further enrage the likes of Malachy McKeon, and he had to be stopped at all costs. We had secreted our respective firearms in the leather casing of the footballs that we brought over.

Let me tell you about Eden Park, the largest stadium in New Zealand's largest city: Auckland. It has been the home of rugby since nineteen twenty-five, and today holds sixty thousand one-eyed, loud-mouthed, football experts. The organizers spent over two hundred million dollars to promote and accommodate intrepid locals and optimistic visitors for the recent World Cup. They did everyone proud, and the supporters had no complaints. Under blue skies, the fans were close to the action in a cauldron of seething testosterone. Of course, the best seats in the house were supposed to be allocated to visiting dignitaries, but they didn't get the really good seats. There were only three of them: for the Governor-General; the Prime Minister; and Malachy McKeon.

I was at ground level, but my trusty binoculars were aimed at the muesli man. He had aged a bit since I last saw him, and he wasn't looking very happy. Most of the other Kiwis were. Their team was odds-on to retain the Bledisloe Cup (Australia v New Zealand), which has been a perennial trophy since the thirties, and was on display at the side of the oval. I lifted the lid and hid my Beretta inside. I needed to have my gun close by.

The preliminaries to the game were quite splendid. Kiri Te Kanawa performed the national anthem for the local team, and Rolf Harris played Waltzing Matilda on the Wobble Board. I had tears in my eyes, and Stormy noticed it.

"Paddy, where on earth did you get that onion burger? It's made you very emotional."

I had hardly imparted my skills advice to the team when all the grunting and groaning started. The Kiwis were stamping their feet and making silly grimaces. This was the Haka, and it was very loud at ground level. I used the diversion to sneak another peek at McKeon. He had a smug look on his face. The All-Blacks were now 3/1 on. Connellan arrived on the scene.

"Paddy, I can't believe the odds. Have you got on yet? I really think that we can win."

"OK, Kevin, if you say so. Here's a gorilla ($1,000). Put it on each way for me."

"You can't bet each way. It's a two horse race. I'll put five hundred bucks on the Aussies to win."

"Fine, but when you are on, I want you to get up to that official box, and keep an eye on McKeon. If the All-Blacks lose, he may go ballistic."

Now, I suppose that I could drag this out, but I really don't want to distress my New Zealand readership. The match was an anti-climax. The Wallabies came out fighting, and mauled the All-Blacks in every possible way. Three of their best players limped off the ground in the first twenty minutes, and the Aussie boys ran home three tries to nothing before half-time. At the interval, there was consternation in the official box. The Governor-General was hyper-ventilating, and the Prime Minister was in the hands of the medics. Malachy McKeon was in a trance.

"OK guys, Paddy and Kevin have honed your skills to such a degree that your performance in that first half was exquisite, but the game is not over until the fat lady sings. I don't want those tattooed tigers getting back in the game. Give it your all, and we will have a glorious victory."

Some of you are not going to believe this when I tell you that the Aussie coach was actually a New Zealander. The Kiwis had overlooked him to be their mentor, and so he transferred his indentures to those nice neighbors across the water. I expect that he will retain his position until I become available.

The Wallabies held firm, and they ran out easy winners, but I was uneasy with what was to come next. The teams were congregating in front of the main grandstand, and the trophy presentation was about to be made. I couldn't find Kevin, and Stormy was massaging the upper thigh of one of the front-rowers. That could take forever.

From the corner of my eye, I saw somebody emerge from the vehicle access chute. It was Malachy with a rocket launcher under his arm. He was intent on taking out the whole Aussie team, and to make matters worse, I was in his line of fire. He stopped, and fiddled with the instrument of destruction. He then raised it into a fire position, and took aim.

Malachy McKeon and his chocolate poison

In three quick bounds, I accepted the trophy on behalf of the assembled group, and dispensed with the lid. My Beretta was still there, but I would have to be a good shot, which I was. Distance might be a problem. I threw the Bledisloe Cup to the ground, and raised my gun. People started screaming, and the television audience was told that we were filming for an upcoming blockbuster. I shot Malachy McKeon between the eyes. As he fell, the rocket was released, but it didn't go in the original direction; it took out Rolf and his Wobble Board. Oh well, every long innings must have an end.

Naturally, Stormy and I strangled a few stubbies that night, and I believe that a grateful nation, back home, also partied with great enthusiasm. We were humble victors, and I even sent flowers to their Prime Minister, who had been rushed to hospital after a cardiac arrest. There was only one person missing from the celebration group, and nobody had any idea where Kevin Connellan was. It was later established that he had absconded with my winnings. When I contacted the Australian Security Intelligence Organisation, they said that they had never heard of him.

STARLET BY STARLIGHT

Marjorie Mayflower wasn't always going to be a star. Her ascent to the heady heights of the Hollywood hierarchy was as sudden as it was unexpected. She had managed a few barely watchable B-grade movies, and then nailed it with a mesmerizing portrayal of gangland matriarch, Machine-gun Matilda. This was my kind of movie, and I think I have seen it about half-a-dozen times. To be able to meet this young lady was something that I was looking forward to. When I say young, she was just twenty-two years old: the perfect age to be a cinema starlet.

We had mutual friends, and I was invited to a knees-up at the home of sometime actor and playboy J. P. Carlton, in Holmby Hills. It was just a stones-throw from the real Playboy Mansion. Marjorie was a stunning piece of crumpet. Her willowy frame was kind of spindly, but those long legs gave her the capacity to be overpowering. Not that anyone would want to put up any resistance. She was wearing a tight silk blouse that seemed to be short on buttons, and she had tucked it into her belt as if she wanted to choke her Brad Pitts. Notwithstanding all that, her babaloos were bouncing around as they do if you are only twenty-two years of age.

"Marjorie, I would like you to meet a very good friend of mine: Paddy Pest from Australia."

"Hello Paddy. How are you? We don't see many Australians over here. Are you an actor?"

There are so many Aussie actors in Hollywood. I don't know where she does her shopping. Could she have failed to notice Mel, Russel, Nicole, Geoffrey, Cate, Guy, Naomi, Hugo or Hugh? I stone-walled, and then gave her my best smile.

"No, Marjorie, I'm an investigator, and the world is my beat. J. P. Carlton is in the gun."

"What, for over-acting!"

"You've got it in one, young lady."

Carlton raised his eyebrows, feigned displeasure, and walked off. Of course, all this was an obvious ploy to put me one-on-one with the hottest dish in the room. I wasn't about to give up this rare opportunity, and invited the alluring thespian for a moonlight walk by the pool. She graciously accepted.

I don't intend to go into the niceties of our intimate conversation. The secrets of my magnetic attraction are not for public consumption, but I will say that the Pest pool-side manner is not unlike my bed-side manner: irresistible. Needless to say, the poppet was suitably captivated, and very much looking forward to our arranged date, which would occur in New York after the St Patrick's Day parade.

Perhaps I should have arranged an earlier time for our rendezvous. There are so many distractions on St Patrick's Day, and sometimes the green beer starts flowing before breakfast. In such cases, an evening liaison can be a long time coming, and one will often arrive all the worse for wear. Fortunately, Marj also had her happy side, and when I picked her up, she was more inebriated than I was.

I had a discount voucher for one of those all-you-can-eat places in the Bronx, but she pooh-poohed that idea. The lady was intent on Italian, and so we went to Frankies Spuntino.

Frankies in Brooklyn hasn't been around long enough to become an institution, but the two guys called Frank, who run the establishment, have been good enough to open two follow-up restaurants in Manhattan. The food is good, and so is the ambiance. However, I suspect that they don't get too many horn-bags in the place. When we walked in, there were immediately two dozen pairs of eyes fixed on my attractive companion. I could have been the Abominable Snowman, and they wouldn't have noticed.

The first person to arrive at our table was the sanctimonious waiter, who proceeded to read out the specials while peering down Marjorie's cleavage. He obviously knew the dishes by heart because he didn't give the printed menu much eye-time. I just knew where he was going to tuck the table napkin.

"Oh! Your fingers are cold."

"Sorry ma'am. Would you like to see the wine list?"

There are some questions that never need to be asked. This is one of them. I glared at the randy waiter, and he scurried off. I couldn't help but notice the large table of men who were not far away. It looked like it was the monthly meeting of Murder Incorporated, and the house staff were fussing over them with all the respect that these people demand. One of the Italian stallions at the table couldn't take his eyes off Marjorie. He was chomping on a fat cigar, and the smoke was coming out of his ears. It wasn't long before a complimentary bottle of champagne arrived at our table, and the heavy with the slicked-down hair wasn't far behind.

"Good evening, Miss Mayflower. Welcome to Frankies. I'm John Stompanatti."

Johnny Stompanatti

I need not have been there. He ignored me completely. However, I still sipped his champagne, and wondered what this goon wanted. As if I didn't know. What I didn't know was whether Marj was aware of this brute's credentials. Johnny Stomp-on-you-face had quite a few scalps on his belt. He had beaten a dozen murder raps, and there wasn't anyone who thought that he might be innocent of any of them. It wouldn't be a good career move if Marjorie encouraged this overture.

Stompanatti's beefy grin disclosed a number of gold teeth, and the waiter must have taken this to be some sort of sign. He slipped a disc into the machine, and the theme from *The Godfather* wafted across the room.

"The champagne — it was very nice of you, John. Would you like to join us?"

Marjorie was glowing in the light of his adoration. It appears that he was a great fan, and was convinced that she was a moral to win an Oscar for Machine-gun Matilda. He promised that he would put in a good word with his friends at the Screen Actors Guild.

"Wow, John, do you actually know people at the Academy?"

"Not really, sweetheart, but most people always seem to agree with what I have to say."

Well, there you have it. In one foul swoop, she had stitched up an Oscar, and found a new friend. I had sobered up pretty fast, and was happy to get out of there. When I left her, she had this glint in her eye, and I knew that she was heading for trouble with a capital T.

I don't know why people who have it all want more. To date, Marjorie had been a model apprentice in the movie business. There were no drug busts, sex scandals, or alcohol- fuelled embarrassments. She had made it to the top quickly, and now came the fork in the road. Johnny Stompanatti was a passenger that she didn't need. The simple truth of it all was that she liked it a bit rough, now and then.

I was to find out, some months later, that the now and then was more often than not. They had moved into a penthouse together, and she became a bit of a hand-bag on his arm. The media lapped it up. Often, she appeared at movie premieres with a black eye or a swollen lip. The inevitable occurred just two weeks after the greatest moment of her life.

"Winning the Academy Award is a great thrill, and there are so many people that I have to thank: in particular, my greatest fan, partner and soul-mate, Johnny Stompanatti."

Johnny and the boys from Murder Incorporated had booked out the front five rows of the Kodak Theater, and they applauded enthusiastically. The likes of Tom Hanks, Tom Cruise and Meryl Streep snarled through the cigar smoke that distorted their view from the bleachers. Not one of them had the nerve to tell the lads from New York that they were in a smoke-free environment.

Just two weeks after this happy event, Marjorie did a runner. I was in New York at the time, and I don't know how she found out where I was. Nevertheless, there she was: under my bed at a not so fashionable hotel in Manhattan. I coaxed her out from down-under, and made her more comfortable on top of the bed. A double shot of whisky calmed her down appreciably.

"Oh Paddy, what have I got myself into? He's a monster. When he finds I'm gone, he'll try and kill me."

This information was disturbing in itself, but what was more disturbing was that fact that he would also want to kill me. We both had to get out of there, fast.

In most stories like this, people who are on the lam always have a friend who has a cabin in the woods. The best I could do was a holiday house at Martha's Vineyard, and I wouldn't need a jemmy. I knew where the key was. On reflection, this wouldn't be a bad hideout. The place was a refuge for the rich and famous, and Marjorie wouldn't stand out, as she would be only one of many celebrities that frequent the island. Being an island, we could also scan the arrivals at the ferry terminal. The Mafioso always stands out in a crowd.

I purchased some clothes from Wal-Mart, dyed her hair, and finished her off with some not-so-stylish glasses. We then made our dash up north, under cover of darkness; and caught the last ferry from Woods Hole. By now, Johnny would be stomping on the floor in a rage.

I must say that I enjoyed my time with Marjorie. Even with her unfashionable eye-glasses, she was a good-looking broad. We managed a few days on the beach, and poked around some of the historical landmarks like the Chappaquiddick Bridge and Murdick's Fudge Shop. We only realized that our location had been traced when we arrived home to find the cottage in flames. The two bodies that were removed from the wreckage were the house cleaner and her husband. Evidently, the cleaner turned on the vacuum cleaner, and the bomb exploded.

This god-fearing Mexican couple was in the wrong place at the wrong time, but I wasn't sure that the perpetrators of this destructive act were aware that they had clipped the wrong people. We needed to be gone before they discovered that Mrs Gonzales had never been to Hollywood. The main road was nearby, so Marj and I hitched to Vineyard Haven, and waited for the next available ferry. I also gave my buddy in Boston a call. It was time to bring in some external help.

"Hey, Declan! Get down here fast. I need a couple of wigs, sunnies and two plane tickets out of here. We'll meet you on the mainland."

Declan had been a drinking pal when I had attended a pick-pocketing course in Cambridge all those years ago. He was street savvy, and definitely had mob connections. The man could handle a piece, and was loyal right down to his bootstraps. However, he was rather casual — a bit too casual for his own good, I'm afraid.

"Don't worry, Paddy. You'll be safe in Massachusetts. The Irish run things in this neck of the woods. Any incursions from those prima donnas from New York will be frowned upon."

We were forty minutes into our flight when the body of Declan Moreland bounced off the grill and splattered on the windscreen of a black limousine on the Boston Turnpike. The Cadillac sped off into the fog without stopping. An eyewitness couldn't remember the license number, but they were definitely New York plates. I didn't hear about this tragic event until we cleared the terminal at LAX, and I kept the information to myself. Marj wasn't quite ready to absorb any death notices.

The studio people were delighted to see her. In the aftermath of Marjorie's Oscar win, opportunities had really opened up, and there were scripts aplenty on her agent's desk. It surprised everyone but me when she decided on a low budget film with a virgin director. The movie required a location shoot in Swaziland, and you can't get further away from New York than that. Unfortunately, John Stompanatti was now a subscriber to The Hollywood Reporter, and details of the forthcoming project had been leaked by the virgin director. I could have killed him, and Johnny still might. This guy takes no prisoners.

If you thought that Mr Stomp-in-your-face had it in for Marjorie because she had injured his pride and reputation, you would be partly right. More worrying for him was the fact that she had acquired inside information into his disreputable dealings, and important evidence that could implicate him in a juicy murder case. If she decided to sing to the cops, this would be a murder rap that he would find hard to beat. So, her card was marked.

I know that you will say that a wife can't give evidence against her husband, but they weren't married. Therefore, he had to marry the actress, or kill her. In her present state of mind, I think Marjorie would have been happier with the second option.

The leading lady wanted me added to her personal staff as a bodyguard, and to accompany the production people to Swaziland. I had to explain that I always charged a premium fee if I was dealing with the Mafia or African head-hunters. You can never get life insurance. The producers countered with a profit-sharing arrangement, and I accepted. This was a bold move on my part as nobody was expecting a smash hit. At least the weather in Swaziland was nice at that time of year.

Lois Davies was Marjorie's mother; you didn't think that Mayflower was her real name, did you? The alcoholic shrew had been added to the star's paid personal staff to fulfill the role of grooming advisor. Lois was a real piece of work. Her curriculum vitae listed a swag of low-budget movies where the heroine sported a beehive hairdo. Lois was the accredited hairdresser on the set, and if there was a limited crew list, she would also do make-up. However, most of the actors couldn't handle her alcoholic breath, and did their own.

As a young girl, she was quite attractive, and did have her admirers. There were lots of propositions, but no proposals. Eventually she found love albeit fleetingly. The wrangler with the spurs that jangled stayed around for a few months, and then lit out for the great outdoors. At the time, Lois had no idea that she was carrying Marjorie inside her: the child who would become the apple of her mother's eye.

Bringing up a child with no money and few prospects! It was enough to drive one to drink. I won't bore you with the details, but the ensuing years were a bit testy for both mother and daughter. Nevertheless, Marj made it to high school, drama school and the glee club. She never looked back, and neither did her mother. Lois is now drinking a better class of booze, and her requirements were written into the film's budget: two bottles of gin per day

The seating arrangement on the plane was as you might have expected: Marjorie, me, her mother and the producer were in First Class. The director and the rest of the production were in the cheap seats. We had safely maneuvered out of Los Angeles air space, and the stewardess had served our complimentary champagne and orange juice. It was time to relax. The captain took over the microphone, and gave us all the flight details and the forward weather conditions. It was his concluding remarks that made us sit bolt upright in our seats.

"On behalf of me and my co-pilot, Vince Stompanatti, we wish you a comfortable flight."

Jesus, Mary and Joseph! Did I hear that right?

"Excuse me, young lady. Can you remember the name of that co-pilot? I think that it was Vince something."

"Yes, Mr Pest. That is correct. Vince Stompanatti! He's from New York. I've never flown with him before, but he seems very nice."

Marjorie had gone a whiter shade of pale, and her mother called for more gin. This was a major development. I had checked out the passenger list, but never thought that the crew could be suspect. After all, they were a family airline.

A later investigation would determine that the company was owned by La Familia: the Cosa Nostra. With a bit of due diligence, someone may have discovered this fact a little earlier, but when you are on the run, time is of the essence. They also had some pretty good corporate hackers who were able to disguise the names of the principal shareholders of the company.

I was impressed that young Stomp-on-your-face could handle the controls of a Boeing Jumbo Jet, but I would imagine that this was a skill learned in recent times. I am sure that his formative years would have seen him tutored in the art of smuggling, extortion, protection and brutal physical persuasion. Marjorie's demise would have been an absolute priority for Murder Incorporated, so they would not have sent a novice to do the job. The young man must have been a Whackmeister.

I ordered another drink, and racked my brain for a solution: if not that, at least an escape plan. On one side of me, Marjorie was sobbing her heart out, and on my other side, her mother was snoring. We were thirty thousand feet up in the sky, but it didn't feel like heaven to me.

Half-way through our flight time, the co-pilot made an appearance. He joshed with the stewardess, and made polite conversation with some of the passengers. He didn't approach our seats, but from the corner of his eye he was able to confirm that the names on the passenger manifest were where they should be. Marjorie was cowering behind the upright seat in front of her. She had met her soul-mate's son before.

The aircraft made it to Johannesburg without incident, and we managed to transfer to our Mbabane flight without any interference from Mr Stompanatti. Still, I guessed that we hadn't lost him, and I was right. He turned up as a baggage handler, and stayed with the baggage until we touched down at Manzini Airport. He then lost himself in the crowd; and it was quite a crowd.

Do I need to tell you that Machine-gun Matilda had been a huge hit in Swaziland, and half the country turned out to welcome the fresh-faced star with the golden hair? That she looked nothing like her characterization was of little consequence. They only had one red carpet in the country, and it was rolled out for Marjorie Mayflower and her friends. Even the virgin director signed autographs. King Mswati gave our girl the traditional kiss on the cheek, and a pat on the butt for good luck. We were all invited to the civic reception in a nearby tent.

I don't know why the writer of this mindless screenplay decided that it should take place in the Highveld of Swaziland, because there was nothing here. I counted a few malls and markets, a bus, one taxi and a hotel, which we had completely booked out. The population was lucky to etch out an existence, and the quality of their sanitation service was questionable. I warned Marjorie not to touch anything unless she had to. I would have liked to have said the same thing to the king because he had his hand on Marj's ass again. I guess rank gets you extra privileges.

If we were not so on edge, the soirée would have been great fun. Certainly, my presence raised a few eyebrows with the unmarried set. Many of these girls were ready to become betrothed, and they must have learned that I had money.

He's a real chick magnet.

Many of the guests were speaking Bantu. Some Zulus and most of the Royal Family were in attendance: they were a happy bunch. It turned out that King Mswati and I had a mutual acquaintance.

Back in the seventies, I had shared an apartment in Melbourne with a young chap from Kenya, who we called Masai Pete. Would you believe that he went to school with the king? This put us on an almost intimate footing: it was just the opening that I needed. I told him all about the plot to kill Marjorie, and the shadowy figure, recently identified as a baggage handler. He told me not to worry. He would make him a Swaziland offer that he could not refuse.

Unfortunately, circumstances invalidated any such offer being made.

Marjorie had been signing autographs for most of the afternoon, and now she was talking to some tribesmen from the surrounding district. They were unusually small, and she had to bend down to hear what they were saying. This unexpected action saved her life.

One of those long hunting spears came hurtling through the air, and sailed over her head, only to find its mark in the chest of the Prime Minister's personal secretary. Pandemonium erupted. I immediately went to the guest of honor, and wrapped my arms around Marjorie. The king was livid. He shouted at his security staff.

"Get that fellow now. I want him in prison, and strung up before sundown. He may be disguised as a baggage handler."

Marjorie was beside herself. So was her mother, who was shouting obscenities at everyone. I did my best to whisk them away to the hotel as quickly as possible. I gave Marj a sedative, and her mom scored another gin. We were safe for the time being, and now that all the king's men were on the case, I felt that I could relax a little. I found a k.d. Lang retrospective in the music library, and poured myself a drink. It had been a long trip.

The next day they found Vince hiding in an outlying area, masquerading as a missionary. What a sham! Under interrogation, the Royal Prosecutor discovered that the man couldn't even recite The Lord's Prayer. They put him in a cell, and were about to throw away the key when he begged for a deal. Daddy could provide a king's ransom, and would personally deliver it. This sounded pretty good to the king, who had recently seen his riches depleted, due to some unsuccessful visits to the Sun City Casino in South Africa.

I had not been party to these negotiations, as we were all very busy with the location shoot, which would take us out of town for two weeks. In fact, I was starting to get a bit upbeat about the production. The young director had some good ideas, and Marjorie's nude cameo with the Hippopotami would be talked about for years to come. Perhaps my profit-sharing points would not be a total loss, after all. Marj and I were both feeling a lot better about life when we returned to base in Mbabane. We were not going to be there for long because most of the crew had already moved on to the location for our next sequence — the Ezulwini Valley.

In my business, you always have to be prepared for the unexpected. Nevertheless, the sight of Johnny Stompanatti seated at the bar of the Kapola Hotel was a total shock. He immediately locked eyes with Marjorie.

"Hi babe, have you missed me?"

The loud thump was Marjorie hitting the floor. She had fainted.

Naturally, the valets and hotel staff came running from everywhere, and Johnny took advantage of the commotion to take his leave. He threw down his drink, and as he passed, he sneered in my direction.

"See you around, Mr Deadmeat."

Oh my God! Did this mean that he still harbored malevolence in his heart for little old me? And what of his son! Two psychopaths on the loose would be more than one hard-working crime fighter could handle. It turned out that Mr Stomp-on-your-face Snr was a guest of the king, and was not staying at our hotel. At least Marjorie would wake up to find that she was not dead — for the moment!

It didn't take me long to bone-up on the current situation. Johnny had arrived with bags of money, and invested it with the King Mswati Superannuation Fund, not incorporated. Vince had been released from prison, but the small print demanded that father and son remove themselves from the kingdom within forty-eight hours. However, there was a rift at the palace. The Prime Minister had not only lost his personal secretary, but also his nephew. They were one and the same. He was bent on revenge, even if it meant that he was at odds with his lord and master. Actually, the king didn't care one way or the other. He already had the money.

The scenario that developed the next day was quite farcical. We hit out for the *Valley of Heaven* in our four-wheel drive, followed by Johnny and Vince in another jeep, and the Prime Minister's cronies followed them. I could see a showdown looming, and I hoped that we didn't get caught in the middle.

It was difficult for Marjorie to concentrate on her lines that morning, and there were numerous takes. This was most unusual because she was a slave to her script, even one as bad as this. The frequency of the dust storms also didn't help, but she got through it all, and we enjoyed a lunch break at the mineral springs. I had a feeling that whatever was to happen would happen that afternoon. I needed to be alert, and as I might have to engage with two of them, I added more firepower to my ankle holster to supplement my Glock automatic. I was giving the Beretta a rest on this trip.

I always checked out the running sheet before we committed to any location, and today's activities were particularly interesting. We would be in the beautiful Nyanyane Valley, and the director was going to shoot the finale to the movie. They never film in chronological order, and the final action scene was to take place on a granite peak, which is actually called the *Rock of Execution*. How spooky is that?

Marjorie was to grapple with the badass villain, and then throw him over the edge. If the producers had known that the Stompanatti boys were in town, they could have saved on talent fees. I knew that these creeps wouldn't be far away, and they would enjoy the significance of this landmark. I immediately warned Pogo Umbunga, who was in charge of the Prime Minister's small military unit. These lads were an elite fighting force, and they didn't take crap from anyone.

I knew that the New Yorkers were a creative bunch, and the diversion that they created at the *Rock of Execution* would have been praiseworthy, if I were not on the other side. They had kidnapped two lions from the Milwane Wildlife Sanctuary, and let them loose just as the director had called action. Five of the African crew ran so fast, they bettered Usain Bolt's land speed record; and the military unit was not far behind them — an elite fighting force indeed.

When the dust settled, there were only four of us left in the game. Johnny and Vince were both carrying sawn-off shotguns, and Marjorie was vulnerable. She was standing in full view: like a shag on a rock. In fact, she was a shag on a rock.

I was only twenty feet away from the mobsters: mounted on a small pony called Gladys. It may have looked ridiculous to these spaghetti-eaters, but I had a gun in both hands, and I was a crack shot.

"Hey, Mr Deadmeat! Why don't you give us your best shot? Then you can ride off into the sunset. Ha ha!"

I shot Johnny Stompanatti in the bollocks. His face became contorted; he made a gurgling sound, and slumped to the ground in a pre-natal crouch. Vince couldn't believe it. He looked down at his father, and then stared at me with his mouth wide open. Before he could raise his gun, I aimed mine, and rearranged his dental work. At least Marjorie would be able to smile again. She jumped down from the rock, and onto the back of my pony. We trotted back to the camp-site.

A postscript is always important in a story like this, but I am reluctant to elaborate too much as the details are rather disturbing. Whereas young Vincent was to meet his maker instantaneously, Johnny was to linger a little longer. Although he had been de-sexed, the Manhattan mauler was not mortally wounded, but he was losing a lot of blood. He tried to get to his feet, and this he achieved quite admirably. Unfortunately, the rampaging lions, who had failed to catch-up to the rest of the crew, returned to *Execution Rock*, and immediately smelled blood.

The remains of Vince and Johnny were returned to New York in a very small box, and I was happy to be the courier. Those at Frankies had no dispute with me, and we all sat down for a glass of wine, and a bit of reminiscing. In fact, I brought along some company, and it wasn't Marjorie. I had met a fine young man in Swaziland, who had just lost his parents, and I had agreed to sponsor him in America. In order to get him a Green Card, I employed him as my food taster. Would you believe that his first meal in New York was a minestrone soup at Frankies? He never had another one.

How was I to know that Johnny Stompanatti had another son?

THE LADY ON THE TRAIN

It was one of those mornings when the rush hour was beyond belief. I am not a daily commuter so my frustration was intense, especially when the train made an unscheduled stop some half mile short of our destination. I was hanging from a strap in the center of the compartment with all the other sardines, fully deodorized, thank God. I suppose that I should also thank God for the pretty brunette who was my closest travelling companion; she had embarked at South Yarra station. With every lurch of the red rattler, her soft body brushed against mine in a rhythmic repetition of intimate suggestion.

She was wearing a long loose-fitting dress, a designer blazer, and an open-neck blouse — certainly *prêt-à-porter,* but definitely not available this side of Paris or New York. Her perfume was discreet and feminine, and possibly only available in small portions. Expensive! Although the train had completely stopped, my loose arm continued to sway, in anticipation of an imminent continuance of our journey. That it periodically made contact with her groin area was a matter of awkward embarrassment for me, and I wondered if I should say something. In the end, I did.

"I'm terribly sorry, but my hand seems to be out of control down there. I hope I haven't offended you."

"Not at all," she replied. "In fact, it has been quite pleasurable. I regret that I didn't wear my high heels today."

You can't be in a sardine situation, and not listen to another person's conversation. So, this response brought stifled exclamations from the surrounding commuters. There were grins, guffaws, and a shocked reaction from an old biddy wearing a Country Women's Association badge. Fortunately, further conversation was stymied by the movement of the train — possibly activated by the silent prayers of the Muslim woman in the hijab head-dress, who was sitting immediately opposite my good self and the lady with the comfortable shoes. She had an eye-line that would have captured the indiscretions as they happened.

It will surprise no-one to learn that the enchanting brunette and I exchanged telephone numbers on the railway platform, and I also discovered that her plans for that evening were open for consideration. I had planned to sort my sock drawer, but this was something that could be postponed for another day. She accepted my dinner invitation, and so I whisked her away to a small tapas bar called MoVida. This is an unpretentious place in the central business district, and perfect for a first date. We had a nightcap at the Supper Club, and I had her home just after midnight.

Her name was Melina, and she lived in a gated community not far from town. A bit posh, I thought, for someone who was an insurance clerk. Then there were the designer clothes and French perfume. These kinds of luxuries were certainly above her pay scale. The secure accommodation may have been warranted. After all, everybody hates insurance people.

The front door was hardly closed, and she had her shoes off. I slipped out of my jacket and tie. She then noticed the light under the bedroom door.

"I don't remember leaving the light on this morning,"

She pushed open the door, and revealed a decorator's delight. The walls were luxuriant with a rich burgundy wall-paper. A Chinese tapestry was tucked away in the corner of the room beside chintz drapes and matching throw-rugs. There were cushions all over the place, and above the bed was an original Tom Roberts painting. The bedspread was all beads and bobs, silk and satin, and there were antique side tables on either side of the king-size bed. I noticed a half-empty bottle of Scotch on one of the tables. A half-full, cut-glass tumbler was being held by a monster of a man. He was stretched out on the bed, totally relaxed amongst the mass of cushions that supported his over-sized head. In his right hand, suitably cradled under his arm-pit, was a Browning twelve-gauge semi-automatic shotgun. It was pointed at us both.

"Welcome home, Melina darling. I see you have company. I hope he doesn't mind some buckshot in his belly."

I sub-consciously crossed my arms in front of my stomach. He didn't look like he was joking. Melina didn't seem in the least perturbed by the presence of this bozo in her bed. Perhaps he had been there before.

"Paddy Pest, meet Mario Mozzarella, the meanest man in Melbourne."

"Glad to meet you, Pest. Now lie down on the floor, and keep your hands where I can see them."

I did what he wanted, but managed to keep him in my line of sight, in case an opportunity should arise. It came sooner that I thought.

"OK, Melina! Frisk him. If he's carrying, I want to see the heater, handle first. Got that, honey-babe?"

Initially, Melina was resistant, but eventually she did move over to my prostrate body, and positioned herself above my head. She was going to bend over, and start the frisk at my ankles. An ankle-holster is common protection for people on both sides of the law, so it was a good place to start.

I think that I may have mentioned Melina's expensive flouncy dress earlier in this riveting tale. From where I was lying, it was worth every penny, and I could only think of the observant inscription on my front door mat: *Wow, nice underwear.* I don't propose to wax lyrical about the quality of Melina's pins, but I couldn't fail to notice the pearl handle of a small pistol in a small holster that was strapped to her inner thigh. Sure, it was a lady's weapon, but lethal, if used effectively.

It only needed a small touch on her calf for me to convey the message that the klutz that she had picked up on Flinders Street station was a little more savvy than she might have first thought. All I needed was a diversion, and she provided that. Her drapes were open, and the starry, starry night beckoned.

"Oh look, a shooting star."

Mario wasn't the smartest pea in the pod, and this diversion worked a treat. I grabbed the pearl-handled pistol, and pushed Melina aside. Before he could raise his shotgun, I let him have it with both barrels. He caught the first bullet in his teeth, which was pretty impressive. I wondered if he might have been brought up in a circus. Nevertheless, the second shot took out his left eye, and he was dead in seconds. The lady and I breathed a collective sigh of relief.

There were questions to be asked, and I wanted to ask them. However, there was no way that my lady friend wanted to 'fess up to a dead body in her bed, and I agreed to help dispose of the villain. We stripped the corpse of all identification, not that there was much on offer. We discovered a membership card for the Collingwood Football Club. He remained a one-eyed Magpie fan to the end.

On each floor of Melina's apartment block there was a refuse chute that channeled down to a garbage skip in the basement. We tossed the body plus the shotgun and the bloodied bed-clothes down the chute. I checked the basement to make sure that the carcass was well hidden in the skip. They would not discover the remains until the council truck reached the city dump, and finding the scene of the crime would be difficult. At least that's what we hoped.

We remade the bed, and tested it for sex. It was the only thing to do. Tomorrow, one could ruminate on this most intriguing day, and I would try and dissect my thoughts and opinions. In the meantime, I needed to re-establish my softer side. I couldn't believe that I had just killed someone that I didn't even know.

The next morning we put together a make-shift breakfast. There were questions that we both wanted to ask, but she got in first.

"Paddy, I am very impressed with the way that you handle a gun. You're not a pro, are you?"

I could have asked her the same question. After all, with those designer clothes and the ritzy apartment, I had wondered if she wasn't some kind of high-end call-girl. I had also wondered why her chintz drapes weren't sashed. I had stewed over that one all night.

In truth, I already had some kind of answer. While she was in the shower, I did what good investigators often do. I rifled her handbag. Her collection of business cards was most edifying.

She was Melina Smith, Mel Jones and M. E. Pappadopolous. Her titles were very impressive — Chair of the Bourse, Investment Adviser to the Sultan of Brunei, and Director of the Santiago Zoo. The lady was a con-artist. My chest swelled with pride.

At exactly eight am, I heard the squeak of a cat flap, and witnessed a large black moggy stride into the kitchen as if he owned the joint. Evidently, he did. She scooped him up, and smothered him with kisses, and then admonished him for being the alley cat that he obviously was. Fancy coming home at that time of the morning! Nevertheless, the pantry door was opened in ten seconds flat, and there was a can of cat food all laid out for the hungry predator.

I have to say that a chill went down my spine. From my experience, women with black pussies are bad luck. However, my horror stories from Singapore and Hong Kong can wait for another day. I needed to get out of there so I made my excuses, and hit the road — not before we had arranged another date for the following Friday. This was a bold move on my part because all I needed was a black cat to cross my path on the night before a big race meeting at Flemington. The following day, Distant Ruler, the Horse of the Century, was going for his eighteenth win in a row, and I had decided to invest some counterfeit money that I had been saving for a rainy day. In the meantime, I had an appointment at the Dionysus Greek Taverna, a popular café and meeting place in downtown Melbourne.

Con Stantinople had changed his name in order to ingratiate himself with his new-found friends in this new country of hope and prosperity. His departure from his native land doesn't bear talking about because the circumstances are cloaked in confusion and disinformation. Needless to say, he left in a hurry, and with bags full of other people's money. He is now known as Con the Greek, and seems to wield considerable influence amongst the movers and shakers in the third largest Hellenic community in the world.

Unfortunately, his desire for love and affection from his fellow travelers has not panned out so well — mainly due to the fact that he keeps killing people: not that they didn't have it coming to them.

His son, Spiro, was the person on my radar. The lad was a rich kid with an insatiable desire for souvlaki and loose women. I suppose you can't hold that against him, especially as he wasn't a bad apple like his father. Spiro did have good connections, and I wanted to pick his brain. If there was something in it for him, he could be quite co-operative.

"Well Mr Pest, you've come to the right place if you are looking for a woman with a black pussy. Her name is Melina Mercurochrome, and she is some kind of financier. If you wanted a seat on the next moon rocket, Melina would be your gal. It is also said that she does her best work lying down.

That's a bad cough you've got, Mr Pest. Would you like a glass of water?"

I didn't want to know anything else, so we confirmed our non-agreement with a playful arm wrestle, and I let him win. It is always best to save victories for important occasions. The Friday date came around more quickly than I had anticipated. I hadn't even studied the form for Flemington.

Women can be quite interesting at times, and at other times they are totally predictable. Melina was hardly predictable, and Friday night was a bit of a whirl, as I remember it. She had decided to show me her Melbourne, and I have to say, I had never consumed so many sticky food items in my life. The Ouzo was good, too. I met all her friends. There were fat Greeks, skinny Greeks, and Greeks bearing gifts. Strangely, none of her friends were female.

We went back to her place, and I collapsed on her bed with exhaustion. The next morning, when I awoke, I was alone. There was a pitcher of juice on the kitchen table, and a bowl of cat food for *Black Bart* to enjoy when he returned from his nocturnal journey of salacious intent.

I had hardly completed my ablutions when there was a knock on the door. Two burly detectives were planted on the door-mat.

"Are you Mr Mal Pappadopolous of this here address?"

"No I'm not. Why do you ask?"

This wasn't good enough for them. The turned me around, and slammed my head into the wall. Before I knew it, they cuffed me, and shoved me toward the elevator.

"Hey, what kind of police force is this? You haven't even read me my Miranda rights."

For this, I copped a severe knee in the groin, and I blacked out. A splash of water on my face brought me back to reality. I was tied to a chair in a dark room. There was a table in front of me, and a bright light was shining in my face. Two darkened shadows were creaking on chairs with spindly legs. Detectives Dickhead and Dumbnut were eyeing me apprehensively. They were both chewing on toothpicks.

I have to say that this scenario was confrontational, but it didn't seem right. The place didn't feel like a police cell, and it didn't smell like one. In fact, my nose picked up on the most delightful aroma that I could have imagined. It was coming from the next room, and was soon empowered by vocal accompaniment.

"Luigi, Carmine; your linguine is ready. Come and get it before it gets cold."

Beefy and Bozo immediately stood up, and grabbed me by the collar. "Are you feeling hungry, Pappadopolous?" They pushed me through a door, and into a sweet smelling kitchen that was redolent of all things marvelous about Italian cooking. On the table were three plates of pasta. Beefy sat me down, and Bozo pushed my face into the steaming hot bowl. When I re-surfaced, dripping with linguine and tomato sauce, they were already tucking in.

"This is great, Fat Mama. You should be on *Master Chef.* Those other guys are amateurs compared to you."

I hadn't had a chance to pay my compliments to the chef, so I glanced in her direction, and received the shock of my life. She was bigger than the Michelin Man. The lady was wearing an apron, but it couldn't hide the layers of fat that were trying to escape from every nook and cranny. Her smile would have been radiant if it didn't set off her four chins and that birth mark with the hairs growing out of it definitely needed cosmetic adjustment. I couldn't help but think that she would benefit socially if she were also a few inches taller, and not so wide.

"Would you like some more pasta, Mr Pappadopolous?"

"My name is not Pappadopolous. It is Pesticide. Patrick Pesticide!"

"What a nice name. I think I like you, Patrick."

My God! I believe that she was coming on to me. I immediately immersed my face in the linguine, and tried to gag on the pungent and aromatic sauce. If it clogged up my nasal passage, it would be a quick and merciful death. No such luck! Beefy grabbed a handful of my hair, and yanked me from the bowl.

"OK, whatever you name is! No more Mr Nice Guy. Where is Mario's two hundred grand? And for that matter, where is Mario? We haven't seen him for a week, and he never misses his mom's week-end linguine."

Get out of here. Fat Mama was Mario's mom. I couldn't believe it. Then again, perhaps it was a breached birth. Let's face it. These were the two ugliest people on the planet, and if one was no longer with us, where was the pain? I pleaded ignorance.

"I don't know what you are talking about, and I don't know what I am doing here. I have told you repeatedly that my name isn't Mal Pappadopolous, and I don't have two hundred grand. I am supposed to be at a meeting. Please let me go."

"It's Saturday, onion-face. They don't have business meetings on a Saturday."

"Who said it was a business meeting?" I meekly replied.

"So, where is this meeting that you're talking about?"

"Flemington!"

"Ahh," murmured the big man knowingly.

"So, you're going to the laundry with Mario's money, is that it? Spread it around all those innocent bookmakers in the ring; and on the hill. Tell us, crap-face. It's the money, or you're in a box."

If he needed to accentuate his impatience, he did it nicely with another kick into my billy bollies, and I doubled over in extreme agony. If only my friend Stormy Weathers was here to help me. She is a whiz in situations like this, and doesn't take this kind of rough play from anybody.

I have told you about Stormy before. We are both employed on a temporary basis by a certain government agency, and I think it is fair to say that we have a very close relationship. Perhaps that is why I didn't think that it was necessary to acquaint her with the existence of Melina whatever her name is.

In the end, I didn't need Stormy. A stroke of luck came my way in the form of Constable Terry O'Connor. The knock on the front door took all by surprise, but the new arrival had to know that there was someone home because we were making so much noise. Bozo nodded at Fat Mama, and she went to the door. Constable O'Connor already had his two-way in his hand and he was checking a car registration.

"Excuse me, ma'am. Do you know anything about that hearse that is double-parked out front? I have already given it a ticket, but there is an irate motorist who claims that he is blocked in. My information indicates that the vehicle in question has been stolen."

I hadn't realized that I had been delivered in a hearse, and I now accepted the fact that they had only stopped off for lunch. I was on a journey to Fawkner Cemetery, and this didn't please me. Constable Plod couldn't see into the kitchen, but if I could make some kind of racket, the noise would alert him. I decided to make a run for the kitchen window; this was a bold plan as I was still tied, and cowering on the floor. Nevertheless, I made the effort, and jackknifed through the plate glass window, making sure that my face received minimum damage from the flying glass. I then exercised my now-famous rumble roll, and was on my feet immediately, and free.

Beefy and Bozo were in a quandary. They had a bead on the cop, but in Melbourne it is regarded as bad form to kill the fuzz. For the first time in their life, they decided on discretion rather than valor, and high-tailed it out through the back door. Terry O'Connor was already on the blower.

"Ten-four, ten-four, I need back-up, now."

Of course, this left Fat Mama to absorb all the flack and she did the best that she could.

"Would you like a bowl of pasta, Constable? It is freshly made."

They couldn't fit the handcuffs around her hands, and they were quite lucky to be able to squeeze her into the paddy wagon. I was released from my bonds, made a short statement, and was at Flemington for the running of the third race.

"Hi there, Paddy. Do you think that Lurch can do it?"

Lurch was the stable name for Distant Ruler, the horse of the century. He was a big beast, but he wasn't so disjointed that he couldn't win seventeen races in a row. On the other hand, Paradoxical Pete was a weed who boasted multiple convictions for illegal gambling and other minor crimes. He wore all of these convictions like a badge of honor. Pete was a colorful personality at the track, and most people believed that he had his wardrobe designed at the Jerry and Ben Ice Cream Parlor. Nevertheless, he was an excellent tipster and he etched out a living by providing good information to bad punters. The Socratic Paradox that has been laid on him relates to his oft quoted answer to those who would seek information at no cost to themselves: *I know that I know nothing at all.*

I knew better than that, and parlayed his question right back at him. His answer was not unexpected.

"Well, Paddy! They have put the grandstand on him, but he does have a nice barrier, and the jock is confident. They have also injected him with the appropriate carrot juice, so he is a *dead bird* (a certainty)."

This was all I wanted to know. It was good information. I slipped Pete a spot ($100), and went on my way. The money was no great loss as it was counterfeit.

The hype for this race had been quite substantial, and they had a good crowd through the turnstiles. The Champagne Bar was overflowing, but I saw a familiar face, so I went in.

"Hello Paddy, fancy seeing you here. I'm sorry about this morning. I had to do some early financial work. Did the cat get home alright?"

"I don't know, Melina. I didn't have time to stick around. Who's your friend?"

"Paddy Pest, I would like you to meet Con Stantinople. Con has a horse racing in the big event. However, it is not fancied by the pundits."

I knew Con's horse, and you wouldn't fancy it at a Balnarring picnic event. What was it doing here against the best horses in the land? 100/1 wouldn't be overly generous odds so I looked hard at its form. I couldn't help but notice that the trainer was bent, the jockey was bent, and even the farrier had done time. It might be an absolute shoe-in.

In the background, I noticed young Spiro. He threw me a wink, and then went back to some serious canoodling with his model friends. He was certainly riding above his weight, and was buying them champagne with drachma, which had been replaced by the euro in 2002. Con produced a glass of bubbly for me, and Mel swanned off with some of the beautiful people. I skulled the champagne, and then made my way to the main betting ring. The Greek community is well represented in the bookmaker's ranks in Sydney, Melbourne, and all parts west. I noticed that they were all short with their price for Ulysses, Con's horse. Most of the bagmen had it at 100/1, although the Young Turk, Stan Bull, was shouting 200/1. Stan had burst on the scene over the previous twelve months, and was a daring and controversial character. He had attracted a lot of big-spending clients.

I think that he was heading for a fall today. The more I thought about it, the more I was convinced that there was a sting on the way. I went straight to the cloak-room, and handed in my ticket. Out came my satchel, full of fake money. I usually withdrew it, looked at it in the toilet, and then returned it to the cloak-room. Today, I distributed it evenly at all of the tote windows. I would get a smaller each-way dividend on Con's horse, but there was less chance that a bookie would smell a rat. They usually do whenever they see me.

Anticipation was high as the big race approached. All of the jockeys for the big race had arrived to find a small plastic presentation pack of Greek salad in their locker. This was greatly appreciated as most jockeys have a weight problem, and salad has little effect on the scales. The only person who did not eat the salad was the Ulysses jockey. You know how it is. Some people can eat anything, and they don't put on weight. The lad had just consumed a double lamb souvlaki followed by some *Baklava*, and washed it all down with some over-proof *Retsina*. He decided against his usual after-dinner cigar in case it exploded.

When the jockeys came into the mounting yard, the crowd had swelled to immense proportions. They were six deep around the parade ring, and history was in the offing. All of a sudden, Distant Ruler's jockey clutched his stomach, and let out an earsplitting scream. He collapsed on the ground, and was rushed into the medic's room. The crowd went ballistic. Rumor and speculation was rife.

I suppose that I should explain that in situations like this, the jockey can be replaced, as they had yet to go onto the track, but there are regulations about what kind of rider can substitute. You cannot replace a high weight senior jockey with an apprentice. In this instance, there was only one hoop in the jockey's room that was eligible, and togged-up.

Joe Klutz had never raced at Flemington before. In fact, he hardly raced anywhere because the only trainer who would put him up was his father, who had a horse in the next race. When he was announced as the replacement rider for Distant Ruler, the horse's price blew from 4/1 on to 25/1. Ulysses firmed to 3/1 favorite, and it was the biggest plunge ever seen on an Australian race course.

The horses were soon on the track and behind the starting stalls. There were just two minutes to post time when the little person on the second favorite clutched his stomach, let out a blood-curdling yell, and fell off his horse. In quick succession, four other jockeys fell to the ground in pain. One was bleeding from the mouth, another had violent diarrhea, and one fellow was writhing on the ground, having convulsions. The stewards didn't know what to do — after all, the whole nation was watching, and they wanted to see a race. Now, there were only two starters.

In the end, they let them go, and Ulysses started a 3/1 on favorite. However, the bookies hadn't counted on Joe Klutz riding the race of his life. He pushed Distant Ruler out of the stalls, and before they had gone a furlong, the big horse was five lengths in front. At the half way mark, he was fifteen lengths clear; he went on to win by thirty-five lengths. Lurch also broke the track record, and received a tumultuous welcome back to the winner's circle. Ulysses finally made it to the finish, and was booed over the line.

It was Stan Bull not Con Stantinople who made the killing that day, and many questions were asked. Stan, the bookmaker, was found to be innocent, but not so, Mr Stantinople. The *E coli* outbreak was traced to the Greek salad, which had been prepared by Con's personal chef. The big man would not be seen on a race track for the rest of his life. He was arrested and convicted, and passed over control of his empire to his son.

Nobody was in a position to further enquire about the whereabouts of Mario's disappearing dollars, but I can confidently inform you that, for a short time, they were in Melina's purse, before being placed on Ulysses at long odds. Back at her apartment, she was philosophical about the whole thing.

"Oh well! It was only Mario's money."

Melina Mercurochrome: the lady on the train

LE MORT NOIR: THE BLACK DEATH

Chateauneuf sur Charente is a small town in France. As the name implies, it nestles on the Charente River, just a few miles from Cognac. It is more of a village than a bustling provincial municipality, and is serviced by a small regional railway that connects this rural community to the larger towns and cities nearby. I was on the morning run which dropped me at the small one-manned station. That man, the stationmaster, saw the train off, and then disappeared into his office. The willowy woman of mystery who remained on the platform must have been waiting for me. I was the only passenger to alight from the train.

As I bridged the gap between us, I was able to absorb many of her features, and I liked what I saw. She was wearing a uniform that was tight in all the right places, and neatly tailored to reveal a slim waist. Her dark hair was swept back into a bob, and her gendarme's peaked hat was neatly tucked under her right arm. She had a rather regimental posture, and her chest was heaving gently as she waited for my arrival. It was the kind of chest that you would love to pin a medal on.

It was apparent that this policewoman would be more than a handful for the most hardened criminal. All the same, I didn't like her chance of catching many felons on foot. She was wearing high heels.

"*Bonjour, Monsieur Pest. Comment allez-vous?* Welcome to Chateauneuf. My name, it is Yvette Baguette."

Most French people would like to be able to converse fluently in English, but they don't usually have the confidence to carry dialogue adequately, so they often combine both languages in the one sentence. I find it quite appealing, and especially so when the conversationalist is a hot babe. I was feeling quite horny. However, I think that she caught me looking at her bazookas, so I decided to be formal and businesslike. I gave her my heaviest bag.

"Nice tie, Yvette. Let's go."

The two-seater was the smallest Peugeot that I had ever seen. It must have been her car as there were no police markings anywhere. Fortunately, the vehicle had a sun-roof because she was a tall lady. We both squeezed in for the ninety-second drive to my hotel, where I was processed with minimum fuss. In my room, the lass made another attempt to make me feel at home.

"*Monsieur Pest*, 'ave you had *le petit déjeuner*? I get you the croissants. Would you like some wine?"

"Thank you, Yvette, but I have already eaten. Perhaps if you let me unpack, we could meet up at eleven o'clock. How does that sound?"

"*C'est bon, Monsieur Pest*. I will return *dans deux heures*."

"By the way, Yvette, please call me Paddy. Everybody else does."

I have always liked women in uniform, and I could tell that this was going to be a beautiful friendship. Over the years, I have established a working relationship with a number of international intelligence agencies, and the results have been good, especially here in La Belle France. When you work outside the borders of bureaucracy, you can stretch the boundaries a bit and crucial leaks are less likely to occur. The French Government had a significant dilemma on their hands, and it was a wise move to outsource the problem to a reliable contractor. There was also an Australian factor in the equation — more about that, later.

Racial harmony has always been a problem in Europe. With the advent of the common market, German reunification, and other frontier adjustments, the place has become a real melting pot. Immigration and refugee issues have also become more prominent, and the quality of life and the amalgamation of different cultures have become serious political concerns. France, in particular, has had issues with gypsies and Muslims. They banned the burqa, and bought themselves into conflict with some really mean fundamentalist terrorists.

It was explained to me that there had been many terrorist plots over the past few years, but nothing as insidious as their present challenge. MI6 had picked up some electronic chatter in London, and passed on their information to Paris. The information was double-checked with people on the ground, and it was soon confirmed that there was a plot afoot. Somebody was going to poison this year's garlic crop.

The President was alerted to the potential catastrophe, but he was initially dismissive. Everybody knows that garlic is resistant to anything toxic, and is usually resilient enough to survive through flood, drought, atomic bombs and insect plagues. A think tank was established, and the brightest minds in agriculture and biochemistry were brought together to ascertain whether there was any need to worry. It was established that there was only one substance on earth that could kill garlic → Vegemite.

Many of you will not have heard of Vegemite. It is a beef extract that is manufactured by Kraft Foods, and devoured by children across the length and breadth of Australia. They spread it on their toast every morning. It is fair to say that there are also some adult Australians that are partial to this highly unique taste. Everybody else hates it.

It was highly improbably that Muslim terrorists could have acquired large quantities of Vegemite, but there was one person who could find out, and the man from the Elysée Palace had authorized my consultancy assignment. The larrikin lad from Down-Under would save the garlic crop.

Professor Serge Bastille was my go-between at the think tank, and he reckoned that they would need many tons of the black mixture to completely cover the crop, which came from three main areas of the country. The Vegemite would have to be melted down, and could either be sprayed on the un-picked crop or injected by syringe into the pods: a huge task. I think that he thought the whole thing was a bit of a joke, and I like a good joke as much as the next person. However, I was being paid, and the least that I could do was investigate in a thorough manner. I did have my reputation to uphold.

"Thank you, Professor. Your input has been most illuminating. I have the resources in Australia to monitor the movement of Vegemite in recent times, and I will get back to you when I have completed my investigation."

My resource in Australia was a young lady called Stormy Weathers. You know her well. Stormy would infiltrate the head office of Kraft as a temporary computer consultant, and search their files. If she needed to seduce anyone of consequence, she could claim the cost of condoms on her expense sheet. I'm an equal opportunity employer.

The foxy lady came up trumps, as usual, and the spread sheets were most revealing. Twelve months earlier, the product was delivered to all

Australian states in great quantities. Our troops in Afghanistan consumed impressive amounts of the stuff, as did Aussie expatriates in Great Britain. Other international sales were poor: five jars to America; three jars to Germany; and one jar to France. Evidently, someone wanted to commit suicide, painlessly.

This year's sales figures were similar, except for one glaring addition: a consignment of a ten ton container to France. The consignee was not known to me, but I would be soon familiar with the destination address. It was Chateauneuf sur Charente.

Before Yvette left me, I asked what she knew of a gentleman called Michel Montmartre. He was the recipient of the ten ton consignment.

"This man is a mystery to us all, Paddy. He lives on an island on the *rivière*, and does not 'ave the social contact with the village people. Not even 'appy Hour! *Mon Dieu.*"

"Perhaps he doesn't drink alcohol. He could be a Muslim. Does he look like a Frenchman? That name sounds a bit fishy to me."

"I think he comes from Paris, but there are many Muslims in this city. I will make the check on the computer. If there is a bad man in Chateauneuf, we must flush him out."

"Good girl, Yvette. I'll see you at eleven o'clock."

Although I had reservations about drinking wine with breakfast, mid-morning was a different matter, and I didn't want to offend my hosts by neglecting their favorite product. When Yvette returned, we retired to a nearby café, and tried to sort this whole mess out. She had some revealing news.

"Paddy, Monsieur Montmartre is not who we think he is. His real name is Abdul-Azim bin Omar al-Ahmad."

"Ahhh, so he's Chinese."

"*Non, non, non!* He is an Arab, Paddy. A Muslim Arab!"

I fall for it every time. You just can't make jokes with people who don't fully comprehend English. My amateurish attempt at humor was totally lost on this innocent flower so I didn't dwell on it. Of course he was a Muslim, and unless he was brought up in Australia, there would be no dietary reason for ordering ten tons of Vegemite. There was no doubt in my mind that this was the nasty conspirator, but we had to tread carefully. After Yvette and I had polished off a carafe of *vin rouge*, I asked the young lady to drive me to the vicinity of Abdul's residence. It would be necessary to arrange a stake-out, but first I wanted to see if his house was pointing towards Mecca.

If you are concerned with security, you can do no worse than live on an island. Strictly speaking, Monsieur Montmartre, or whatever his name was, was not totally isolated. A strip of causeway connected his acreage to the mainland. It was big enough to accommodate a large truck, and by the looks of the tire tracks, it had recently seen some heavy traffic. I wondered if we were too late.

"OK, Yvette! I'll tell you what we are going to do. Nothing untoward is going to happen until after dark, so let us come back with night binoculars, and watch for any action. I want the gendarmes back at the station on stand-by, should we need to storm the island. Meanwhile, I need to contact Professor Bastille, and find out the latest. If the terrorists have made demands, they would have received them by now."

"That is a good plan, Paddy. I will wear my camouflage ensemble."

I was keen to see Yvette in her camouflage gear. I reckoned that it would be designed by Dior or someone like that. I was going to wear my Fletcher Jones drip-dry trousers, and roll-neck wool sweater. It can get cold when the sun goes down.

"Hello, Professor! This is Paddy Pest in Chateauneuf. Have there been any developments in the case of the Vegemite Villains? We have the prime suspect under observation, but all is quiet on the western front."

"It is diabolical, Paddy. They have already injected a number of produce cases, which were sent to *le President*. Already, two of his food-tasters are dead, and he has invited the leader of the opposition to dinner, tonight."

"Settle down, Professor. Vegemite doesn't kill humans. It only kills garlic. What are you telling me?"

"I am telling you that the certifiable cad has perfected a lethal poison that uses Vegemite as its base ingredient. Omar al-Ahmed is a biochemist, Paddy. We sacked him from the Université d'Orléans, and he has gone feral."

The simple solution would have been to warn the peasants that eating garlic was a health hazard, but who wants a simple solution. These people even refuse to believe that the smelly stuff is unsocial. It would be down to me and my charming assistant to save France from a fate worse than death.

It was horrifying to think that the Froggies were prepared to dice with death rather than forgo their intake of garlic, but such was their life choice. I told Yvette as much as she needed to know, and we settled down for our evening of surveillance. As expected, her camouflage ensemble was stunning. I was feeling horny all over again.

"So, Paddy, this *homme terrible* dilutes the Vegemite here in Chateauneuf, and ships it to all parts of France, where his cunning confreres inject the individual liquid into the garlic. This is unbelievable."

"It certainly is unbelievable, Yvette. You would have to have a sick mind to think this one up. Of course, Abdul-Azim is a biochemist, so that must tell you something."

"The chemical laboratory is in his 'ome, do you think?"

"I do think that, Yvette. Why don't you head off, and get your gendarme buddies? I am going to break into his mansion."

"Oh Paddy, please be careful. Sometimes you can be a little impulsive, no?"

"If you say so, *ma chérie.*"

Breaking into the mansion was a breeze. The big gate was forever opening for the convoy of trucks that were arriving from all parts of France. I slipped in under cover of a slow moving vehicle.

The entrance to Abdul's island home was at the end of the causeway, but there was no sentry on the gate. I expected some kind of security, and it wasn't long before they appeared: two massive Great Danes. They came bounding my way, but Paddy Pest is never caught unawares.

Because this kind of thing happens quite often, I always carry a pound of rump steak with me. However, I wasn't sure that it would be necessary. Omar al-Ahmad and I probably worked off the same list of great Danish heroes, so I used the friendly guy approach.

"Hi there Hamlet, Hans. Nice dogs. Give Paddy a kiss. There, there. Nice dogs."

Hamlet and Hans

Shakespeare's Hamlet was the prince of Denmark, and Hans Christian Anderson was the prince of story-tellers. If there were any other great Danes, Omar and I were probably not familiar with them. It was good to be on a first name basis with the animals, but you can never be too careful. I gave them the steak anyway. It was laced with Valium.

There were three trucks parked in the circular drive outside the mansion entrance, and the drivers were all bonding on the grass verge. When I say bonding, I mean they were smoking foul-smelling *Gauloise* cigarettes, and telling dirty jokes. You can recognize a dirty joke no matter what language people are speaking. I slipped past them, and made my way to a side entrance. The door was open so I went in, oblivious to the possible consequences. Fortunately, the room was empty. It was very much a commercial kitchen.

There was a large electric stove slapped up against one of the walls, and a gigantic range hood that would provide exhaust relief for the many meals that had been cooked here. There were two ovens by the stove, a rotisserie, and also a couple of round ceiling racks that were home to many stainless steel pots and pans. A long wooden table took pride of place in the centre of the room, and it looked like someone had been interrupted. There was a big chopping block beside the table, and the ingredients for the evening meal were on show. Either someone was a big eater or else guests were expected. The pantry door was ajar, and beckoned to the nosy and inquisitive. I was all of that.

The pantry that I was looking at was full to the ceiling with exactly the same thing: endless shelves of Vegemite. I suppose you can fill a lot of shelves with ten ton of product, but this revelation gave me hope. Perhaps the evil biochemist had yet to initiate mainstream manufacture of his molecular molestation. I wondered if the President's delivery was just a trial run.

I heard a noise. It came from the basement, and I would recognize an Arab laugh anywhere. I have played cards with Omar Sharif, and he hardly ever lost. I made my way to a door that was almost open, just off the hallway. A spiral staircase descended into a dungeon of sorts. A single light-bulb illuminated the passageway below. There was another door, and beyond it, more laughter. I was about to walk into the devil's lair.

When you sneak around as much as I do, you have to be prepared for any contingency. I could see that the hinges on the door were rusty, and the last thing that I wanted was a squeaky door to announce my arrival. I just happened to have a small can of lubricating oil in my pocket.

Contrary to public perception, oils are oils, and I wasn't fussy which brand I used. I lubricated the hinges, and slid effortlessly through the aperture. Unfortunately, it was a false door, and I immediately fell thirty feet, and landed on a pile of discarded Vegemite cartons. I was stunned, but none more so than when I looked up to find myself staring down the barrel of a Smith and Wesson Monster Magnum. I had only seen this handgun in the movies, but this wasn't Dirty Harry that I was looking at. It was a dirty Arab.

"So, what have we here?" grunted the grotesque midget with the garlic breath. At least he was still eating the obnoxious onion, so there was still hope for the rest of France. One of his cohorts came forward, grabbed me by the collar, and dragged me into the main part of the room. I was thrust onto a distinctly uncomfortable hard-backed chair, and forced to confront a gaggle of gruesome gorillas: fanned out in front of me in a semi-circle. Two of them were wearing white coats, and looked like nerds. The other three were hard men: thugs to be sure. I came up with the best explanation that I could think of.

"I am collecting for the Red Cross. There was no one upstairs so I thought I might find someone down here."

For this explanation, I copped a right cross from one of the thugs. The other one kicked me in the shins, and the midget cocked his revolver. I have never been a good liar. I figured that the tall swarthy one in the white coat was Abdul-Azim bin Omar al-Ahmad.

He didn't look like a physicist. Then again, who does? You could tell that he was an Arab because he had one of those goatee beards that start under your bottom lip and then leapfrog onto your chin and spread around both sides of your jaw line. He had dark brooding eyes and some pretty bushy eyebrows. His hair was disheveled, but he had plenty of it. He was on the wrong side of fifty, but I couldn't find a bald spot. Having said all that, he wasn't a handsome man, and I didn't like the way that his blood vessels were starting to enlarge. He produced this blood-curdling laugh, and stepped forward with a sinister sneer on his face.

"Who are you, and what business do you have here? And what kind of stupid accent is that? Are you with the police?"

"I will be shortly, Abdul, old chap, and so will you. We're onto you and your diabolical scheme. My government doesn't like what you are doing with Vegemite, and neither do the children of Australia. We are all united in wanting to bring you down. By the way, Professor Bastille sends his regards."

It was quite a show of bravura, considering my position, but it was the message from Serge that really blew his fuse. His face went red, and he hit me with all he had. It felt like a king hit from a queen, and I licked my lips provocatively. It was obvious that I had touched on a nerve — professional jealousy I expect.

"Jamal, Karem, get that liquid extract loaded now. We've got to get out of here. Mustapha, check out the front gate, and repel all intruders. Tariq, you come with me. We have to set the explosive devices. It is time to blow our safe house, and dispose of this interfering infidel. Allah Akbar; God is Great."

When they all went off, I was left to my own devices. As I had been securely bound to the chair, escape didn't seem a likely option. I couldn't help but think that God would have to be great to get me out of this one. I presumed that the explosives would be on a timer, so I was hoping that Yvette and the constabulary hadn't stopped off for a *vin de soir*. I must admit, I had my doubts that the locals would be able to cope with three Muslim extremists who had obviously been trained in a terrorist camp. I wondered if the pert policewoman would regret that she chose to wear her high heels with her camouflage ensemble.

In point of fact, Yvette was already at the front gate, and she saw Mustapha coming. He was such a small fellow; it was difficult to get him in her sights. Nevertheless, she rattled off a few rounds from her SIG Sauer pistol, and he dropped. She and the other gendarmes would have no trouble with the Great Danes. They had awakened from their Valium-induced nap, and were licking the face of the fallen Mustapha. Perhaps they were buddies, or else they were partial to his garlic breath.

At the entrance to the house, the three trucks were on the move. With Mustapha gone, there was no guard for the front vehicle, and a fat, forty-five-year-old desk sergeant with a penchant for Bouillabaisse and Beef Bourguignon, tossed a hand-grenade into the cabin. The vehicle swerved menacingly, and then disappeared off the causeway into the river. Those in the truck behind were shocked. Karem, the invincible one, had once been praised by Bin Laden for his dedicated loyalty, and he stood high above the cabin roof, proudly brandishing his Kalashnikov AK-47. Unfortunately, he wasn't able to get a shot off. He couldn't avoid the overhanging branch from the gardener's favorite Sycamore tree, and was swept off the truck, and into the river. Chateauneuf's favorite desk sergeant scored a further bulls-eye when he lobbed another grenade into the second truck.

I'm afraid that this is where the good news ended. The final truck, with Omar al-Ahmad on board, made it through the barricade, and lit out for an unknown destination. Certainly, there was a highway alert sent out, but Yvette was aware that there was a more important priority — rescuing me.

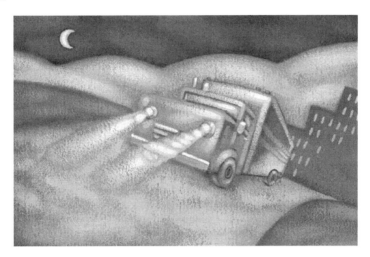

Omar escapes

She couldn't do this herself because she had broken one of her heels, so she sent the desk sergeant to the house to search for yours truly. Unbeknown to everyone but me, the clock was ticking, and there was only ten minutes before an almighty explosion would send us all to the Promised Land. Normally, this would be time enough, but Sergeant Camembert entered through the kitchen entrance, and discovered the meal ingredients on the kitchen table. It was only my plaintive cries from the basement that alerted him, and I was rescued with less than one minute to spare. The house went up in a ball of flames, and I looked forward to showering Yvette with my appreciation — preferably in the shower.

In the aftermath of the firefight at Terrorist Island, the media got hold of the story, and the plot became public knowledge. The gendarmes at the small village police station at Chateauneuf were handed bravery awards, and Yvette became a page three girl in all the dailies. She turned out to be the hottest French babe since Joan of Arc. Of course, she wasn't burnt at the stake, and just wanted to get on with business — as I did.

This wasn't over by a long shot. The road and air search failed to locate the missing truck, and this meant that a mad man and his malevolent mixture were still on the loose. All consumers were advised to check their garlic for syringe marks and a black tinge, but the noxious nerd was creative. If he decided to spike their black sausage, it would be undetectable.

We caught a break when someone reported that they had seen a jar of Vegemite in a kebab restaurant in Toulouse. It was Yvette who brought me the news.

"Paddy, someone has sighted a jar of Vegemite in a kebab restaurant in Toulouse."

"I think we need to check it out, Yvette. It's a bit of a trek to Toulouse. Can your small car make it alright?

"*Mais oui,* of course!" she spluttered, indignantly. "This is a French car. It will never let me down. *Le voyage* to Toulouse, it is nothing."

Unfortunately, Ms Baguette had failed to respect Mr Peugeot's maintenance suggestions, and the car blew a gasket near Marmande, burst a water hose in Condom, and ran out of gas just short of Cadours. As we pushed the vehicle towards the local service station, I couldn't help but notice the crops that were growing by the side of the road.

"*Mais oui,*" said the attendant at the pump. "This is garlic country. Our blue garlic, it is the best in all of France."

He breathed on me as if he needed to confirm this assertion. I paid for the gas, and we continued our journey. It was twenty-five miles to Toulouse. I had failed to notice the jar of Vegemite that was open beside the oils and lubricants in his garage. He was using it to black-wall some motor cycle tires.

The El Forli kebab joint was a bit of an oddity. We had run a background check on the establishment, and discovered that it was owned by Li Ling Lung Ho, a Lebanese businessman whose Asian appearance was decidedly deceptive. I wondered if this was a name of convenience, because when we arrived at the restaurant, the customers and the service people all looked Arabic. The jukebox only seemed to feature Middle Eastern melodies, and every tune sounded the same.

Eventually, Yvette found an Edith Piaf classic, and slammed her money into the slot. Her action only elicited dark and dangerous looks from the few patrons that were hunched over their kebab wraps. When I caught sight of the latest patron, who had just entered the premises, I immediately turned my back to the door, and buried my head in the Toulouse edition of *Allah Akbar*, the magazine. It was none other than Abdul-Azim bin Omar al-Ahmad. He walked straight through the short-order kitchen, and into the nether region of the restaurant.

This was an incredible stroke of luck. It was obvious that El Forli was a terrorist hang-out, but what would we find behind the white-washed walls of this ignominious excuse for a downtown diner?

"We must be careful, Paddy. They may 'ave a cache of weapons back there, and we are but two peoples."

This was the first time that I had ever seen Yvette on the back foot. I think that she loses confidence when she is not wearing her high heels. I squeezed her bottom, to show my support, and immediately agreed with her.

"You are going to have to go for back-up, sugar lips, but make sure that you check the water and oil before you leave. We can't afford any stuff-ups."

I gave her a quick peck on the cheek, and she blushed noticeably. I probably lingered a little longer than I should on her departing form, but I wasn't the only one. One of the customers had his mouth open, and garlic sauce was dripping down his chin. I shuddered to think what thoughts were going through his mind.

From the unseen area of the restaurant, I heard that same Arab laugh that had taunted and tormented me. As I cocked my weapon, I promised myself that it would be different, this time. There would be no pussy-footing around. I barged through the swinging door with my Beretta at arm's length. The scenario that presented itself was not what I had expected.

Al-Ahmad was seated at a table with a steaming hot bowl of lentil soup in front of him. An elderly woman with a distinctive mustache was holding the soup pot, and there was a small child bouncing on Al-Ahmad's knee. I would never be able to take him out without injuring her. I wondered who she was.

"Not you again. Who are you? You're becoming a bit of a pest."

"My name is Paddy Pest, and you are a dirt bag. I have come to arrest you on behalf of the Government of France. I will also serve you with papers on behalf of the Kraft Food Company. They are not happy with the way you have misused their product. Please step away from the table, and separate yourself from that delightful young girl, who probably has no idea what a monster you are."

"Monsieur Pest, this is my grand-daughter, and you are right. She is a delightful young girl, and that is why I am introducing her to this yummy product called Vegemite: the liquid version, of course."

My heart froze. There on the table was a vial of the insidious black liquid poison that he had brought from Chateauneuf. He was going to sacrifice his own grand-daughter in order to make his escape. This mongrel was the vilest scoundrel that I had ever come up against, and he was playing me on a break. There was no way that I could gamble with the child's welfare. Her whole life was ahead of her, and she hadn't even had the opportunity to sample Vegemite in its natural form. They have even released a variation with a cheese mix.

Abdul-Azim backed up to the kitchen door, clutching both the little girl and the container that was full of liquid death. His ever-faithful companion, Jamal, was probably waiting outside with the keys to their transport. I had to move quickly, but his human shield was all over the place as she kicked and struggled in his vice-like grip. I saw an opening around his groin area, but my shot would have to be accurate: otherwise, I would hit the girl, perhaps fatally.

On page forty-seven of the crime-fighter's manual, they say that you should never shoot anyone in the groin unless they are foreign, or they have mistreated one of your lady friends. This situation ticked all the boxes, more or less. I raised my automatic, and was about to squeeze the trigger when Madame Mustache wrote herself into this kitchen drama.

The old cook had been out of my line of sight, and I had never considered her as a player. This was a big mistake as she was still holding the cauldron of hot soup. In an inspired moment, she poured the whole lot over me. I screamed in pain as the searing hot liquid burnt my sensitive white skin. My gun dropped to the floor, and so did I: like a sack of potatoes. She then decided to finish the job, and whacked me over the head with the empty soup pot. I went out like a light.

It was very embarrassing when Yvette arrived with back-up. I was lying on the floor with my head in a soup pot. All the same, her ministrations were first class. Cradled snugly in her arms, I could only whimper as she ran her fingers through my lentil-riddled hair.

"*Mon cher*, you is in pain, no? I will 'elp you with your distress. All France feels *votre douleur*. We will apprehend this monster."

If all of France was feeling my pain, they must have a gigantic headache. Nevertheless, I struggled to my feet, and asked for a report. I had only been unconscious for a short time.

"There 'ave been developments, Paddy. Sales of garlic 'ave plummeted and *le President* 'as urged the peoples not to be afraid. It is good to eat the oignon, but we must first check for the black tinge. *Monsieur President est un homme courageux.* He 'as eaten a whole pod of garlic on live television."

I could imagine how many votes that kind of thing could get him, but I was more interested in the whereabouts of Omar al-Ahmad and his supply of *Black Death.* Yvette was on top of that also.

"We 'ave him under surveillance, but he is behaving erratically. We is waiting your instructions."

This chick should be bottled. She is amazing. So was the story we had just heard from the traffic warden. Evidently, Abdul had ditched his grand-daughter by the side of the road, and set off on a motor-cycle. Jamal was driving, and the mad professor was sitting backwards in the side-car with an automatic machine gun. He was spraying everyone and everything. The highway patrol had received instructions to back off.

"We cannot see the liquid vials, Paddy, but we think they is in the compartment in the side-car. We do not know his destination, but the motorcycle is moving *très vite*: very quickly"

"Yvette, get me a map of the area, and I need a helicopter. Get me a helicopter, now."

The wait for the chopper seemed like an eternity, but we were eventually airborne, and I was able to get a close look at Omar al-Ahmad, who looked rather disheveled. I had always doubted the quality of his hair product, but now confirmation was there for all to see. It was all frizzed-up, and he looked every bit the mad professor that he was. The motorcycle and side-car were painted black and so were the tires. I had seen this machine before: in a garage in Cadours. They had painted the whole bloody unit with Vegemite extract. The man was as mad as a cut snake.

The motorbike was certainly leaving town, and they had plenty of company. The law was in pursuit, but at a discreet distance. The cavalcade of pursuing police vehicles was reminiscent of the O.J.Simpson motorcade in Los Angeles. I could see where they were heading, and I confirmed it on my map: the Pech-David water purification plant. These people drained water from the Garonne River, and provided a drinking alternative for the people of Toulouse, and surrounding districts. The monster was going to poison their water supply.

"Paddy, will we get there in time? There is no landing facility nearby. They are closer than we are. For them, it is only a short distance to the perimeter of the plant."

She was right. We would lose valuable time by trying to land. We needed to stop them before they could reach their destination, but we had no artillery. Madame Mustache had bolted with my gun, and Yvette had left her pistol in the car. She didn't want any bulges in her ensemble that weren't supposed to be there. I looked around the cockpit for alternative weapons, but could only find a plastic bag full of shopping. No wonder the chopper was late. The pilot had been in the supermarket.

I managed to liberate two cans of foie gras, some jam jars and a small bottle of Pinot Noir. How ironic that we were going to try and hit them with some wine that was made from a black grape. The pilot brought the helicopter down, and hovered over the motorbike, which was fast approaching its destination. Yvette dragged the door open, and I pelted everything I had at Jamal. I think that it was the glass jar of marmalade that hit him in the head, and he lost control of the handle-bars. The front wheel jack-knifed, and the bike and side-car cart-wheeled three times before smashing against rocks at the side of the road. An ever-widening black stain seeped out from beneath the side-car, and I could see how malignant it was. All the vegetation immediately died. The wreck ended up a short distance from the entrance to the facility's major water storage.

The pilot put the whirlybird down as close as he could to the wreckage, and Yvette and I jumped out.

"Look, Paddy. It is Abdul-Azim. He is not dead."

The girl had twenty-twenty vision. It was indeed the awful Arab, and he was staggering around the wreckage, looking for something. He found it, and I realized that he had discovered a vial that had not been destroyed. With manic determination, he sprinted for the water deposit, with me in hot pursuit. I wasn't particularly worried, as one vial of the stuff surely couldn't do much damage to the whole water supply. I was horrified by what I saw next. I was transfixed to the spot. Yvette came rushing up, completely out of breath.

"*Mon Dieu!* It is 'orrible."

Abdul-Azim bin Omar al-Ahmad had dedicated his life to science, terrorism and breakfast alternatives. Now, he decided to end it all. He opened his mouth, threw down the black liquid, shouted *Allah Akbar,* and threw himself into a watery grave. Yvette crossed herself, and produced an entreaty to the Virgin Mary. Somehow, I figured that this was one lady that al-Ahmad would never get to meet in the afterlife.

The police arrived with underwater gear, and pulled his body from the pond. His corpse had gone totally black. Vegemite is pretty potent stuff.

"*Sacré Bleu,* the body! *C'est noir.*"

"You are right, Yvette. It is black and blue, and even Jamal will be a little sore."

The only remaining terrorist had been knocked out, but was now hand-cuffed, and in the hands of some pretty fierce looking interrogators. I was sure that he would be able to help them with their enquiries. For me, that was the end of the story. I took a congratulatory call from the President, and headed back to Chateauneuf with Yvette. She had already been awarded her bravery award, but such distinctions were not available to me. However, the town council put on a function for yours truly, and I was awarded the keys to the village. This was mostly ceremonial as no one in Chateauneuf ever locked their doors.

Priscilla and Michaela were two powerbrokers on the council who fussed over me and sought my advice. Between us, we came up with the idea that we could rebuild the Arab's mansion as a garlic and cheese museum. They put a committee together, and I suggested that Sergeant Camembert be appointed Chairman of the Cheese Board. They thought that this was appropriate.

Kraft Foods is a substantial cheese manufacturer, and they were also keen to get behind this initiative. As a sweetener, they gifted the town a year's supply of Vegemite. That evening, I caught the last train to La Rochelle and home. Yvette was there to see me off. She was out of uniform, and I was out of my mind with desire. I had never seen a woman with so many accessories.

Yvette Baguette

"*Au revoir, mon cher.* I will always remember *le Vegemite.* I do not like it, but I will always remember it."

She kissed me three times, and walked away. The stationmaster blew his whistle, and the train trundled off. I didn't look back.

PEST AND THE CANADIANS

You are aware that Stormy Weathers and I are a bit of an item. We hang around together quite a bit, and this day was no exception. We are in the same business, and both find it necessary to carry a piece; she has a Heckler and Koch 9mm P30, while I usually rely on my Beretta. At this particular point in time, we didn't have our guns on us, due to the fact that we were both stark naked. I knew that Stormy wanted to say something, but this was impossible. Her mouth was gagged, as was mine. They had tied our hands behind our backs, and we were both suspended from the roof in some kind of harness.

I had always liked Fisherman's Wharf, but this warehouse was not on my tourist map. The trap-door below us was presently closed, but I had the feeling that this was a temporary state of affairs. Was it my imagination, or was that the gnashing of teeth that I could hear below? The sharks like to congregate around the wharves when they feel like some dinner. I was hoping that they were Catholic sharks that didn't eat meat on Fridays.

One week earlier, we had met these Canadian guys, Linas and Devin. I told Stormy that I thought that there was something fishy about them, but she would have none of that.

"Hey, Paddy, let's invite them out to dinner. They really are a lot of fun."

"Gee, Stormy, I thought that this was going to be our special time — just you and me and a Lobster Thermidor. We've even booked the honeymoon suite at the St Regis."

"Now, there's no need to get crabby. We can still do all that, but wouldn't you prefer to go on a pub crawl? We could meet the guys downtown, somewhere."

The streets of San Francisco

In the end, Stormy and I picked up the guys, and headed for the Gold Dust Lounge on Union Square. We then made stops at Lefty O'Doul's and Tommy Tequila before I managed to isolate one of the lads for a heart-to-heart. They had put pressure on Stormy for a loan of five thousand bucks, and I was keen to learn what commission they expected to pay.

"This is dead set money for jam, Paddy," said Devin, who was certainly eager, if not financially embarrassed. The fact that he had not approached his bank manager indicated to me that there was a certain degree of illegality about the sure-fire earner. Not that this would deter an old greaser like me. Stormy was already keen, but what did she care? It would be my money that they were playing with.

"My cousin in Vancouver has access to an unlimited supply of legitimate designer watches that fell off the back of a truck. His brother is a marine trader who exports Atlantic Cod to a company here in San Francisco. The cunning devil guts the fish and secretes the watches within. We have a lot of end clients, but no working capital. You are looking at a three hundred per cent profit margin, Paddy."

I was also looking at five years in the slammer, unless I could establish myself as a silent partner. Furthermore, I was worried about the opposition who were tinkering around in this market. They don't like competition, and they all had Italian surnames. I was skeptical, but not totally cold on the idea. When one is a committed crime fighter, you can sometimes have misgivings about breaking the law. A few more bar stops, and I would probably be clearer in the head — or not.

We moved on to the Rockit Room and Ruby Skye, and by the time we had last drinks at Hemlock Tavern, I was in. I promised to produce the lettuce before lunch on the following day. Linas and Devin were waiting at our hotel before the midday chimes had stopped ringing. The first shipment under our auspices was on its way, and they introduced us to their California cohort, Charlie Pentzer, who sold cockles and mussels from his seafood restaurant. To my mind, his place looked a bit fishy, and Charlie didn't look like he could lie straight in bed.

I have nothing against guys who wear a rug, but it irks me that most of them think that nobody notices. Charlie had blonde hair and black eyelashes. He also had a hair lip which may have been the result of a confrontation with his fishing hook. When he opened his mouth, his teeth were all yellow. Fortunately, he had made a fashion compensation for this state of affairs. He was wearing a brown tie.

Charlie Pentzer's lips were definitely not kissable, and I was glad that we were only business partners. I made my reservations known to Stormy, and waited for our first shipment of watches to arrive. They were eventually fenced out to various commission agents. This was Tuesday. On Wednesday, both Linas and Devin were dead. You just can't beat bad luck.

You have to be very careful when driving around the wharf area. Their four-wheel drive vehicle was found with the fishes, but although the local police wanted to call it an accident, the coroner was not convinced. Both had been gutted, and they found a heap of Atlantic Cod in their stomach cavities. I thought that Stormy would be shocked, but she was just outraged.

"Paddy, we can't let these bastards get away with this. The boys were honorable men who were up for a little honest competition. We have to avenge their deaths."

As Tonto said to the Lone Ranger; "who is we, white man?" I couldn't believe that Stormy was prepared to take on the mafia over a couple of Canucks. As for honest competition, she seemed to have forgotten that the whole scheme was cloaked in dishonesty. Nevertheless, how can you argue with a woman and why would you want to? I put forward another scenario.

"You know, Stormy, it may not have been the mob that sanctioned or performed this little ritual. Charlie Pentzer had everything to gain by eliminating the middle man. You take two pieces out of the pie, and his cut increases markedly. Plus, I still believe that restaurant of his is a bit fishy."

"It's a fish restaurant, for God's sake."

"All the same, let's snoop around a bit. I feel like a bit of snooping."

We decided to dine at Minnows and Man-eaters, Pentzer's restaurant. It was a cavernous kind of place on the waterfront. A large fishing net hung from the ceiling and the walls were adorned with object d'art of a seafaring nature: everything from shark's teeth to a picture of Moby Dick. I thought that this was rather fallacious, as all of Dick's adventures had taken place on the other side of the country. The table cloths were traditional red and white squares, and the menu was quite comprehensive. We started with oysters, mussels and some clam chowder. I had John Dory for the main, and Stormy opted for the chili crab. We were contemplating the sardine dessert when the proprietor joined us.

"I was shocked to hear about poor Linas and Devin. Nobody expected this. Do you think that there was a fake watch in the consignment, or did we step on someone's toes?"

"Charlie, these are ruthless people. You step on their toes, and they chop off your legs. I would like a list of all the fences, commission agents, and anyone who might be involved. We'll suspend further shipments until I can get to the bottom of this."

"Good on you, Paddy," chimed in, Stormy. "I knew that you wouldn't take this lying down. Let's get 'em."

Charlie Pentzer went a bright shade of red, made his excuses, and retreated to the kitchen. Was this a show of guilt or fear? That was something that I would have to find out. I paid the bill, and we left the premises. A less observant person would not have noticed the shadowy figure who was seated at one of the outside tables. The goon still had his hat on, and could not have been more conspicuous if he was wearing spats and carrying a violin case. While we walked, I asked Stormy to retrieve her mirror, and check her make-up. Sure enough, he was on the move. I wondered whether there would be a second tail on the other side of the street.

There is a real art to having someone followed. You can follow from the back or the front or you can orchestrate some elaborate relay team.

The whole thing depends on how smart they think you are, and whether you are dealing with British Intelligence, the FBI or Maxwell Smart. As I am more in the latter category, I doubted whether the Cosa Nostra would want to diminish their resources by putting two men on the job. After all, they were probably busy with their daily grind of intimidation, murder, smuggling, loan sharking and other forms of racketeering. Who would worry about silly little me?

My plan was to lose the tail, and end up following him. The best way for us to determine whether there were two of them was to split up, so I sent Stormy back to the hotel. The man with the hat stayed with me. It was just what I wanted. I was keen to see how good he was.

People often look at me and come to the conclusion that I might be a little soft. This is not so. I maintain a training regime that keeps me fit and healthy, and I thought that this would be a good time to compare my aerobic capacity with one who probably diets on spaghetti and vino. I strode out manfully along Taylor Street for two blocks, but then had to slow down. The spaghetti was taking its toll, and my tail was dropping behind. I decided to make it easy for him. I jumped onto the cable car at Bay Street. This is the only conveyance that I know that is slower than walking. Unfortunately, he didn't make it. A big black limousine pulled up beside him, and he staggered into the passenger's seat. I diligently noted the license plate.

When I alighted from the tram, I crossed the road to a nearby shopping precinct. The thug in the limo was taken by surprise, and this gave me precious seconds. He slipped out of his vehicle, and tried to follow me but to no avail. I was lost in the crowd of shoppers. The gangster could only throw up his hands in disgust, and return to his car. Meanwhile, I had doubled back and found a cab at the taxi rank. I was now three cars behind him, and feeling smug all over. Of course, cabbies just love the old follow that car routine, but I brandished some dollar notes in front of his eyes and he became enthusiastic. We followed the limo all the way to North Beach, where he was deposited outside a low-life night-club called Pussy Galore. There was no mention of Ian Fleming in the advertising. I hoped that his estate wasn't missing out on lucrative copyright royalties. I have a writer friend who gets very uppity about things like this.

Those creative people from the Beat Generation are probably sitting up in their wheel- chairs, now that I have mentioned North Beach, but it is no longer the refuge for Italian immigrants that it was. Nevertheless, I could still detect a whiff of olive oil and stale garlic in the air. Most of it was coming from the aforementioned club.

As I walked along Broadway towards Columbus, I phoned through the license plate of the limo to a mate at police headquarters. Within minutes, he had a name and address: Franco Fedele c/- Pussy Galore Gentleman's Club. I now knew who had it in for us, but I wondered why he would be so upset over a few designer watches. Perhaps he had too much time on his hands.

My buddy with the badge was little Johnny Weston. Well, that's what we all called him when we danced over a few rip tides together in the eighties. I don't think any of our group missed one surf carnival from Makaha to Malibu, and Jack was the boss. In those days, Aussies dominated the sport, but if he had put his mind to it, he could have been a contender.

The people of San Francisco were lucky to have Jack Weston on their side. He was smart, personable, and boasted a pretty good arrest record. However, you could no longer call him little, and I expect that his first wife Celia had something to do with that. For the first few years as a junior detective, his lunch box was overflowing: mostly with double cheese baloney sandwiches. His baldness was down to his second wife, Dot. She exacerbated stress levels that were beyond acceptable levels. He blames his impotence on wife number three, who he recently divorced — I can't even remember her name.

Over the phone, he still sounded fat and bald. All the same, the man knew how to background a suspect, and I was now a lot wiser concerning the persona of Franco Fedele.

Yes, he was a Wiseguy, and may even have been Capo Bastone, an underboss in the Bay Area. The thug had gained his infamous reputation on the back of some outrageous financial racketeering, and then progressed to prostitution, GBH and probably murder. The perennial cheroot that forever dangled from his mouth made him even more unsocial than his abrupt manner and rude habits. He sometimes spat at women if they rejected him, and it was a wonder that he didn't run out of saliva. He was that ugly.

Of course, I was only looking at an image on my iPhone, and had no desire to get up close and personal. I decided to return to Stormy at the hotel — possibly due to the visions that I was having of a bubble bath for two with caviar and champagne.

When I returned to our suite, Stormy was well into her private ablutions. She had goo all over her face, and two cucumber slices over her eyes. I grabbed a beer from the bar fridge, and turned on the TV: *World Wide Wrestling* was on, my favorite.

I awoke the next morning to see my friend surveying her melons. She always preferred fruit for breakfast, together with yoghurt and dry toast. I was glad to see that the kitchen staff had also catered for me: eggs over-easy, flapjacks, raisin bread and strong black coffee. Because her healthy start to the day was always over before my breakfast, Stormy often tried to distract me with a gratuitous striptease or something equally as disarming. This morning, she was only interested in getting a report on the previous evening, so I filled her in.

"I'd like to get into that club, Paddy. We could find out whether he was running a legitimate business, or it's a front for something else."

I can tell you that Pussy Galore had more front than Macys, but why shouldn't it? It was a topless bar. Did I tell you that Stormy is the manager of a similar establishment in Melbourne? Her input would be invaluable, but that gangster who followed us would recognize her for sure. I wondered if disguise might be an option.

I didn't have time for further deliberation. What came next was a bolt from the blue. In fact, it wasn't a bolt, but a hail of machine gun bullets. My coffee cup shattered in my hand, and I reacted swiftly. Grabbing her ladyship by the waist, I dived for the floor, and we scrambled under the bed. Another round of bullets rearranged the feature wall, and those mock Dali paintings were no more. Beneath the bed, I clutched Stormy so closely that our lips were almost touching. She read my mind.

"No, Paddy. I have already told you. I am not interested in sex this morning."

Damn! Oh well, it appeared that we would live to fight another day as the machine gun had stopped its death rattle. I didn't want to climb out from under the bed, so I took a peek outside the window via the wall mirror. There, hovering beside the smashed glass and burning curtains of our panoramic suite was a Sikorsky S76 helicopter, with its side door open. Squatting there with the gun in his hands, and a big grin on his face, was the man with the hat. When he didn't hear or see any movement from within our room, he motioned to the pilot, and they flew off into the morning sun.

Surprisingly, management was most apologetic, as if it were their fault. They quickly gave us another room, which was all very well, but the snitch that shopped us probably worked on the front desk. I decided to finish my breakfast in their dining room where, once again, I broached the subject of disguise with Stormy. If you want a gay old time, San Francisco is a magnet for show business people, and there was bound to be any number of costume rental companies around. We formulated a bit of a plan. It wasn't a very sophisticated plan, but we didn't have much to go on.

"Stormy, it's too early for the night club to be open. I want you to masquerade yourself and stake out Fisherman's Wharf. I am going to catch up with my pal at police headquarters. We are going to scrutinize Franco, and see what he is up to. The mobster is probably a late riser, but he has to eat lunch somewhere. We'll catch up with him there."

It was hard to camouflage Jack Weston because whatever he wore, he still looked like a cop. We found a costume place on Market Street, and togged up. The end result was a cross between the Blues Brothers and Dirty Harry with a mustache. Dirty Harry disguises were popular in this town. The man did so much to redecorate the city with his .44 Magnum.

Jack helped out with Franco's whereabouts, and this wasn't hard. Everybody knew that Fedele dined every day at Joe DiMaggio's Italian Chophouse. When this iconic eatery recently closed, the Italian mobster was happy to transfer his indentures to the new kid on the same block — Original Joe's.

Everybody knew Joe DiMaggio. He was a slugger for the New York Yankees, but he was a son of San Francisco who married a daughter of Hollywood, Marilyn Monroe. They talk about Joe in revered tones around the Bay Area, and if you were Italian, you were more than welcome at his restaurant. However, life moves on, and so did Franco. He was already inside the restaurant when we arrived.

The mafia man was seated at a corner table, and it was a rare day that he wasn't surrounded by sycophants and other toads. Jack and I were on the other side of the room, but we could have direct eye contact with those at table number one, if that's what we wanted. The California cop gave me a rundown on Franco's table guests.

"The guy in the hat is Salvatore Volk, the wolf man. That is what the name means in Russian. It is rumored that he has an Italian mother, and most people believe that she was one of the Berlusconi girls, who was served by Satan. He rarely leaves Franco's side, and only takes off his hat at funerals. There have been plenty of those."

"I have a bit of history with Sal, Jack. You would probably beat him in an egg and spoon race."

Franco Fedele

This cryptic comment was lost on my friend, so he proceeded with his commentary.

"You may have noticed the three stunning looking girls at the table. Do not underestimate them. Each of them is a martial arts graduate, and their skills with a semi-automatic are impressive. We call them Franco's Flip-Flops. They know how to kick ass."

I couldn't wait to tell Stormy about this. She was the best ass-kicking female that I knew, and I was certain that she would be delighted to lock horns with America's best. There was one other fellow at the table, and he looked out of place; he was dressed like a fisherman.

Over the course of the next ninety minutes, there was a lot of laughing that came from the corner table, but every now and then, Franco and the fisherman locked horns in some kind of debate. The others pretended that they weren't there. Eventually, the man in the waterproof dungarees excused himself from the table, and left the restaurant.

This provided us with a dilemma. Was he an important link in this chain of criminality, or should we concentrate on the main man? As the number of diners was starting to thin out, I had the feeling that we were starting to look conspicuous. We paid our bill, and followed the mariner out of the building. The fish must have been biting lately, because he had valet parking whereas my hire car was on the kerb with a parking ticket attached to the windscreen. It was just behind Franco's limo, with no parking ticket. Jack Weston just shrugged his shoulders.

I had hardly turned over the engine when a tray truck came out of the car park, and turned into Union Street. Thank God for advertising. It had the name *AAA Seafood Trading Company* emblazoned on its side, and a bumper sticker that declared that *Fish is the Dish*. I was sure that I had seen the name of that company somewhere before.

"It's on the first page of every local telephone directory, Paddy. They supply to most restaurants in the Bay Area. However, I didn't know that they were mixed up with Franco Fedele."

Jack told me that the company had a warehouse on one of the wharves, and I immediately rang Stormy and told her to meet us there. I presumed that Mr Triple A would be heading home to his Hake and Halibut, and I was dead keen to find out what other treats were housed in his warehouse. Sure enough, he pulled up outside a long oblong building that backed onto the water. It seemed that he owned or leased this pier. There, bobbing on the rippling surface, were two fishing vessels; each was branded on the bow with the AAA Seafood Trading Company. There was hardly anyone around, except for a little old lady with white hair. She was sitting on a bench, eating her sandwiches. I immediately confronted her.

"Hi Stormy, nice disguise. Has anyone come on to you yet?"

She grunted in disbelief, and wondered how I had recognized her so easily. The truth was that she couldn't bring herself to dispose of her designer shoes. What old lady wears Christian Louboutin stilettos? What old lady has legs like Stormy?

I could see that Jack Weston was impressed, and he even offered to drive her home to her hospice. 'Frisco cops are like that. They are forever horny. I told him to put a cork in it, and we all crept around the perimeter of the premises. The owner had gone in through the front door, but we would be contemplating something far more sinister. We found a side entrance, and I produced my trusty lock-opener.

"Hey buddy, a Swiss Army Knife! I have been trying to get one of those on eBay. Are they good?"

A small click confirmed to Jack that they were, indeed, very good. The door slid open with nary a sound, and we slipped into the warehouse like three blind mice. Fortunately, there was lighting, but it was rather dim. We had cover because there were crates and boxes all over the place. They didn't keep a neat shop, and some of the plastic containers were as slippery as a butcher's prick.

"Gee, Paddy, some of these fish containers are as slippery as a butcher's prick."

Stormy had picked up some embarrassing colloquial expressions on her recent trip to New Zealand, but I was more interested in those cartons that didn't smell like fish. I threw Jack my knife, and he proceeded to lever open one of the boxes. A drizzle of white powder oozed from the package. We all knew what that meant.

* * *

I suppose there comes a time when I am going to have to tell you what this is all about, and it may as well be now. You already know that Franco Fedele is not a nice man, and it looks like Pedro the Fisherman is up to his gills in some kind of illicit activity. We were only minutes away from discovering the nature of this shady endeavor.

You've heard of Jonah and the belly of a whale? This was all about Pedro and the bellies of his fish. He was importing the heroin from Columbia, and he and Franco had all the bases covered. The required bribes had been paid, and the business was flourishing. Enter Linas and Devin with their penny ante scheme: using the same technology. However, they weren't greasing any palms, and it was only a matter of time before U.S. Customs wised up to their arrangement before coming down hard on all the other fishermen.

The Canadians had to be terminated: and all who moved with them. Pedro, whose real name was Umberto Peroxide, already had a sheet with law enforcement, and he would be the first person that they looked at. Jack couldn't wait to contact the drug squad, and went outside to make his call. We should have gone with him.

I don't know whether any of you have ever been coshed with a large sea bass before, but it can hurt. Stormy was in even more trouble. She had a gigantic eel around her throat. This was no way to treat a little old lady. I lashed out at my attackers, but it was a hopeless gesture. We were outnumbered, and they had an unlimited supply of marine weaponry available. We were overwhelmed, and they then imprisoned us in their freezer. It was cold.

It didn't look good as far as our continued existence was concerned. The two of us snuggled together in an effort to share the body warmth.

There was so much that I wanted to say to Stormy and one thing in particular. Once again, she read my mind.

"No Paddy. Definitely not."

I don't know how long it takes for one to expire with a severe case of hyperthermia. I think that we must have been close. My teeth had stopped chattering, and I was starting to nod off when the door opened, and some swarthy sailors repatriated us from the cold store. I still couldn't control my functions, and faded to black. I awoke dangling from this bloody harness. There was my favorite ass-kicker, swaying beside me.

The slam of a car door and the sound of voices alerted me to the fact that we would shortly have company. Footsteps became increasingly louder, and soon there was a small crowd immediately beneath my kerbangers. We were lowered into their midst; there was nobody there that I hadn't seen before.

It was a reunion from Original Joe's. Franco was looking quizzical. Sal was sneering, and the three girls were giggling. The fact that Jack was not with them was a good sign. With a bit of luck, the place may already be surrounded.

In point of fact, the drug squad was tied up elsewhere. One of their own was having a farewell lunch, and they had all turned off their cell phones. To Jack Weston's chagrin, it turned out that they were at Alioto's, a Sicilian restaurant, not any distance from the AAA warehouse.

"Who are you, scumbag?" came the inquisitive demand from the crime boss of Columbus Avenue. "What have you got to do with those Canuck cretins, and why are you snooping around in my friend's warehouse? Sal, bring me that bolt cutter."

Oh dear! This was not going the way that I had hoped. Bolt cutters definitely give someone the edge if they are looking to control the situation — especially if the other person is naked.

"Leave him alone, you bully," shouted Stormy. "Without your weapons and your hard man, you're a pile of shit. I could take you in ten seconds."

Oops! There goes any chance of conciliation or appeasement. The lady is a bit of a straight-talker, and in one foul swoop she had diverted his attention away from me. He had hate in his eyes as he approached her with the bolt cutter.

"I'm going to cut your tits off, young lady, and it is going to take less than ten seconds."

This was starting to turn ugly, and I couldn't imagine Stormy with less than perfect boobies. I had to do something. I then saw our only chance; it was a gamble, but one I had to take.

The trap-door was open in preparation for our forthcoming dispatch, and I decided that we should go early. My girl was between a rock and a hard place. She was teetering on the edge of the open manhole (in this case, it was a woman hole), and the sleazebag was coming at her. I yelled at Stormy to jump. She disappeared into the abyss before Franco could get to her, and then he was on the edge of the trap-door. He turned around to find me charging at him. With my hands still tied behind my back, I hit the sinister Shylock amidships, and we both tumbled into the water beneath. On the way down, I shouted "J-aaaaaack!"

This was perfect timing. Not being able to rouse the drug squad, Lieutenant Weston had recruited half a dozen traffic cops from point duty, and they descended on the warehouse, blocking all means of escape. He heard my cries, and threw a mongrel dog into the water to appease any sharks that might be in the area. This was followed by some life-buoys that he purloined from a sea-shanty café. We were OK. I was treading water, and Stormy had her legs tightly around Franco's neck. At any other time, he might have enjoyed it.

When the drug squad returned to work, they were severely embarrassed, and didn't probe too hard. They concentrated on the cocaine haul, which was quite significant. Of course, Sal and Franco went down for the murders, but my association with Devin and Linas was never really investigated. I just told them that they were two guys that I met on a cruise.

Stormy and I stayed in San Francisco for a while. There was a Lobster Thermidor to consume, and Jack Weston was having a small party. He had been bumped up to Captain, a promotion richly deserved. The dinner was hosted by the station chief, and they celebrated at Original Joe's. Even some of Franco's Flip-Flop girls came along. They had heard that the portly policeman was recently divorced. Let's face it; a good man is hard to find.

Just ask Stormy.

PEST AND THE TERRIBLE TWINS

Melinda and Joan were raised on a small farm in Georgia. Their folks were down-home dirt farmers, but there are no personal records to illustrate the difficulty that such an upbringing might evoke. It wasn't until they were fifteen years of age that the twins were subject to public scrutiny. They had just hacked to death the newspaper delivery boy. The young ladies had just received some bad news in the daily news. Do you think that they over-reacted?

As you might expect, the local press were all over it. The national media picked up on the story later, when they learned that they were twins. That's the twisted logic of the media.

It didn't take the judge and jury long to determine that Melinda and Joan were bonkers, and psychotic to boot. They were put out to pasture at the *Scarlett O'Hara Home for the Mentally Disturbed*. It was a sojourn that only lasted three years. They stabbed a guard, and made their escape in the laundry van. When I say that they stabbed a guard, I mean it. They do everything in tandem. She was found with two kitchen knives in her back. However, I think that it was shock that killed her, if her last words were anything to go by.

"I can't believe it. They were such nice girls."

The youngsters had been on the run for over twelve months, and local law enforcement felt that the trail had gone cold. This is when the regulators reached out to a recommended investigator, who was a bit of a bulldog: me. However, the police chief had initially been a little apprehensive.

"They say that you are the best private detective in Austria."

"This may be so, but I actually come from Australia; Melbourne, to be precise."

"Get out of here. Did you know that we have a Melbourne just down the way in Florida?"

"I did know that. Most of my mail goes there."

Working with someone for the first time can be difficult. The Chief of Police was obviously skeptical about my credentials, and here I was, foisted on him. I suspected that co-operation might be minimal; especially as a quick result could severely embarrass the Atlanta Police Department. After all, they had let the trail run cold.

"I'd like to give you more help, Pest, but with the budget cuts and all, I can't spare any people. However, if you can catch up with these femme fatales, we can mobilize the troops pretty quickly. Good Luck!"

That was it. I was back out on the street with his blessing, and nothing else. At least, I was escorted to the front door by the cutest little gal in uniform that you have ever seen. Marg Scanlan gave me her telephone number in case I got into trouble. I assured her that I always get into trouble.

My first stop was the scene of the crime. Although Joan and Melinda had split, their parents stayed on in their modest timber farm house. Some of the neighbors treated them with outright hostility, and others were loyal and true. It was a rather downtrodden Jill McCrone that met me at the door.

I could tell that the last four years had been hard on her. She was an attractive blonde, forty-something housewife, but the worry lines on her forehead, and the bags under her eyes gave away the fact that there had been a lot of crying and soul-searching in recent times.

"They were lovely girls," she said "but I guess that they just snapped. The paper boy, Andy Rule, was in the wrong place at the wrong time. They had just heard that they had been dumped from the cheer-leaders' squad. It was the most important thing in their lives."

I could understand that. I liked cheer-leaders, but most of the community liked paper boys. There wasn't much sympathy for the terrible twins. After their escape, they cut loose in the nearby town, where security was rather lax. They stocked up with provisions, and then stole the sheriff's recreational vehicle. It was found abandoned by a bus stop in Savannah, two days later. Since then, the only sighting of the twins was in a bar in Colorado Springs, but the informant was not a good witness. He was so wasted, he was probably seeing double.

The sisters seemed to have disappeared into thin air, and I figured that my only chance of finding them was if they were to re-offend, in same way. I was hoping that it wouldn't be another murder. Just as I was beginning to despair, a report came out of Houston, which caught my eye. There had been two bank robberies in different parts of the town, at the same time of day. In each case, the description of the female participant was identical. I made my way to the airport, and caught the Texas Flyer. Police Chief Godkin had paved the way with an introduction to the local authorities.

"We're certainly baffled by this one, Mr Pest. We haven't seen a female bank robber on our patch since Bonnie Parker. And you say that they might be twins?"

Neil Imlach was the most senior detective in the armed robbery squad, and I could tell that he had a wise head on his shoulders. There was also a fair bit of dandruff, but I didn't like to say anything in case he was sensitive. He certainly was casual. Although the uniform boys were all buttoned up and looking ultra efficient, Neil was cool in a garish Hawaiian shirt of outlandish colors. The perps would see him coming a mile off, but they wouldn't know what was hanging from his trouser belt: one Smith and Wesson .40 caliber semi-automatic handgun; one pair of standard issue handcuffs; a baton; an X26 Taser; a canister of mace; and usually a couple of donuts from the nearby diner.

The man was prepared for anything, and he was also very accommodating. He escorted me to an acceptable hotel, and helped me settle in. I promised that I would keep him informed of any progress that I might make. My first visit was to the library. I wanted to catch up with the local news.

I trolled the social pages of the Houston Chronicle for the last twelve months, and it wasn't long before I scored a hit. There in the middle of some fund-raising benefit was a Texas dude with a blonde on each arm. Joan and Melinda had certainly matured over the last four years, and they were more beautiful than ever. I jotted down the name of their escort, and returned to police headquarters.

"We don't have to access any records for this one, Paddy. Chuck Lenegan is one of the richest men in the area. He has a spread just north of here, and it is a big ranch."

"How big is a big ranch?"

"Well, if you were on horseback, it would take you all day to ride the boundary of his property."

"I used to have a horse like that. I would like to see the place, but perhaps I'll try a different transport system."

I didn't like to be conspicuous, so the Piper Cherokee that I hired at the airport came with an advertising banner, which proclaimed that you should eat at Luigi's Pizzeria. We did a few turns over Lenegan's ranch. It was big alright and well guarded. The house was a mansion. Through my binoculars, I could also make out some dogs and a few people around the pool. It looked like Joan and Melinda were permanent residents. I decided that I would take a closer look after everyone had gone to bed.

I slipped over the outer wall well before dawn. It would take another thirty minutes to get to the main house. I was glad that I had brought my fold-up bicycle, and certain other accessories that would make James Bond jealous. The dogs would be first to investigate my arrival, and I was ready for them. I hit each Rottweiler with an anti-bark dart, and laid out the poisoned steaks, which they demolished in a less than a minute. I gave them time to slip into the nether world, and then proceeded to the edge of the house. The guards seemed to circumnavigate the house once per hour, and the crunchy pebbles gave me suitable warning. The guard house was by the first tee of the golf course, which reverted to a club house during the daylight hours.

It didn't take me long to get into the mansion; my Swiss Army Knife picked a window lock, and I turned on my night goggles. Fortunately, I had also brought along my Sonnombulator. This is space technology at its best, and I had nicked the unit from Cape Canaveral, when I was there, last year (Pest Takes a Chance — it is never too late to buy a copy).

The small featherweight aluminum box disburses sound lasers that collect and isolate snoring noises, and indicates whether they are male or female; also at what distance and height. I determined that both girls were on the second floor, and that they were sleeping alone. The other possibility was that Lenegan was sleeping with his wife, and she didn't snore, but this was long odds. They were divorced.

The first bedroom that I entered belonged to Joan or Melinda. How does one tell? After all, they are twins. She was naked on the bed, and her bed clothes were in disarray. It was a hot night, but it was obvious that she was a restless sleeper. In between her intermittent snoring, she moaned and groaned and tossed herself around. With my infra red glasses working perfectly, I scanned the room for any definitive proof of her identity; not that I had any doubts that this innocent looking rose was one of the Andy Rule murderers.

In the corner of the room was a hat-stand that was overloaded with bonnets and scarves and other furry headgear. There was a small desk with an open lap-top on it. The screen saver was the usual Harry Potter garbage. Hanging on the walls was an assortment of posters of Johnny Depp, Lady Gaga and Wonder Woman. This was a typical teenager's room. On the back of an open wardrobe door was a group photo of the Dallas Cowboys' Cheer Squad. Two of the girls were in the gun. They had hair-trigger rifle sights painted over their hearts

I suppose that I could have stayed around and opened a few drawers, but I thought that she might wake at any moment so I moved into the en suite. One should have been more careful, but I didn't see the rubber duck on the floor. It was one of those squeaky ones. It let out a yelp when I stood on it, and the restless sleeper sat bolt upright in bed.

"Who is there? What do you want?" There was no sound, but the flapping of the curtain by the open window. Perhaps there were uninvited ducks in the swimming pool. I could see through the crack in the door that she was still in bed, and looking quite terrified. The silence was broken with a small knock on the door, and the other twin poked her head in the door.

"Joan, is everything OK? I had a premonition that something was wrong."

What is it with twins and their extra sensory perception? A small intrusion and Melinda has come to the rescue. Not only that; a small four-legged critter padded into the room, and jumped up on Joan's bed. She clutched the Welsh corgi to her bosom as if there were no tomorrow. From my vantage point behind the crack in the door, I thought I could see a look of satisfaction on the mutt's face. Lucky devil!

What came next frightened everyone. The old Klaxon alarm, when repeated, provides fair warning that something is amiss. Downstairs there was shouting, and lights started to appear in all parts of the mansion and its surrounds. The guards had obviously found the drugged dogs. This was not looking good for me. Joan quickly slipped into her robe, and the girls departed the bedroom. I was right behind them at a discreet distance. They went downstairs. I tried to find an alternative refuge.

I found myself in the servants' quarters, and ducked into the only room that didn't have a light shining from beneath. It was the butler's room, and he was just beginning to stir from a deep sleep. I noticed some sleeping pills on his night table. I put him back to sleep without recourse to that kind of thing. To be safe, I pushed a couple of pills down his throat, tied him up, and hid him under the bed. I then borrowed his wig and pajamas, and settled in his bed for a well earned rest. I knew that the guards would enter the room, and see the pill box. I would be safe until later in the morning.

Later in the morning, I moved the comatose butler to a less obvious hiding place. I put him under Chuck Lenegan's bed. The residents and staff were all downstairs, having a meeting to determine what this was all about. I was able to eavesdrop at the top of the stairs. I could even see part of the action. They had this fat Italian guy strapped to a hard back chair, and were beating the crap out of him.

"OK, Luigi, one more time. What were you doing flying around my place in a light plane, yesterday? There is no point lying. We saw your ad."

"I tell you, Mr Lenegan. I only pay for weekends. It is not my aircraft. You must talk to the pilot, or the airport manager. I pay little but give them free pizzas for the service. You must believe me, Mr Lenegan."

"OK, I believe you, Luigi, but we must keep you here until we clear this up. Sonny, take the pizza man down to the cellar, and let him try a bottle of my very special Chianti. After lunch, I want you and Mickey to take the Merc and visit our friends at the airport."

He threw the car keys to his hard-assed bodyguard.

I don't have to tell you that this opened up the possibility of escape for me. There was no point in hanging around until nightfall because I had no more meat for the dogs, and I am sure that they would have discovered my foldaway bicycle. While the kitchen staff was serving lunch, I slipped out to the driveway, and with my infra red goggles and Swiss Army Knife at the ready, climbed into the rear of the Mercedes, and closed the trunk. About an hour later, the luxury vehicle pulled into the car park of the Houston Hobby Airport. I gave the lads a few minutes to walk away, and then got to work on the lock with my knife. I was just finding my feet when the racy lady from the booking office walked by. She was obviously returning from lunch.

"Hello, Mr Pest. Don't tell me that you are back for another joy ride? Flying can be quite exhilarating, can't it?" she said, as the top button of her blouse involuntarily slipped out of its eyehole. The upward pressure of her breathing was too much for the under-rated pearl clasp, and I was dragged along the footpath in the aftermath of my interest.

"No, not really; I have misplaced my hat, and I thought I may have left it here."

"Well, let's look in the office, shall we? We do have a lost luggage room. You can't get by without your hat, can you?"

I could see that Lenegan's thugs were talking to the pilot on the tarmac, so the office would probably be a safe place to be. I didn't expect them to walk in the door a few minutes later.

"Why, there he is, there. Hey, Mr Pest; these gentlemen would like to talk with you."

Calling them gentlemen was a bit of a stretch, but I went along for the ride.

"What can I do for you fellas? Did you find my hat?"

"We want to know what your interest in Mr Lenegan's ranch is, and why you buzzed us yesterday. This is private property, and the boss doesn't take kindly to snoopers."

From the corner of my eye, I could see the office staff taking refuge behind the booking desk, and I knew what was coming. Sonny's right cross didn't quite make it. I ducked, and spun him around in one movement. The kidney punch hurt him, and so did the knee in his nether region. He dropped like a sack of spuds. Mickey was going for his gun, but he was as slow as a crippled crab. I broke his nose for him, and slammed him into the frequent flyer counter. The kick in the groin was just for good measure. They were totally disabled. A soft voice called out from behind the desk.

"Mr Pest, I think we've found your hat."

I collected my hat, and retrieved the car keys from the designated driver. Lenegan would not be pleased when the lads returned; all bloody and bleeding, and with his favorite set of wheels missing. I immediately drove the car to the worst neighborhood in the city, and left the vehicle with the keys in it. I hoped that the boys in the 'hood liked German wheels.

As I expected, Sonny and Mickey were dead-meat. Literally! As Joan and Melinda looked on, the Rottweiler dogs savaged the juicy bits of their corpses. They would probably only need one Chicago overcoat (coffin) for the two of them. It was a public demonstration that enhanced Chuck's reputation as a man who doesn't abide failure. This was all lost on the girls. They just got an exhilarating thrill from this kind of stuff, and their libido increased markedly. Joan turned to Melinda.

"Are you feeling randy, Mel?"

"I am, dear sister, but you can borrow him for the afternoon, if you like. He is over by the pool."

Randy Rapadopoulous was Lenegan's pool boy, and he also did other odd jobs. He had a room over the garage, and often entertained the teenage girls. It was a risky adventure, but the fellow was not known for his brain capacity. However, he did have quite a bod, and that was an adventure of discovery that the girls enjoyed.

At some time in the late afternoon, Chuck got word from one of his city cohorts that his Mercedes had been seen in Hillcroft. This is not an up-market area, and he would probably have to reclaim the vehicle from a young gang leader. As these kids were usually more bark than bite, he wasn't particularly worried. Melinda hammered on the door of Randy's room.

"Joanie, get out of there. Chuck wants Randy to drive them into town. I mean like now." The blonde bombshell was not prone to urgency, but Randy was. He pulled on his pants, and combed his hair. You've got to look your best if you are driving for the boss. With Sonny and Mickey gone, there was an opening for a chauffeur, and it sure beat pool cleaning.

An hour later, Chuck, Randy and two gunmen were cruising the streets of Hillcroft, looking for anyone who might know where the Mercedes was. They came across a sizeable group of youths near a suburban youth center. The guys slowly exited their vehicle, and walked over to the group, who were all pumped up, and kitted out like Pancho Villa. You get that with Mexican gangs.

For Chuck, it wasn't difficult to isolate their leader. He was leaning against the wall with a sweet-pea on either side. They seemed to be attached to his arms. The tooth pick that was protruding from his mouth was overdramatic, to say the least. Chuck explained that he was looking for his car, which had been seen in this area. The gangster was quite polite, but the young punk chose to be aggressive.

"Why should we help you, fart face? We don't like Gringo's around here."

Chuck took out his .45 revolver, and shot the young fellow between the eyes. The girls screamed, and everyone bolted. When the pandemonium was over, the killer turned to find a very young boy standing beside him; as cool as you like.

"Well, young man. You seem to have more balls than the rest of them put together. Would you help me with my enquiry?"

"Sure thing, mister, but it will cost ya."

A big grin came over Chuck's face. He saw in the young lad, a version of himself at the same age. He responded gratuitously.

"Randy, give the kid twenty bucks."

With the completion of the transaction, the young lad mounted his bike, and sped off. Chuck had an address for the leader of a rival gang. He was so tough; he still lived with his mom and pop. They would visit him, that evening.

* * *

They found the Mercedes parked out front in good condition, and the doors were locked. If the vehicle was owned by the Police Commissioner, it would be on blocks, devoid of any saleable spare part. There is a certain respect afforded those who carry a big stick. The delegation from Rancho Lenegan knocked on the front door. It was a small walk-up terrace with the possibility of a getaway down the fire escape. Chuck sent one of his henchmen out back with the instruction to block all exits.

A tall hard-boned woman answered the door, and she was pushed aside as Chuck and his entourage burst into this humble abode. In the foyer, they were met by a man wearing glasses with a newspaper in his hands. He assessed the odds, and decided to be co-operative. His son was upstairs, studying. Yeah, right!

"Freddy, there are some folks here to see you. They say you have the keys to their car."

Freddy appeared at the top of the stairs. He was wearing an Abercrombie and Fitch T-shirt and faded jeans. His dark hair was slicked back, and he had a smirk on his face. Quite frankly, he looked like a jerk. However, he was a smart jerk, and decided to remain at the top of the stairs.

"I don't know what they are talking about. As you know, my choice of transport is a Harley Roadster."

Chuck took a deep breath, removed his trusty firearm from inside his jacket, and put a bullet through daddy's brain. His recently widowed wife started gagging, and Freddy went as white as a sheet, but had the presence of mind to run for the fire escape. A shot rang out, and everybody heard the body fall to the ground. This was too much for the lady of the house. She went into hysterics, and Chuck decided to take pity on the neighbors. He shot her as well.

Randy was dispatched to recover the car keys from Freddy's room, and they all left the house well pleased; and well fed. They had found an excellent Green Zebra tomato salad in the kitchen. If they didn't eat it, the crime scene investigators would.

The end of this little episode would have its climax a short while later. Randy had a bit of trouble getting the car started, but on the third attempt the engine turned over, and the Mercedes exploded in a ball of flame. In fact, both cars were totally destroyed, and all the occupants were DOA at the local hospital. Someone had it in for Freddy, but this was a turf war that had snared a bigger fish. Senior Detective Imlach would be well pleased.

He found out about the explosion before I did. The names of the victims were announced on the television news, and the girls and I probably saw it at the same time. They were at a downtown pool hall, and I was in my hotel room. I rushed over to police headquarters. The saucy sisters rushed to the Amtrak station. No luggage! No goodbyes! They boarded the first train to San Antonio. There was no life in Houston without Chuck's protection.

Unaware that the terrible twins had departed the city, I hitched a ride on the police paddy wagon that departed for Rancho Lenegan. In the light of day, I must say that the compound was not unlike J.R.Ewing's Southfork Ranch, although the people were a lot nicer. With many of the nasty residents gone, the survivors were mostly the house staff. I made a point of apologizing to the butler, who had been found under the bed by the maid. However, I could tell that we would never be best friends.

No-one knew where the girls had gone; perhaps a beauty parlor or a disco. Somebody seemed to think that they were part of ten-pin bowling team. An older, less generous member of the staff suggested that they were on the streets, on the game. Then again, Melinda had called her a slag, so there was probably retained resentment there. What is it with women? Why can't they get along?

"There's not much for you, here, Paddy" said Neil Imlach. "If the girls have heard about this tragedy, I can't see them returning to the ranch. We have them in the gun for those robberies, and you know too much about their other skills. We'll put out an APB, but you will just have to keep your fingers crossed."

Back in my hotel room, I decided to report back to Chief Godkin in Atlanta. He was impressed that I had tracked down the girls, but not so impressed that I had lost them. Nevertheless, he authorized the continuation of my contract, so I accessed the Amtrak journey planner, and tried to figure out where the girls might have gone. The airport and hire-car companies had already been checked out, but there was one important reason why they might travel by train; you don't have to give anybody your name.

Amtrak's Houston outpost used to be called Grand Central Station. It is not so grand, anymore. There is one side platform, an island platform and two active tracks. Other tracks and platforms have been abandoned. Just a reminder of the good old days! The station master would have to remember two stunning looking female passengers, unless he was gay or senile. He was neither, and his tongue was still hanging out when I provided a description.

"I remember them well. They were such lovely girls; although they did seem to be in a bit of a hurry. They asked whether the train could leave fifteen minutes early. We only do that kind of thing for George Bush and other *Good Ol' Boys*."

I could see that San Antonio was a major stop on the route, but one could transfer to the Texas Eagle service, and be in Dallas eight hours later. My mind raced back to that poster on the back of Joan's wardrobe door. Was there about to be two vacancies in the cheer squad? I hoped that I was wrong.

So, it was to Dallas that I traveled. A quick kip, a bit of a freshen-up, and there I was: outside the Dallas Cowboys facility at Valley Ranch. The cheerleaders had a dance studio within the complex, and if auditions were taking place, this is where I would find the escapees. I wondered if the targeted high-kickers would end up with a debilitating injury in order that the twins make the finals. I really was at a loss. After all, they were such nice girls. Everybody said so.

During my initial investigation, I had tried to find some rhyme or reason for their unsocial activities. Everybody told me that the McCrone twins were not devoid of talent. They were dropped and disbarred from other groups because they caused friction in the team. They also caused a lot of broken bones, and were generally regarded as bad luck babes. In Texas, they take cheerleading very seriously. In 1991, Wanda Holloway from Channelview was charged with hiring a hit man to murder the mother of one of her daughter's competitors. The kids were both thirteen years of age.

I don't know whether Joan and Melinda have ever been to Channelview, but I don't think that they would be hiring a middle man. They would do the job, themselves. I wished that I had taken more notice of the wardrobe poster. I was hoping that Neil Imlach had retained it as a souvenir. I rang him.

"Neil, I need to know the names of the two targeted girls on the DCC poster. Do you still have it?"

"I gave it to my son. He knows all of them by name. I'll track down their addresses, and get back to you. How are they looking after you up there? Have you been to the Old Texas Book Depository?"

"I'm happy with my Kindle, Neil. Perhaps when I am sure that it is safe!"

"Come on Paddy, take a chance. Even the Kennedy's have been back. It's a great town if you've got a few hours to kill."

I wasn't sure that his choice of words was appropriate, but I knew that he was trying to be an ambassador for the Lone Star State, and let's face it; the eyes of Texas would be upon him if the terrible twins cut up rough. The girls had been living under his nose, and with the Johnson Space Center just down the road; you would have thought that they could even have picked up on Joan's small tattoo. While I was in her bedroom, I found it quite mesmerizing.

When Neil's list arrived, two names stood out. Heidi Schmutt and Erika Eriksson were certainly second generation Americans at best, and although they might be sold on hamburgers and pumpkin pie, the twins would probably see them as European interlopers who had stolen their birthright; a place on the Dallas Cowboys Cheerleaders squad. These ladies would need my protection, and after another glance at their pictorials, I was glad to give it. I hurried over to Heidi's house.

It was a large contemporary apartment, actually, and Heidi answered the door on the third ring. She was wearing a tank top that would make a tank commander blush. My eyes slowly drifted down past her exquisite navel to a pair of hipsters that looked like they had been painted on. Her ensemble was minimal, but effective. The pink pumps that she was wearing set everything off just fine. A small dog was panting at her feet. He had a pink ribbon around his neck.

I didn't want to alarm her so I broached the subject of her safety with all my renowned delicate discretion.

"Hi there, Heidi; my name is Paddy. Somebody is trying to kill you. Can I come in?"

The cheerleader was not alone, and her room-mates were both stunning blondes. One was draped across the settee, reading a fashion magazine. The other was perched on the edge of a chair, painting her nails. She flashed me a smile that would stop a raging bull. Introductions were made, and I accepted the offer of a low-fat beverage.

Although the others were not part of the plot, I included them in the briefing because I think that it is important for youngsters to be aware of the perils associated with cheerleading. I also explained that I didn't think that Joan and Melinda would be fussed with a bit of collateral damage.

"Gee, Paddy if there is any collateral damage we'll get the landlord to fix it."

I let that one go through to the catcher, and asked to see their bedrooms. They needed to re-arrange their pleasure palaces because having beds under windows is too easy for a bomb throwing maniac: male or female. I think that they accepted the rudimentary protection advice that I gave them, but was it enough? The twins were tough teenagers, and they were imaginative.

I said my goodbyes, and this included a hug and a kiss from all of the girls. I couldn't believe that I was getting paid for this. Still, somebody has to do this kind of thing, and I did have another call to make. I would shortly be on overtime.

Erika Eriksson was not so accommodating.

"Who the hell are you, and how did you come up with such a cockamamie story? Are you a pervert or something? Get out of here."

Naturally, I was taken aback to think that someone would think that the little man from Melbourne was some kind of pervert. After all, I was on a mission of mercy, and this kind of welcome was beyond the pale. I stared at the closed door for a moment, and then retreated to a nearby cantina where they served the largest Blue Margaritas in the world. Perhaps I would return to visit Erika Eriksson the next day.

That night, a semi-trailer, carrying inflammable liquid, ran off the highway, rolled down an embankment and landed on Erika's house. The occupants were burnt beyond recognition, but dental records confirmed the residents as Erika, her lesbian lover, a cockatoo and two goldfish. Obviously, they didn't have dental records for the goldfish, but as they were in water, they were preserved. However, I think they may have died from renal failure.

All of the cheerleaders attended the funeral and Heidi was particularly nervous. I offered to move in with her until these demonic dames were apprehended. Yes, you guessed it. Melinda had acquired a trucker's license in Houston, and had probably seduced the driver or drugged him. His was the only corpse that was smiling.

It was hard to convince the chief cowgirl that this was more than an unfortunate accident, and there was no way that she was going to let me interfere with the forthcoming auditions. They don't even let parents into their sacred auditorium during the try-outs. The Dallas police were a different story. They had been briefed by Atlanta and Houston, and they don't like crazies on their streets. They had the area staked out all the way to Fort Worth.

For what it is worth, I didn't think that the sisters would show. They must have seen the increased police presence, and who would gamble their life on the chance to parade around with a few pom-poms? Well, what did I know?

They were first sighted in the registration queue, and I don't know how they got that far. Then it was the rest room. They went in as blondes and came out as redheads. You can do that kind of thing if you are a woman. I left my observation point, and rushed down to ground level. The noise level was unbelievable, and so was the standard of conversation. Every second person was texting, and I was carried along in the crush. Unfortunately, a big brute of a doorkeeper put an end to my journey.

"Sorry, fella; it is ladies only from this point."

I don't have to tell you how this ends. Both Joan and Melinda breezed through their audition, and ended up as two of the most promising recruits. The also-rans were dismissed, and the main contenders were transported over to the main stadium to absorb the reality of how the real thing might feel. They arrived in advance of wailing sirens and general police activity. If Joan and Melinda had been aware that Dallas' most infamous law enforcer, Colly Baybee, had personally taken over the woman-hunt, I think they would have surrendered immediately.

Baybee had an arrest record that was second to none, and he wasn't one of those new age technocrats with no street cred. He was big, burly and brusque, and had bullied his way from the mean streets of Avery and Alvarado to Amarillo and Abilene. He made detective in Houston and captain in El Paso. He was now the longest serving police officer in Texas, and probably the most obnoxious. Two little chicky-babes from the east coast would be no problem for Colly Baybee. His sergeant handed him the loud-hailer, and he took up a position outside the front entrance to the stadium.

The Cowboys stadium is a marvel of twenty-first century creativity. It is futuristic in design, and resembles a football with its ass blown out. There is a large light-well above the arena, and multi-storied walls of glass and curved panels give off a sheen that is a beacon to all those who worship at the well. The domed roof sits comfortably on top of this tabernacle of testosterone, overlapping the structure below; which incorporates angular steel girders of every size and description. It looks like a beetle waiting to be circumcised.

The cheerleaders were in the main arena when the police arrived. I wasn't far behind. The girls were clustered around their guide, who was pointing out some of the architectural marvels of the stadium. When they broke ranks, they found that they were surrounded by a SWAT team. They don't do things by half in Dallas.

Were the terrible twins there? No, they weren't. They had slipped away somewhere on the concourse, but the sisters had not left the building. Everyone was sure of that. All of a sudden, one of the cheer squad shrieked out.

"Look, its Joan and Melinda."

All eyes looked to the ceiling, and sure enough, the girls were picking their way through the maze of lights and aerial ropes that typify the grid support that is necessary to put on a game of night football. It looked like they were trying to get onto the roof. In fact, there was no doubt that they were going to get on the roof. At this stage, cell phones all around me were buzzing, and I was pretty sure that the media would be onto this in a flash. By the time I made it to the apron of the stadium, there were helicopters in the air; some were police choppers, but the news boys were also well represented. They were all strafing the roof with their searchlights.

The girls had made their way around to the front of the big dome, and were butt-sliding their way down to the overhang of the front portal. There was a flat surface there, and they were going to use it as a stage. Sure enough, they stood up, straightened their uniform, and started their pom-pom routine. Some of the officers below started clicking their fingers, and one of them whistled. He has since been demoted to beat duty.

You have to hand it to the sisters. They wanted national acclamation, and now they were getting it. Across the nation, television programs were interrupted with a live cross, and they were showing the world what a few gals from the back-blocks of Georgia could do.

Unfortunately, the television audience got more than they bargained for. When they had finished their routine, the two lovely girls waved at the assembled crowd, totally ignoring the ranting of the fellow with the microphone. The sisters embraced, and then Joan did a one-and- a-half with pike off the roof, and splattered herself on the pavement. Melinda followed with a perfectly executed swan dive, and landed on the policeman with the loud-hailer.

Mel and Colly Baybee! Who would have believed it?

The terrible twins

A TALE OF TAILS

The *House of Butterflies* was a pleasure palace in a predominantly Polish precinct in Philadelphia, Pennsylvania. However, the only poles in the immediate vicinity of this three-story brothel were those that supported their power lines. Madam Chu Yu imported her indentured labor from her home province of Guangdong. The girls were shipped directly to the docks, where they were whisked away in the back of a Chinese laundry van to the *House of Butterflies*. The ladies received free board and lodging, and could expect to pay off their debt to Madam Yu within seven years. That's a long time to be lying on your back.

You may wonder how I know all this, and I can understand why you would ask. In truth, it was one of those quirky coincidences. The building is such an imposing edifice; you just have to detour off the main street to take in all the charm and grace of this Gothic masterpiece. The old-world residence is set back from the road at the end of a winding path, and I just happened to be in the vicinity when I heard this ear-piercing scream. As I looked up, I saw a naked lady fly over the balustrade on the roof, and plummet to her death below. She hit the ground with an almighty thump, not ten feet from me.

Lights came on, doors were opened, and on-lookers flocked to the scene, to see what they could do. I was already there, and it was obvious that the poor thing was dead. I still felt a bit embarrassed for her, lying there on her back, completely naked. I did what any decent chap would do. I took off my hat and placed it over her private parts. I then dialed the emergency line

In the meantime, quite a crowd was gathering, and it was hard to keep them back. A very inebriated gentleman, who was an assertive drunk, looked down at the naked body and my strategically placed hat, and tried to take control.

"OK folks; the first thing we gotta do is get that guy out of there."

"Excuse me, pal. This doesn't concern you. Would you mind moving on?"

When the law arrived, I noticed that the lead detective was a woman, and I gave her my business card. A male would have flicked it into the dirt, but she was most amenable.

"Well Paddy, I don't know how you can contribute, but we will probably need all the help that we can get. Follow me and stay close."

Inside the house, all the girls were gathered in the vestibule, and they were in various states of undress. Most were sobbing, and the madam was doing her best to keep them under control. Detective Inspector Woodley isolated the lady of the house, and plied her with questions. She was a pretty brutal interrogator. As you might expect, the Chinese woman was inscrutable.

"Girl come off street. Ask for job. I hardly know her. She must be having shower, and fall out window."

I mentioned to Woodley that I saw the young thing come off the roof, not through a window. Madam Yu glared at me.

Naturally, we searched the premises, and the roof was our first port of call. It was decked out like a Hawaiian island, and it seems that one could book out the area for a private orgy on a sunny day. There were no high-rise buildings in the vicinity, so privacy was assured. On weekends, they did a yum cha themed luncheon: very tropical.

However, it looked like this had been a private party, and only one of the partygoers had been accounted for. The forensics people would later determine that she had been bound, prior to her demise, with a neck-tie. I hoped they didn't look too hard at me. My tie was very tropical.

The detective thought that it was strange that there were only a few gentlemen on the premises, but I didn't. The victim's scream had hardly completed its echo, when there was a stampede out of the house. I suspect that Inspector Woodley may have recognized one of the fleeing males, Police Commissioner Lovell.

Forensics is an important part of a murder investigation, and we were keen to absorb the early findings. It was determined that the missing neck-tie was made of silk, and might be a club tie. There was an imprint on her skin of some kind of emblem. I certainly hoped that it wasn't the Jockey

Club. Then again, one of those little monkeys had murdered my best bet only last Saturday. It wasn't beyond the realms of possibility.

Their other discovery was equally as tantalizing. The victim had a Tong tattoo on her bottom. I wonder if this crime was more than a sexual dalliance gone wrong. Talk about a co-incidence! I had been admiring Inspector Woodley's rear end when I learned of this snippet of information from the dude from the Coroner's Office. She turned around quickly, and caught me out. Damn! Women must have eyes in the back of their heads.

I am a glutton for punishment. There are semi-naked broads all around me, but I am ogling the cop in comfortable shoes and the cashmere cardigan. That tight skirt was plain, but there was no disguising what it was covering. Her police badge was neatly clipped onto a wide leather belt, and her white blouse was set off with a single strand of pearls. She wore little make-up, and had the bluest eyes. Her blonde hair was short, and would never get in her way. Everything spelled out efficiency, and I suspected that she was no pushover for the male jocks at the station.

"Hey, Komoneski! Stop flirting with those chicks, and start searching the rooms."

"Yes ma'am."

"And don't call me ma'am."

Wow! I just love assertive women, and I wondered what Officer Komoneski might find during his room search. One of the pole dancers might be a relation.

Woodley and I got together to compare notes and I caught a whiff of her perfume: Christian Dior's enigmatic seduction fragrance, Poison. An obvious choice, I suppose, for a homicide cop. She was intrigued by the tie angle, but she thought I was the best person to look into the tattoo on the girl's butt. We needed to check every one of the hookers to see if there were any other gals who were doing it for the Tong. It would be a long and thankless task, but she left the Polish policeman behind to help me. He was delighted.

"By the way, Paddy, you can call me Janet. For now, I have to get back to the station."

"You can call me anytime, Janet. Why don't we meet later, and discuss the case. I hear that Finnegan's Wake never runs out of beer. What do you say?"

"Sounds good to me. I'd like to meet your Irish relatives. Shall we say around six?"

She was off in a flash, and I managed one last glance as she sashayed over to the police car. The nervous cough that emanated from behind me indicated that Officer Komoneski was ready to begin our arduous undertaking.

A few hours later, after much giggling and gasping, we had completed our task and found two babes with Tong tattoos on their tails. Surprisingly, one of them was Madam Lash, the only non-Chinese employee in the house. Josie wails on cue, but she doesn't sing for anyone. We got nothing from her. The other one, Phuk Yu, may have been related to Chu Yu, but we would get nothing out of her. She didn't speak English or Polish.

The House of Butterflies

I enjoyed the social diversion with Woodley at Finnegan's. I treated her to a Guinness Pie, which came with the usual trappings of French fries, mashed Murphies, scallop spuds and a good luck voucher, signed by a leprechaun. We decided to finish off the night at her place, and because it was such a mild night, I thought that we might walk to her apartment, a few blocks away.

It didn't take long to realize that we were being followed. Even with a skin-full of stout, those eyes in the back of her head were still working. She sensed it. I could feel it. We hastily decided on a plan, which was a no-brainer. We turned into the nearest lane, and cowered amongst the dust bins. The guy must have been a rank amateur. I hit him on the head, and Woodley flicked his legs from under him. He hit the deck like a sack of Finnegan's potatoes.

I have to say that this loser wasn't your average low-life. His finger-nails were expertly manicured, and his after-shave, although overpowering, was expensive. If that wasn't a Zegna suit that he was wearing, it was cut from the same cloth. However, the most riveting part of his wardrobe was his neckwear. He was wearing a silk tie with a club emblem, front and center. I dragged him to his feet.

"OK, sleazebag! What does The Right Worshipful Grand Master of the Most Ancient and Honorable Fraternity of Free and Accepted Masons of Pennsylvania want with Paddy and Janet? Let's hear it, dickshit."

He spat at me, which, I have to say, wasn't very neighborly. Woodley stepped forward, grabbed his nuggets, and squeezed hard. He let out an almighty howl, and then became quite conciliatory.

"The Grand Poobah wants to see you both. I have a car around the corner."

As if on cue, a slinky black limousine silently rolled up to the entrance to the lane. The windows were all blacked out, and I half expected Justin Bieber to emerge, or at least Miley Cyrus. The limo was just for little old us, and we all boarded through the rear entrance. Mr Sleazebag sat next to the bar, but he didn't offer us drinks. I was beginning to think that this wasn't going to be a friendly meeting.

The Masonic Temple in Philadelphia is a most impressive building. It has been around since seventeen eighty six, and sits in all its magnificence opposite City Hall. Naturally, I thought that we would be heading there. I was wrong. It doesn't take twenty minutes to get to North Broad Street, and those blacked out windows didn't come down without the approval of the creep who was sitting opposite us. The alarm bells started ringing in my head. I looked at Woodley. She was on the same wave-length, and we both knew that we had to take fast action as soon as the car stopped. Our hands were already on the door handles.

* * *

When you are telling a story, you can always move things along, and in so doing, sometimes the reader will know what is going to happen to the prospective victims before they do. So, here it is.

Janet and I had a date with death, and that big black limousine was going nowhere except to a deserted building site of the Acme Construction Company. They were putting up a block of high-rise apartments, and they had some serious machinery in action. The piece of equipment that will interest you the most was the crane that transferred the huge concrete blocks onto each floor. You would have to be a civil engineer to know how heavy each block was, so just think humungous.

If you have had any experience with unions, or people in labor-intensive industries, you would know that the knock-off whistle means *down tools,* and all work ceases at that time. The driver of the main crane, Tony Pellicano, had a hot date that night, and he needed every spare moment to scrub up nice. So, he left his crane in suspension. That humungous block of concrete was just hanging there, and there it would stay until his relief operator, Michael Dennehy, furtively returned to the site, and released the concrete onto the black limousine, and its occupants below.

This was a bold plan, and it might have worked if the dunderhead in the limo had dead-locked the doors, but he didn't. As soon as the car came to a halt, Woodley and I scrambled out of the vehicle, and with only a moment to spare. The concrete block came crashing down, and completely flattened the Cadillac. The two Masons inside would now be part of someone else's masonry. There was nothing left but rubble and a flattened limo.

Woodley was quick to her feet, and produced her Colt Detective Special revolver. Dennehy was fast out of the crane cabin, but had been counting on a leisurely climb down to the ground. This was not to be. The deadly dame picked him off with one shot, and he plummeted earthwards. Dead on arrival! I told you that this was one tough lady. She didn't even read him his Miranda rights.

The rest of the evening went as you might expect. We booked in for a sauna and massage at the *House of Heavenly Hands*, and then went back to her apartment for a night of sexual gymnastics. I was hoping that this intimate sojourn would not affect our professional relationship because we still had a long way to go with this case. Nevertheless, we had an important lead, and I was looking forward to meeting the Grand Master of the Masonic Lodge on my own terms.

The fact that he was Chinese surprised Janet, but not me. I would almost bet on the probability that he had a Tong tattoo on his tush. He was a robust little fellow of indeterminable age; I guessed around fifty years. I don't know whether he still worked out, but there was definite muscle tone on show. The general quality of his attire indicated that he was wealthy. If that suit that he was wearing wasn't a mix of Himalayan Pasmina, then I'm no fashion guru. I felt distinctly under-dressed in my drip-dry slacks and moccasins. His gold cuff-links were glinting in the sunlight that streamed into the room, and I had the feeling that he was trying to deflect the rays into my eyes. Some of these Oriental people have no shame.

"Mr Pest, Ms Woodley, extreme salutations! We don't see many lady on these premises, although we do boast one female member. What I do for you?"

I had a strong urge to tell him to cut the crap, but this is not the right way to tackle such an adversary. I have dealt with gangs and triads in Hong Kong and Guangzhou, and these people are difficult to intimidate. You have to outsmart them. If that doesn't work, just shoot them.

I might say that this huge place and all their hoolygooly didn't intimidate me. A few years ago, I had become a Mason in order to recruit some heavies for a heist that I was planning (Pest Takes a Chance — still a superb gift idea). I was well-versed in their disciplines and my membership was still current. I gave him the Masonic hand-shake. He was taken aback, but smiled courageously.

"We have sad news regarding one of your vehicles from the Lodge's car-pool. It was involved in a fatal accident, and your membership has been reduced by two people. You may wish to identify the occupants, although their remains are minimal."

Woodley produced the match-box with Mr Sleazebag's gold tooth in it, and I threw the driver's ID onto the table. Mr Wang went white and, without warning, he wailed and wafted uncontrollably. His outburst was in a foreign dialect and could well have been profane.

"Jimmy, my best driver! I am devastated. How it happen? I want to know everything."

Of course he did, but we weren't in an explanatory mood. Janet gave him due notice of the coronial inquest, and the both of us departed the building. We had locked horns with the guy who wanted to kill us, and that was enough for now.

When things go wrong, I am a great one for returning to the scene of the crime. In this case, it was a wonderful crime scene. We had two dozen of the prettiest suspects that I had ever seen, but we really didn't have a prime suspect. Phuck Yu was definitely in the gun, but she wasn't co-operative, and it wasn't just because of her language difficulty. She had attitude.

By now, there were immigration officials crawling all over the joint, and Madam Yu was complaining that she was getting a bum rap. She claimed that she had a personal agreement with certain people in high places, and nobody doubted this for a moment. The wily woman of the night would need all her negotiating skills to get out of this one.

I suggested to Woodley that they put a tail on Phuck Yu and Josie, the one with the whip. If they were feeling threatened, they might seek refuge with their Tong friends. Need I say that my intuition was right on the ball? They fled the house through a side door, and the flatfoots followed them into town. Their destination was no surprise to me — The Grand Lodge of the most Ancient and Honorable Fraternity. It was time to call in the cavalry.

I hope that during the course of this remarkable tale, you don't feel that I have in any way diminished the role of Freemasons in our society. They do many good deeds, and just because there is a bad apple at the top, you don't need to shake the tree. Of course, the brethren are not big on equal opportunity, and because it is a male-oriented society, I will probably not renew my membership. Some of those initiation ceremonies definitely need a feminine touch.

Getting a complete field team together at short notice is achievable if you've got good cause. Even then, the go word needs to be bounced off the boffins at the top, and that would mean that Commissioner Lovell might be involved. Given his covert assignations at the *House of Butterflies*, Woodley and I thought that a smaller squad might be able to do the job with more discretion. Some of her pals were off-duty at *Pinocchio's Pizzeria and Bowling Alley*. She made the call, and they turned up in their bowling shoes, armed to the teeth.

I told them that the important thing to remember was that we should tread softly, and that is how we entered the lodge. The task force would not waste anyone unless they started shooting first. We entered the building en masse, and presented at the reception desk. I think that it was Woodley's brother who announced our credentials.

"We're the *Police Academy Bowling Club*, here for our match with the *Masonic Gutter Crawlers*. Can you direct us to your lanes?"

"You're in the wrong place, buddy. You should be over at the *Lucky Strike Alley*."

The other security guy was a little more alert, and saw this for the charade that it was. He went for the alarm as I jumped the barrier and king-hit him. His compatriot went red in the face, and fainted. That saved us some muscle.

From here on in, it was to be stealth and opportunity. We dragged the comatose guards into the broom closet, and left a sentry at the reception desk. Monday night football was playing on the idiot box, and he would enjoy that. The rest of us split up, and ascended to the executive floor in separate elevators. We emerged silently, and listened for any movement. The air was redolent with suspense and foreboding, but there was no one around. The crack team of off-duty policemen followed me to the room that we had visited earlier in the day. From within came the sound of music. I hadn't listened to Julie Andrews for years and one forgets what a sweet voice she had.

Woodley gave the signal and we all barged in, guns at the ready. There was no one there. What a bummer! Nevertheless, my nose for trouble started twitching, and I noticed that the resident's high-backed, black swivel chair was turned away from his desk. I spun it around.

"Holy crap," exclaimed Janet. "Nice bod," said her brother.

It was Phuck Yu. She was half sitting in the chair, fully dead. She was also completely naked apart from the club tie that was still wrapped around her neck. It was clear to me that this Wang character was an absolute brute. He must also have had a handy clothing allowance. He was going through Ferragamo ties like they were noodles.

Desirable but dead

This unexpected murder was a startling discovery, but through it all, Wang's high-end hi-fi pumped out the melodic sounds of Salzburg's favorite family group. The emotional strains of *Edelweiss* cut through the room in a timely reminder of better times. Phuck Yu was still warm so she may have chosen her own requiem.

Now my ears were twitching, and for good reason. There was an extraneous sound reverberation that was over-riding the show tunes. I recognized the start-up hum of a helicopter. It was one of those choppers that fart a few times before the engine kicks in. I turned down the volume on the music machine, and rushed to the window. The others followed. It was a small Bell 407 with those gutsy Rolls Royce turbos. Wang was away, and wishing us good riddance. His two-fingered salute said it all. Don't mess with the Masons.

Janet put out an all-points bulletin on this miserable Mason, but it was not yet over in his North Broad Street ivory tower. A loud whip-crack attracted our attention, and there she was: Josie, the tempestuous Tong terrorist. Dressed in a body-hugging leather ensemble, this femme fatale looked a terrifying sight as she guarded the exit with grim determination. The whip was presently idle, but it would not be dormant for long.

"Holy crap," exclaimed Janet. "Nice bod," said her brother.

I know that you are impatient to learn the mysteries that surround Josie's inclusion in this tale of tails, and why a determined Anglo Saxon lass would let a ching-chong tattooist mess with her posterior parts — not that the tattoo wasn't elegant because it was.

I am happy to oblige. In truth, I haven't been privy to this information for very long.

In actuality, Josie was not completely Anglo Saxon. Her father was an American GI Joe, and her mother was a Chinese albino called Sie Sun Soon. The soldier was on leave, and he couldn't leave her alone. She was only fifteen years of age, and when the relatives learnt of their one-night stand, he was run out of town. The pregnancy became a matter of disgrace, but Sie refused to terminate, and raised the child amongst the squalor and grime of a Guangdong ghetto. No wonder she became beholden to the evil and immoral hoodlums that lived off the misery of others.

The good thing about all this was, because of her heritage, she was the only working gal at the *House of Butterflies* who had a Green Card. This was important to the Tong. She was free of any deportation fears, and could travel within the Philadelphia community with equanimity. Although she did make house-calls, most of her clientele came to the *House of Butterflies* in order to exorcise their demons. She could dispense pain like no other.

I had to remind the guys that we wanted a live prisoner, so they put away their guns, and tried to take her down by hand. Woodley's brother went first, but his effort was farcical. She whipped the buttons off his pants, and his trousers fell down, as he did. The muscle-bound sergeant was next, but he fared no better. She coiled the whip around his throat, and pulled. He was sent sprawling into the hi-fi unit with a crash. Julie Andrews immediately sparked up once again. Woodley didn't look like she was enjoying this.

It was left to Officer Komoneski to save the day. He calmly unzipped his bowling ball bag, and removed the round piece of sporting equipment. With pinpoint accuracy, he lobbed the ball into the air, and it came crashing down on Josie's toe. She screamed in agony, and dropped her whip. It was all we needed. Everybody pounced, and she was soon safely ensconced in handcuffs. They lead her away to the slammer.

Woodley and I searched Wang's office. Surely there was some clue that would shed some light on this nefarious business. We found it in his bar fridge. There was any number of different sized boxes, all neatly stacked on the shelves. They were tagged with some pretty prominent names, including Commissioner Lovell. Janet's nose was also working overtime.

"It smells like cheese to me."

And cheese it was, Philadelphia's most popular export: cream cheese. I slipped back the wrapping and taste-tested the contents. It was laced with heroin.

So there you have it. Wang was not only importing girls into Philly, but also high quality smack. The hookers with tattoos on their tails were distributing it through the *House of Butterflies*. Madam Yu was probably involved. When she wasn't snarling, she had quite a cheesy grin.

The word came through that Wang's helicopter had been sighted at the Kraft cheese factory. Before we left, I took one last look at his desk, and there on his blotter were the words *Vat 69*. There was a circle around the notation.

Many of you will not be familiar with the Kraft cheese factory in Philly, but it is an enormous place. There are over six dozen structures that accommodate ingredients for many products. Some of them are very runny. The factory churns out all kinds of taste treats: from Cherry Berry Cake and Caramel Swirls to a Nacho starter kit. They also do Bonox and

Vegemite, but these products are kept in double-steel containers — the smell can be overpowering for the uninitiated.

I was sure that Wang's drug supplies were stored in Vat 69. He would want to recover them on his way out of town. It appeared that Woodley wasn't convinced.

"Gee, Paddy, it might just be the Pope's telephone number."

I pushed her into the driver's seat of the lead car. This little lady had a lot to learn about Catholics, and their relationship with Chinese-speaking Masons.

"Get us to the cheese factory, wench. And fast."

Janet found one of those portable sirens from somewhere, and put the pedal to the metal. She could burn rubber with the best of them, and when the gate-keeper saw that our on-coming vehicle was not going to stop for the usual pleasantries, he dived for cover. She crashed through the barrier, and I directed her towards the building designated as Whisky 1. I didn't need to tell her that this is where she would find Vat 69. The second vehicle was about sixty seconds behind us. I was sure that all the lads would be locked and loaded.

Although large, the facility had been designed with great fore-thought. The storage structures that enclosed the vats had been built in a semi-circle around the administration building, so that the bean-counters would never have to walk far to check on their employees. There was a large lawn recreational area in front of this admin building, Alfa 1. It was here that Wang had parked his helicopter.

The manic Mason and two of his stooges were in the open courtyard, and heading for the chopper. They were pulling a trolley that was stacked with three large boxes. Janet slammed on the brakes. She then dove-tailed the vehicle into the gap; we were now between the man and his ticket to ride. The crafty oriental saw that we had stymied his exit strategy. I saw that she had put us in harm's way. Where were the other guys?

You can tell when you're going to be in the middle of some serious heat. We both saw a stocky figure appear at the side door of the helicopter with a Thompson machine gun cradled in his arms. We scrambled out of the car as glass exploded about us. The people at the police repair shop would need all their expertise to put this one back together again. At least, the Elvis dash-board doll seemed undamaged.

The barrage of bullets that came from the trolley area was only small arms fire, but we were pinned down. I then heard the wail of a siren, and the boys from the bowling club arrived, guns blazing. Their volley at the trolley found its mark. One of the thugs dropped, and I then saw the door of the chopper close. It looked like the pilot was not keen to sustain any damage to his flying machine. He cranked up the rotors, and lifted out of there.

Janet produced a loud hailer, and gave the Chinaman an ultimatum.

"It's all over, Wang. Step out with your hands up, or we shoot you."

There were still no Miranda rights forthcoming. You've got to think that this lady is not one for political correctness. Nevertheless, Wang would not have been interested. He abandoned the trolley, and left his pal to formulate some kind of rearguard defense. I saw him sprint for the door that would take him into the Tango 1 building. He had led me a merry dance, but the end was nigh. Where else could he go? I followed him into the cavernous depths of the storage facility.

It was only after I had entered the building that I realized that he still had a home-ground advantage. Tango 1, 2 and 3 housed the export divisions of the company, and the product shelves gave up their cargo destination; Cantonese Cheesecake, Beijing Blueberry Pie and Changchun Cheese Wedges were just some of the delicacies that were about to be freighted out. I would have liked to sample some of the products on show, but I could see that Wang was getting away from me.

There was an exit at the rear of the building, and he had disappeared through that door. I emerged into the sunlight, and ran smack-bang into an open-topped vat that contained something that didn't smell nice.

Wang was half-way up the steel ladder that was attached to the outside perimeter of the structure, and I had no idea what he had in mind. Nevertheless, I shrugged my shoulders, and started climbing. Because of my superb physical condition, the climb was easy enough, and I did gain on him. The worst part was the smell. I knew all about Little Miss Muffet and her curds and whey, but nursery rhymes had been written before they invented smell-o-vision.

There was a wide boardwalk on top of the vat, and Wang had disappeared over the rim. It was then that I heard the sound of a chopper. The crafty devil! They were coming back for him. It sounded as if the airborne rescue was some distance away, so I still had time to apprehend the monster. Well, I thought I did.

I made sure that I didn't look down as I made my final steps on the ladder, and gingerly placed my rubbery legs onto the firm wooden plank that was the boardwalk. What I saw next was quite a shock.

There in front of me was not the man I expected. Wang was further along the gangplank. This geezer was also oriental, but far more terrifying. I had no idea where he had come from, but I was sure that he harbored no feelings of goodwill towards me. He was carrying no weapon, but his hands were primed for action. The fellow was crouching in one of those Kung-Fu positions, or else he suffered badly from sciatica.

Apart from his posture, I thought that he was quite presentable. His colorful brocade jacket was high in the collar, and I could tell that it was tailor-made. His trousers were loose-fitting, and a bit short, but you can get away with that if you are not wearing any shoes. Of course, he would never get into the Lily Pond night club in New York, but I didn't think that was on his mind.

As he closed in on me, I could smell his after-shave. It was very manly, which contradicted his hair-style: a braided plait that disappeared down his back, and tied with a ribbon just above his butt. Naturally, I goaded him.

"Come and get me, Nancy-boy. You know you want to."

His eyes narrowed; he was almost squinting. The big scar that highlighted his otherwise inscrutable face seemed to blush with anger, and he let out a roar as he charged. I side-stepped him with ease, and gave him one behind the ear. This outraged him.

His next move was predictable, but effective. He came in low, and nobbled me below the knees. He must have been a kick-boxer. I couldn't maintain my balance, but bounced back from the now-swinging boardwalk before he could apply his coup de gras. Nevertheless, his follow-up karate chop sent shivers of pain through my shoulder. He was getting the better of me, and I needed to get in close. I figured that he had never been in the boy scouts, or any Affirmative Action group, so he would not know what was coming. I sank my knee into his crotch, and it worked a treat.

You are probably wondering how we could have maintained this ferocious fight on an unstable platform that was swinging precariously. I have to say that it wasn't easy, and either one of us, or both of us, could have gone over the side at any time. I might have drowned in dairy.

When the oriental hard man hit the rickety runway with a thud, the structure was swaying dangerously, and I have to say that I relaxed ever so slightly. It was enough for the Chinaman. He reached out, grabbed my ankles and pulled. I rolled uncontrollably with the gangplank, and was heading into oblivion, when my natural reflexes saved me. I reached out and caught the lower part of the handrail.

When you are hanging from your fingernails, delicately suspended above a watery grave of curdled milk, you have to think that the pendulum of peril is not about to swing in your favor. The last thing that you want to see is a grinning Chinaman, who is trying to unlock your desperate fingers from the vice-like grip that has almost glued you to the handrail. Fortunately, I am prepared for situations like this, and I owe it all to my pal, Stormy Weathers. Being such a beautiful lady, Stormy has always attracted a lot of unwanted attention, and so she took it upon herself to manufacture her own brand of Mace. I always carry a small spray can in my top pocket, and it is really effective.

I don't want to give away any trade secrets, but I can tell you that the basic ingredients are possum piss and wombat poo. The gaseous spray stings like hell, and disorientates the victim. Mr Fu Manchu didn't know what hit him. He screamed relentlessly, and ran around in a daze. Eventually, he slipped over the edge, and into the ocean of goo below. It was the Cantonese Cheesecake.

I am sure that Mr Wang was grateful for the diversion that his employee had caused, and was probably confident that he was on his way back to Shanghai. The helicopter had arrived, and he was now hanging from the rope ladder that they had thrown him. However, they were not yet in full-flight mode, and I had one last chance to end this. I reached for my Beretta, which had not been dislodged during my little skirmish with the Kung-Fu killer. With one shot, I severed the left side of the ladder, and with my second shot, I split the rope on the other side. Wang plunged to his death, and I hoped that he had his mouth open. I am sure that I had heard him say that he would die for some Blueberry Pie.

In telling this tale, it is important to mention that very few Kraft employees were involved in this subterfuge. Most of them are hard-working shift workers who relish the opportunities that such a high-profile company provides. Nor were management involved. The end of the production line caused the problem. The quality control supervisor was a Mr Gnot: Tong spelled backwards. It was a little bizarre that his whole staff was Chinese, but now you know why.

The procedure was simplicity itself. Gnot injected the heroin into the slabs of Philly, and his team separated the tampered product into defined lots. The largest consignment was addressed to the Grand Poobah at lodge headquarters on North Broad Street. In all the years that they were doing this, only one slab of contaminated Philadelphia Cream Cheese slipped past the watchful eyes of the vigilant Tongs. It ended up in Commissioner Lovell's lunch box. That's how he became hooked.

As a postscript, I can tell you that it took ten years for Janet Woodley to become Chief Commissioner, and it was generally accepted that the promotion was richly deserved. She still hasn't been able to commit the Miranda warning to memory, but retains the admiration and respect of all those who have worked with her. Whenever I visit Pennsylvania, I often drop by. She is still a good-looking woman.

The *House of Butterflies* is still in existence, but there has been a generational change. The Chinese are out, and the Poles are in. Officer Komoneski was also promoted, but decided to accept an early retirement package. He purchased the three-storied house, when it was sold under the Proceeds of Crime Act, and installed himself as manager. Most of the girls now have a K tattooed on their butt.

THE BIG SPLASH

I was on-deck, at the front of the ship, when the incident occurred. In my imperious way, my chest was heaving in sync with the westerly wind as I sucked in the cool night air. It was a shame that no one could see me. I was looking quite sartorial in my hired tuxedo: a traditional but stylish design with a notch lapel and pocket handkerchief. Most of the other guests were wearing white linen slacks and marine loafers, but I am never one to conform.

Howard Bunt's motor yacht was one of the best there was, and he often used it to entertain his friends and contemporaries. On this occasion, he was hosting a fund-raiser for one of his political cronies, and everybody who was anybody was there.

Who is Howard Bunt, you ask? Just the biggest industrialist in the whole wide world, that's who. Incidentally, you should have asked *"Who was Howard Bunt?"* It was he who went over the side while I was communing with nature: all seventeen stone of him. It must have been a big splash.

I think that I must have been the only one to question the immediate assumption that it was suicide. After all, he had his finger in so many pies; it would have been easier to jump off the gravy train. With great dexterity, I started doing what a private eye does best: sniffing around. I didn't have to go far to find a clue. On the deck outside his stateroom, there was a shattered bottle of vodka near the railing, and I immediately thought of Gregoria Killanova, Bunt's mistress. Surely, she would not have received an invitation to the social function. Not with Barbara Bunt in the same room.

Scrawled on the outside cabin wall were two dates, written in lipstick. They were Howard's birth and death dates. The obituary was chillingly short: *good riddance.*

Although the news of the big man's demise swept through the gathering, it didn't reduce the momentum of the party. By co-incidence, the entertainment troupe was called *Vodka and Lipstick,* and the boys on the balalaikas were really belting it out. For a while, I considered them suspects, but they were just happy Cossacks, and I couldn't see them wasting a full bottle of vodka on anyone, much less the man who would sign their checks. However, Mrs Bunt did provide cause for concern. She was doing *The Eagle Rock* with her late husband's bodyguard. He would not get a bonus, tonight. Or would he?

I knew that the captain kept a list of guests on the bridge, and they needed to report the disappearance to the port authority and the New York Police Department. I flipped through the neatly typed list until I came to the name that I was looking for: Gregoria Killanova. What I didn't expect to find was the name of her escort for the night: Igor Igoravitch, the cultural ambassador at the Russian Embassy. This is a colloquial term which means that he is the local head of their Federal Security Service: formerly, the KGB.

I left the bridge deep in thought. These were worrying revelations. However, I didn't have long to ruminate on possibilities and probabilities. Somebody bashed me over the head, and I went out like a light.

* * *

Keel-hauling is an insidious punishment, and I am not surprised that only pirates and other unsavory characters still utilize it. I awoke in the backwash of the boat. My hands had been tied to my body, and a tow rope attached to my feet. The vessel was doing knots, but I was the one who was in a bind. I didn't have any trouble breathing because I surfaced every thirty seconds or so. A family of dolphins must have thought that it was a game because they all joined in the race. That is until the great white shark arrived, and scared them off. He stayed with me for a while, and then got bored. He had probably already had his dinner, or was affording me the professional courtesy of a like-minded predator.

I could hear the sound of rotor blades, and saw a helicopter approach the vessel. The New York Police Department had arrived to investigate the great man's disappearance. The craft slowed down, and the engines idled while the chopper made its approach. This was my chance. As I floated to the back of the yacht, I managed to push myself in the direction of the fearsome looking propellers. My timing needed to be exact, and my foray into the diameter of death required pinpoint accuracy. The propellers could cut my bonds, or convert me into a jar of pesto.

I went in feet first, and hoped that I would not be on the end of any backwash from the boat. Too much momentum would be disastrous, and although the propellers were only idling, they would still chew me up if I got it wrong. Harry Houdini — come on down. I took a deep breath, ducked into the diameter of death, and let the sharp blades of the propeller snip my bonds. If time wasn't of the essence, I might have gone back for a toenail trim.

A rasping, grinding noise warned me that the boat was about to get under way, so I quickly slipped out of the tow line, and hitched a ride on the anchor chain, which was now being raised. In situations like this, I am like a rat up a rope, and it wasn't long before I had slipped aboard the vessel, and found some dry clothes: a borrowed tux. Thirty minutes later, I was back at the party, and feeling ravenous. The barman gave me a vodka martini with two olives. I always like to keep up my green intake.

I could smell her before I saw her: the scent of a woman. All power to you, Al Pacino! It was some kind of musk fragrance that first attacked my sensitive nostrils, and she arrived shortly afterwards. The arriving apparition was a slinky brunette who, although tarnished by time, still managed to turn heads. She was wearing a long cocktail gown that was decorated with a colorful motif that seemed to say "I'm here, and ready to party."

From my position at the bar, I thought I heard an acid comment from one of the female guests. "Gregoria, where is your underwear?"

If she heard this snide remark, she gave it no mind, as she brushed a strand of hair from her face. Her wayward locks had been swept back to an accommodation of sorts at the back of her head. It was a severe coiffure that accentuated her prominent cheeks and Slavic bone-structure. Her make-up disguised the bags under her eyes, and rather blotchy skin tones. Too much vodka can do that to you.

My eyes drifted down south, and I immediately discounted the possibility that she was hiding a cosh somewhere under that figure-hugging tropical dress that she was almost wearing. The commentator had got it right. She wouldn't need to rinse her smalls, this night.

"Hello comrade. Are you here with yourself?"

"I certainly am. Patrick Pesticide is the name. Everybody calls me Paddy."

"I am Gregoria Killanova. I will kill anyone who calls me Greg."

I could well understand that, but I was confident that I could handle this soviet seductress. As long as she didn't call in Igor! His reputation as a brutal interrogator was well founded, and I saw him lurking in the background. I gave the lady my most charming smile.

"Tell me, Gregoria. What is a fine looking Georgian girl doing in a place like this? Did you know the deceased?"

"Ahh Paddy! You have been to Russia. That is good. Bunt is of little consequence. We got together occasionally."

Gregoria Killanova

There was so much more that I wanted to know, but our interchange was interrupted by one of the lackeys from the Hill St Blues. The detective in charge of the investigation wanted to see me. His name was Sipowitz, and he was a surly Polak with an attitude problem.

"I've heard of you, Pest. I believe that you're a minor celebrity."

"And you too, detective. I hope that we can work together."

Under the circumstances, he was quite co-operative. Usually, the boys in blue don't take to private gumshoes.

"I'm happy for you to schlep around as long as you don't get in my way. Capiche!"

"Capiche!"

I told him about the Russians on board, and he told me the results of the forensics. They had found strands of Mr Bunt's toupée attached to the glass remnants of the vodka bottle. I have never been a fan of cranium rugs, but I do know that insecure people use them to get ahead. I am sure that in this case, it had been a vanity thing. It was obvious to me that Sipowitz was neither vain nor insecure. Nevertheless, I thought that he could lose a few pounds.

While Barney Google went off, looking for eye-witnesses, I tried to make contact with the widow. Barbara Bunt was certainly no beauty, and I could understand why her husband might want to fish in another pond. I don't think that I would be out of order if I commented on her fearsome facial features. Naturally, the widow's countenance looked rather grim, but it was more than that. She had this permanent hang-dog expression that made her whole face look like the south end of a north-bound camel. Her piggy little eyes seemed to be cowering under two massive mounds of mascara. They looked out over a hook nose that would make Peter Pan squirm. Her bloated lips were living proof that Botox is not always the right answer.

There was no meat on her bones, but that jewel-encrusted designer dress that she was wearing might appeal to a pawnbroker with panache. I think that he was already by her side, or was he just a gigolo?

I introduced myself, and offered my commiserations. She gave no indication that she was surprised or shocked by the tragedy.

"Thank you for your kind thoughts at such a harrowing time, Mr Pest. Did you know my husband well?"

I hate it when people get straight to the point. Of course, I didn't know the old geyser well. My invite was forged, and that's the ways we do things at Pest Incorporated. I got by as best I could.

"He was a kind and considerate man, and his death was a great shock to me. Was he a troubled soul; perhaps an incurable disease that he couldn't live with?"

She stared at me in disbelief, and walked off with her companion in tow. Her retort filtered back through the sound barrier of a balalaika riff.

"Only if it was a social disease!"

Well, there you have it. Howard Bunt was a scoundrel. I was not surprised. Of course, this didn't make the little woman a murderer, but she was a candidate for consideration. I hadn't even approached any of his business associates, who might share an equal loathing of the man mountain. After all, you don't make squillions without stepping on a few toes.

Ari Ben Canoodle was a big man in his own right, and it was rumored that he was a prominent Middle East arms dealer. He lived on a Kibbutz and owned a substantial orange grove. So, you would have to believe that he was an authority on naval matters. Even with his large frame, he would be able to maneuver himself around this vessel, and remain inconspicuous. I had no valid reason to suspect him, but he did have a guilty look on his face, and his over-defensive response to my innocent observation was intriguing.

"There is a heavy dew around, tonight. Do you think Mr Bunt could have slipped on the wet deck, and fallen overboard? Or was he pushed?"

The Jewish arms dealer went red-faced, and started to sweat. He did not possess the demeanor of an innocent man.

"Until I came here, I haven't left my cabin. You can't pin this on me, Pest."

"I was only commenting on the weather, Mr Canoodle. There is no need to take it personally. However, do you have a witness that can give you an alibi?"

"I'm afraid not."

The fact that Canoodle had a cabin was interesting in itself. The other guests were just here for the soirée. I wondered if, in fact, he did have an alibi. There were a couple of professional party girls on board, and Bunt liked to dish out favors to clients and potential customers. Ari Ben's desire for anonymity could be understood as his wife was a second-tier agent for Mossad. It wouldn't be advisable to piss her off.

There was at least one more potential culprit, and he was sulking in the corner of the room. Or was he just intoxicated?

Barabbas Bunt was the big man's son from his first marriage, and the next of kin always come under scrutiny after the death of a wealthy parent. In this case, the estate and ancillary assets would be enormous. I must say that I didn't take to him much. His face was puffy and his eyes were red and watery. His diluted pupils stared out at me, but I don't think that he saw much. He was on something, and they weren't happy pills.

If I could find some extenuating circumstances, I would. After all, it must have been an on-going burden to carry a name like that. Barabbas was the low-life who escaped the crucifixion in favor of Jesus of Nazareth. The Jews having been trying to live down this decision ever since. Still, this was no excuse for the sailor-boy suit that he was wearing: with a scarf, would you believe? The word *effeminate* immediately came to mind.

I am sorry that I mentioned Jesus because I don't think that the young man was very religious. Certainly, his profane language would exclude him from even the most tolerant communities. And I can confirm that he was very drunk. I had to slap him around a bit to bring him into the real world.

"Who the hell are you?" he spluttered, seconds before he up-chucked into a nearby champagne bucket. I retreated with caution as he continued to cough up unmentionable residue from his stomach cavity. When he was ready, I moved in for the kill.

"I'm investigating your father's death, Barabbas. You can tell your story to me, or I can hand you over to the authorities. What's it to be?"

He looked at me with distain, and produced a contemptuous sneer. If this was his best defense, he would be putty in my hands.

"How were you getting along with your old man? Was he going to cut you out of the will? Did he suspect that you were a pervert and a pedophile? You can answer these questions in any order, but you don't have much time. We'll be pulling into dock, soon."

His response was completely unexpected. He up-chucked again: this time, all over the sleeve of my borrowed tuxedo. He then ran from the room, and it wasn't putty that was left in my hands.

Arrangements had been made for the vessel to be tied-up in an isolated part of the harbor, but no-one was going to be allowed to disembark. Sipowitz had been pretty thorough with his investigation, but we were no closer to solving the crime. Word came through that the coast guard had recovered the body, and were transporting the corpse to the city morgue. We could only wait on the coroner's report.

In a moment of madness, I concluded that some more time with Gregoria would be worthwhile, and I followed the musk fragrance through the kitchen, and into the accommodation area. Bloody hell! Everyone had a cabin except me.

As I stepped into the companion way, I saw Igor Igoravitch outside a half-open door. I presumed that it was Gregoria's cabin, but I had no way of knowing.

Little has been said about Igor during this compelling tale, and there is good reason for that. The man is a complete mystery, and that is not surprising when you consider the clandestine life that he has led. You don't get to be the Russian Cultural Ambassador without chopping down a few tall poppies. It is no surprise to me that I have never seen him at the opera or the Bolshoi Ballet; however, I do believe that Barabbas had a season ticket to both.

Igoravitch lightly tapped on the cabin door, and waited. From within came the words that he was waiting to hear.

"Will you walk into my parlor?" said the resider to the spy.

The cabin door closed, and I crept closer. Who could have anticipated what was to follow? There was an explosion, and two shots rang out, followed by a cry of pain and some unrepeatable Russian swear words. I heard a body thump to the floor, and smoke from the explosion must have set off the alarm. If we were a submarine, I am pretty sure that we would have been in dive mode.

I couldn't get through the closed door, but one of the crew did. I hadn't seen an axe action like that since the Wood-chop Final at the Royal Melbourne Show. The interior of the cabin was a shambles, and Igor was slumped at the foot of the bed. He was as dead as a Dodo. The incendiary device was just a diversion. The shooter had escaped through the open porthole, and disappeared into thin air. I sniffed around a bit, but if there had been any after-smell of musk, it had been diluted by the stench of the smoke-bomb. At least, I knew that I was looking for a murderess. That sexually explicit welcome resonated in my brain.

"Will you walk into my parlor?"

To think that it could have been me! I absolutely love parlor games, not to mention flexible females. She had to be some kind of spider-woman to get through that porthole. This case was getting more mysterious by the hour.

Igor's murder opened the floodgates. Embassy officials from both countries swarmed all over the ship, and the CIA arrived in numbers. The head spook was a guy called Felix Marmaduke. The man dragged me aside, and confided that he was a fan. He said that he had even been to Melbourne, which he had — Melbourne, Florida. I guess that I was a little surprised that he would want to confide in me, but he did. He said that Killanova was one of theirs, and she was from Georgia — Augusta, Georgia.

Given that the lady was nowhere to be found, I had to accept that he was probably telling the truth, and she had been spirited away. Still, I wasn't sure that I liked her for Bunt's murder. Sipowitz had to be the original Sgt Plod as he ploughed on relentlessly. He had received an analysis of the lipstick that had been scrawled on the cabin wall, and the coroner had been on the phone. There was a development. We rushed over to the city morgue.

"Hi there, Mr Pest, I'm Amelie Bonnet, Deputy Coroner; lovely to meet you."

The pleasure was all mine. This was a serious bit of skirt, and smart, too. To think that they had her locked down here with all the stiffs! I was pretty stiff, myself, and I was only half-dead. She didn't waste too much time on formalities, and got down to the business on hand. I like that kind of assertive behavior in a woman.

"Firstly, I can tell you that the deceased didn't die from the blow to his head. The vodka bottle probably only stunned him. If you look closely, you will see a puncture mark just under his Adam's apple. This was the fatal blow. It came from the steel-tipped heel of a stiletto shoe. The shoe size was seven and a half, it was blue in color, and the assailant was left handed. After the attack, the perpetrator vomited in the victim's ear. My analysis of the contents of the said ear indicates that the perp recently enjoyed a fish dinner with scallop potatoes, creamed broccoli and Tartare sauce. It was washed down with a 1994 Sauvignon Blanc from the Loire Valley."

Oh my God! I was in love. She was so good, and I was sure that she could be bad if she wanted to be. I left her my business card, and returned to the ship with Sipowitz. We passed Igor's remains on the way out. I had the feeling that Amelie's autopsy on the Russian spy would be easier. However, as the CIA agent had a license to kill, there would be few repercussions for Gregoria, who would probably melt into the background. It was obvious to me that Igor's killing was just another CIA/KGB type spat, and had no connection with the Bunt murder. I suspected that my next clue would come from the kitchen.

The caterers had prepared fish for the soirée, but there were no scallop potatoes or broccoli on the tables. I wondered if the lunch menu was different. The guests had not arrived at this time, and this would reduce the number of suspects to friends and family. Sipowitz elected to visit the kitchen, and check with the chef. I had my own agenda. There was only one person that I knew who was a serial vomiter. Fortunately, I alerted the policeman to my destination.

Deputy Coroner, Dr Amelie Bonnet

Barabbas Bunt had been given his own permanent cabin on the good ship *Baby Doll*. It was part of the deal that he had with his father in exchange for his silence concerning the industrialist's extra-marital activities. Given that everyone already knew about his extra-marital affairs, including his wife, you would have to think that the lad had got himself a good deal. All Pest had to do was find out if he recently had a good meal.

I used my skeleton key to enter the spacious stateroom that was his living accommodation. I left the door propped open in case I needed a quick getaway. I couldn't help but feel that the cushion that I used was not what you would expect to find in a man's quarters. It was all brocade, and had tassels hanging from the middle; the kind of thing that you would find in a Turkish brothel. Oh dear! I wonder if I have said too much.

There was a closed door that connected to the living room. I heard giggling through the light timber frame, and headed in that direction. Unfortunately, I knocked over one of Bunt's objet d'art, and it crashed to the floor. What a klutz!

The giggling had stopped, and I knew that I had announced my arrival. However, I couldn't turn back now. I twisted the knob silently and slowly pushed the door open. I had every reason to believe that I was now in the dying room. Barabbas Bunt and Ari Ben Canoodle both had their backs to the wall, and they were both pointing dangerous weapons at me. Bunt's firearm was innocuous, but Ari was a big man, and his Smith and Wesson double-action revolver was a feather in his hand.

Having said all this, my initial reaction was shock rather than fear. Barabbas was wearing a dress, and Ari was decked out in a teddy with black suspenders. This is not a good look for a fat man. They were both rouged-up, and there was a bottle of vodka on the table. I expect that I would find a pair of blue stilettos if I looked in the closet. However, I wasn't the one who was calling the shots. It was Canoodle who spoke first.

"You're a smart man, Mr Pest, but your investigation will all come to nothing. Once we have disposed of you, Gregoria Killanova will get the blame for poor Bunt's demise. You have bitten off more than you can chew."

I thought that this last statement was rather ironic as they had been undone because of what they ate for lunch. I said as much, and immediately regretted it. They now knew that Sipowitz was a player. What neither of us knew was the motive behind the crime, and it was left to young Bunt to explain.

"My father didn't approve of my lifestyle, and disinherited me some time ago. He kept me on in the hope that I would change my ways, and I went along for the ride. However, I needed ready cash, and so I have sold all his secrets to Ari, here. The sex was just a bonus."

Any further explanation was curtailed due to the fact that he had to go to the bathroom to throw up. I had the feeling that my time was also just about up. Canoodle raised his arm, and aimed the weapon at my head. Out of the blue, there was an almighty foghorn noise. The Queen Mary was in port. I took advantage of the diversion, and jumped for the safety of the settee. A hail of bullets followed me, and many of Bunt's priceless artifacts shattered into many pieces. Sipowitz was already on his way when he heard the commotion in cabin seven; he arrived, primed for action. The New York cop burst into the room with both guns blazing. He took out Canoodle, and destroyed the rest of Bunt's artifacts in one barrage. We found Barabbas in the bathroom with his head in the toilet.

That's about it, really. The Russia/America thing was glossed over as it usually is, and Barabbas confessed to his father's murder. The whole thing turned out to be less complicated than it seemed. The young man went along to his father's cabin in his drag gear, and pleaded tolerance. Surprisingly, old man Bunt mellowed, and they reconciled. Then they had a barney over whether it was appropriate that Barabbas should go to the party dressed as Marlene Dietrich in a sailor outfit. They took their argument outside, and as the youngster was already three sheets to the wind, he did the inexcusable. He hit his father over the head with a vodka bottle, speared him in the throat with his stiletto, and threw him overboard. Does he need anger management or what?

Sipowitz and I remain good friends. After all, he did save my life, and he was a most co-operative partner in a complex investigation. The other players in this little saga were not so memorable, although I do have fond memories of a very cute Deputy Coroner, and a good CIA agent with a bad Russian accent. I hope to be invited to Augusta, next year, for the Masters Tournament, and maybe we can hook-up.

I will be there with myself.

THE BOY WONDER

It was ten am and I was in Chief Commissioner Green's office. Rita Green was the youngest and prettiest police chief the city had ever seen. In fact, she was the only woman in charge that they had ever known. Rita and I go back a long way, and when things get tough, the lady often calls in the marvel from Melbourne to help out. She was running late, and I was all alone. I amused myself by looking out the window on a bleak day in Boston. There was a small cough behind me, and I turned to confront a rather fresh-faced young man.

The boy must have been no older than twelve. He was of average height for a person of this age, and was sporting a contemporary haircut that would probably appeal to pre-teen girls. He had a fair complexion, and his face was devoid of blackheads or blemishes. The kid didn't seem to be self-conscious in any way, as he bounded over to me, and introduced himself.

"You must be Paddy. My name is Joel. Do you play chess?"

Memories of my golden years at reform school came flooding back. I could always take the warden in less than thirty minutes, but now alarm bells started ringing. The young man seemed to be some kind of under-age hustler. I pleaded ignorance.

"Not really, Joel, but I do play a pretty mean game of *Scrabble*."

This information seemed to dampen his enthusiasm for any kind of interest in my companionship. However, further conversation was unnecessary because the police chief came bustling into her office, full of apologies.

"I'm sorry gentlemen. Breakfast meetings with the mayor never finish early."

If Commissioner Green was breaking bread with the Lord Mayor, there was sure to be serious trouble on the horizon. They don't get on at all well. I presumed that everything would be revealed shortly, but I wasn't prepared for what came next.

"It appears that you have already met Dr Haire, Paddy. Has he told you what this is all about?

Whoa, hold on, what did she say? Dr Haire! The guy is barely twelve years old. Then it came back to me. I remembered an elite faculty at Harvard that is rather hush-hush. All the students are child prodigies, and they positioned their facility near the staff kindergarten so they could mix with people their own age. I unscrambled all this retained information and hardly missed a beat.

"Yes, I have met young master Joel. A doctor, eh?"

"Actually, I'm a forensic scientist, Paddy, and a child psychologist. They've just seconded me to the police department. Things were a little dull over at Harvard. I'm glad to be here."

The child psychologist bit I could understand, but the rest was a blur. It turned out that he wasn't a bad sort of bloke, and not the type to miss his mommy. The bad news was that he was the under-twelve chess champion of New England. I wondered if he needed a manager.

"We've got a serial killer on our hands" said the police chief, in her best matter-of-fact voice. "We've seen nothing like it since *The Strangler*, all those years ago."

In the early sixties, the city was traumatized by the deeds of one, Albert DeSalvo. He killed thirteen people, all single females. They were mostly throttled with a silk stocking, or stabbed. The crimes were called the Silk Stocking Murders, and Albert was forever designated as *The Boston Strangler.*

However, the Boston Police Department were only looking at three murders, and after quickly glancing at the case files, I queried why they were so quick to tag the culprit as a serial killer.

"Gee, Rita, there's nothing similar about these crimes. There is no association between the victims, the MO is different in each case, and there are three possible motives. Why do you think the killer is the same person and a serial killer?

"I'll tell you why, Paddy. Victim one was Kerrie Bartholomew, a twenty-five year old office worker who lived alone. She was stabbed in the back while eating her Coco-Pops. Her face fell into her cereal bowl, and she drowned in the milk."

"So, the knife through her heart was just a superficial wound."

"Apparently so! Victim number two, James Cahill, was a middle-aged casting director, whose routine stop was a healthy breakfast at McDonalds, every morning. He always sat at the same table, near the loo. The hooded killer came out of the toilet, and decapitated him with a machete. He then dropped the weapon, and calmly walked from the restaurant. We are calling it a Mac attack."

"Have you questioned any out-of-work actors who can't get ahead? They always blame the casting director."

The whiz kid, Dr Haire, decided to go into bat for the Commissioner, and chipped in with his forensic opinion.

"You just have to look at this serial killer possibility, Paddy. The third victim, Annabel Carter, was the CEO of a breakfast food corporation. They found her hanging by her tights in the company boardroom, just after midnight. Because she wasn't wearing any knickers, there may have been some kind of assignation."

"So, she was sowing her wild oats?"

"Very droll, Paddy, but I am afraid I have no experience in that area."

What is it with these nerds? They have their heads stuck in a book when they should be out having fun. Usually, I get allocated an assistant who is a blonde bimbo with big knockers, so this was a new experience for me. I didn't know how long I would be able to cope with Dr Smarty Pants. Rita decided that we had seen enough of each other for the first day.

"Paddy, Joel has to get back to campus to watch *Inspector Gadget.* Why don't you both catch up tomorrow, and go over the case files in more detail.

I'll afford you both all the resources of the Force, and hope that we can catch this demonic person before he strikes again."

Alas, this was misplaced optimism. The next day, Dr Joel and I were having brunch at *Hooters,* when I got the call. There had been another murder.

Gwenda Leheny, the victim, had been one of Annabel Carter's most trusted lieutenants. As a bran manager, she was responsible for most of the packaging that came out of Boston. It was disturbing that she was found, curled up in a jumbo sized packet of Bran Flakes. Her tongue had been cut out, and shoved up one of her unmentionable orifices.

This was all starting to look like a disgruntled employee to me, especially when Joel announced some interesting news that he had gleaned from the case files.

The first victim, Kerrie Bartholomew, was also employed by the Best for your Bowels Food Company, and James Cahill was a consultant, who worked on their television commercials. I decided to take a look at some of these commercials. Joel had other plans. He and his egg-head buddies had been invited to the Mayor's gala day-in-the-park on Boston Common. This outing is usually put on for underprivileged children from orphanages and primary schools, and they take over Frog Pond and the carousel. I gave him five bucks for a hot dog, and slipped over to the advertising agency.

James Cahill was an outstanding casting director, according to the overly theatrical art director that I was introduced to. Bran Flakes commercials had won accolades and awards everywhere, from Cannes to California, and much of it was down to shrewd casting. Supposedly, the fellow had a good working relationship with most people, and he couldn't think of anybody who had it in for him.

"Well, there may have been twenty or thirty, but that is quite good for this industry."

This information didn't help me narrow the list of suspects. The commercials were very slick and quite humorous at times. One of them did raise my level of interest. The cartoon character was keen to get to his breakfast; so he lopped off the top of the pack with a machete. Certainly, Dr Joel would need to analyze and evaluate this information, so I decided to catch up with him on Boston Common. I found the young genius in the sand-pit with some of the other kids.

"Sorry to interrupt you on your day off, Joel, but I have some breaking news. That's quite a sand castle you're building, there."

"It's a replica of the Grand Palace in Bangkok. Very typical of what they did in the eighteenth century, Paddy: gold towers, defensive walls and, of course, a temple for the Emerald Buddha. We bet the lads from St Vinnies that we could finish it by five o'clock. Can I meet you at Cheers at five-thirty?

Yes, the Cheers bar really does exist. In fact, there are two of them in Boston. We decided on the original Bull and Finch Pub at Beacon Hill. It's a multi-story building with the popular bar in the basement. Upstairs, they have built a replica of the television setting, and you can close your eyes and think of Sam, Diane, Norm, Frasier, Woody, Cliff and Carla. While waiting for Joel, I closed my eyes, and tried to imagine what could have motivated this cold-blooded murderer to do what he did. Or could it be a she? I guessed the forensic scientist would have thoughts on that little conundrum. Joel arrived promptly at five-thirty with a big smile on his dial. I bought him a soda, and proceeded to wipe the smile from his face.

"The casting director was hated by at least two dozen people, and there was a machete in one of the cartoon commercials. What is the possibility that this crime could have been committed by Popeye or Daffy Duck?"

"Very unlikely, Paddy. What is more likely is that a real person was substituted for the cartoon character, and he or she took umbrage. It could have been their big break in show business."

"I note that you don't discount the possibility that the killer could be female. Are you being politically correct, or do you have a theory?"

"The lab reports that there were traces of perfume found on the machete, and the footprint analysis indicates that the attacker has small feet."

"My nephew, Antoine, has small feet, and he wears perfume."

"The killer could be your nephew, Paddy."

The family would love that. If the fact that he was a raging queen wasn't bad enough, now the possibility that he is a serial killer. Thank God that they didn't learn that he voted Liberal in the last election. This would have really tapped them out.

"What about the first victim, Kerrie Bartholomew? Can you really see a woman stabbing someone in the back? It's just not ladylike, if you know what I mean."

"I know exactly what you mean. Although, Lucretia Borgia and Lizzie Borden weren't particularly ladylike, were they?"

For someone so young, he had a good take on history. Of course, Lizzie may well have been historically maligned. She was found not guilty, but someone gave her father and step-mother forty whacks with an axe, and this also happened in Massachusetts. I was now ready to look for a female badass.

It wasn't so bad, shooting the breeze with this wunderkind, but I was aware of my responsibilities, and I couldn't keep him in a drinking establishment after seven o'clock. I ran the lad back to Cambridge in time for the dormitory call, and then arranged to hook-up with Rita Green. The police commissioner had a lot of Celtic blood in her, and we decided to meet for a Guinness or two at Gerry Burke's Irish pub in Jamaica Plain.

"It's been a long time since we sat down with a cold one, Paddy. I think it was the Naked Nymphomaniac case, wasn't it?"

Ahh, memories! Yes, I remember that case very well, and it was nearly as perplexing as this one. We raised our glasses to old times, and I proceeded to update her on the current situation.

"Dr Haire thinks that the perp may have been a woman."

"Get out of here. I find that hard to believe."

"Well, the killer has small feet, and apparently wears perfume."

"My hairdresser has small feet, and he wears perfume."

Now, here was a lead for Antoine next time he was in town. I made a mental note, and then gave her Joel's standard retort.

"Your hairdresser could be the killer."

Rita at the salon

She just snorted, and ordered another round of drinks. I could tell that this was going to be a long night and it was. We ended up back at her place, and I licked up the last of her last-option linguine. We were in a good mood, and even laughed at Letterman. The Late Show can be quite amusing when you are totally inebriated, but sometimes one tends to nod off during the commercials.

I awoke the next morning to find that there was no longer any food in her kitchen, and suggested that we breakfast at McDonalds.

"You mean McDonalds, the scene of the crime."

"That's exactly what I mean, Rita,"

We acquired a table near the roped-off area that was the crime scene, and ordered from the service bar. She had juice, some yoghurt and a low-fat latte. I opted for a double cheeseburger and fries. No salt! I think my frustration was affecting my blood pressure.

"What we need is the wonder dog, Inspector Rex. He would be able to sniff the perfume, and then take us directly to the villain."

It was then that I noticed that she had a tear in her eye, and it dawned on me that there was a regular resident that I had failed to see at her house: her faithful companion, Fluffy.

"Rita, what is it? I am sorry. Has something happened to Fluffy, your wonder dog?"

"Oh Paddy, it was absolutely terrible. I was going to a police seminar in New York, and he came to the airport to see me off. He was sniffing around one of the jet engines, and it started up, and he was sucked in. All that was left was his tail. I have had it embalmed, and it is now on the mantelpiece."

"Gee, Rita. That's too bad."

Where I came from, there was a similar story when one of the local dogs put his snout in the mince mixer at the butcher shop, but this was a far more gruesome tale. It seems that the airplane was one of those corporate jets, and I certainly hoped that it wasn't owned by the Best for your Bowels Food Corporation. This would put Boston's Police Commissioner in the loop as a major suspect. After last night's little romp in the hay, I can definitely confirm that she has small feet. This is in direct contrast to other parts of her body.

When Rita's tears had dried up, she looked at her watch, and scurried off to police headquarters. My destination was the offices of the aforementioned breakfast food company. The Vice President greeted me. He was a picture of everything that you would expect a VP to be; he wore an expensive designer pin-striped suit, a conservative tie, gold cuff-links and mirror black shoes. Simon Feely was the very model of a model public relations expert, because that was his role in the company. He admitted as much, but refused to confirm that he had put considerable spin on the company's interpretation of the police report. They were saying that their CEO had been wearing *No-Knickers*, a commercial underwear brand that was available at retail stores around the country.

"Mr Feely, I can confirm that Annabel wasn't wearing *No-Knickers*. She wasn't wearing any knickers."

"Well, that may be so, Mr Pest, but you know how it is with serial killers. Sometimes, they see a pair of black knickers as a trophy, and take them with them."

"I don't believe that the police released any information concerning the color of the undergarment in question."

"Well, the lady was wearing black for our board meeting, and you know how women like to co-ordinate. I know that my wife does."

This guy was good. He was really thinking on his feet. Nevertheless, I immediately added his name to my list of suspects, which was now growing like Topsy. I also needed to know what he knew of the first murder.

"I have to ask you this, Mr Feely. Was Kerrie Bartholomew your secretary, and were you having an affair with her?

"Well, er, ah ...yes and no."

"Sir, in my business, we expect a definite answer to a direct question. Was she your secretary, and were you having an affair with her?"

"Yes, she was my secretary, but I wasn't having an affair with her. Is that clear?"

I thanked him for his time, and left the building, but not before I checked with the security guard. Did the company keep a private jet at the airport?

"They sure do, fella. It's a Falcon: top of the range with two crew and eight passengers. It has three turbofan engines, and cruises at over 800 km/h. They occasionally hire it out, if you're interested."

I could tell that this bozo was on a commission. Nevertheless, he told me all I wanted to know, and it didn't look good for Rita Green. It was time to catch up with my favorite forensic scientist, and so I pointed the hire car in the direction of Cambridge. Naturally, I saluted as I passed JF Kennedy St, and smiled as I wheeled into Gerry St. I wonder if they named it after our host at Doyle's Irish Bar.

The faculty building was similar to others in the Harvard precinct: a weatherboard colonial structure with a porch and front garden. There were colored shutters on the windows, and the place had a lived-in feel about it. As the forensic scientist/child psychologist escorted me down the hall, we passed two very young co-eds, who smiled broadly at the handsome nerd.

"Good morning, Joel" they said in unison. It was a harmonized greeting.

"Nice girls! I think they might be a bit sweet on you."

"Kate and Genevieve, Paddy. They are completing their thesis on *Human Relationships in a Post-Modern Era*. They like to practice on me."

He ushered me into what looked like some kind of sitting-room. It was elegantly furnished. The heavy burgundy-colored damask curtains on the windows were securely clasped with a sash, and a long teak sideboard took up much of one wall. There were lamps, clocks and landscape paintings throughout the room. He offered me a place on the settee, which was luxuriant with deep cushions and a throw rug. The lad sat opposite me, and took out his pipe. I was shocked.

"Aren't you a bit young to smoke?"

"I only use play-dough for tobacco. It gives me a sense of superiority when I am talking to someone. Don't be offended, Paddy. Our tutors advise us to do it."

Bloody hell! Where do these people come from: the English aristocracy? I had a good mind to tell him where he could put his pipe, but I thought better of it. Just give him the facts, man.

"Joel, the public relations man at the company was bonking the first victim, and he has seen his boss in her underwear. I am not so sure about the female angle. Rita Green has small feet, and uses perfume" I also told him about the dog episode.

He picked up his plain-glass spectacles, and looked over the rim at me.

"This is only circumstantial evidence, Paddy. We don't have enough. However, if it looks like Rita is up for a charge, let's make sure that we get paid first. The police admin section can be a horror ride."

What a guy. I really liked the cut of his jib. Some might recognize a small sign of avarice there, but you do have to be practical, don't you? I'm sure that Rita would want us to be rewarded if we had her arrested. She's that kind of a dame. Of course, what we really wanted was a confession, but that didn't look like happening. Or did it! Joel's face suddenly became contorted, and I think that this meant that he had just had a great idea.

"Paddy, perhaps we can get a confession. Tell me, are you a gambling man? Do you like risks?"

"I'm up for anything. You know what they say: if you win, you're happy; if you lose, you're wise. Lay it on me, Dr Haire. What have you got on your mind?"

"Well, my friend, did you know that more than half of Boston is Catholic? If the monster is a *Mick*, he will want to go to confession."

"And we will have all the confessionals bugged. What a great idea!"

"And if he isn't a Catholic, we can use the tapes of the other folks to blackmail people. It could be a great money-spinner."

Did I say that this kid didn't have an avaricious bone in his body? He had ideas that Al Capone could only dream about. Of course, some of these brainy types are not very big on the practical side, but, within minutes, he had two seven-year-olds from the applied science program in the room. They were going over plans on how to bug all of Boston's confessional boxes. I needed a drink, and excused myself.

Around Harvard Square and the surrounding district, there are quite a few drinking establishments. Students really do need to rejuvenate after a hard day on the swat, and if you want to pick up a member of the opposite sex, this is the place to be. It was lunch-time, and they must have seen me as a tourist because they gave me a yard of beer, and said that I could keep the glass. What did they expect me to do with the glass if there was nothing in it?

There was a nice feel about the bar that I was in. It was very convivial, and the animated conversation of the large crowd washed over me. There was a football game on the telly, and I think they may have had their version of a rabbit raffle. There was also a quiz for all the patrons, but it wasn't easy: stuff about Pythagoras and other Greek Olympians. I found myself a corner table, and ordered a Reuben sandwich. It arrived within minutes.

I had to consider my position in terms of the proposed assault on one of the Catholic Church's long-standing institutions, not to mention the illegality of it all. Certainly, I am not like the FBI. I haven't taken any silly oath, and I have been known to bend the law, if it suits me. All the same, if we got this wrong, I could have my Purgatory pass down-graded. My thoughts were interrupted by the arrival of a kid with a can. He rattled it in front of me.

"Excuse me, sir. Can you spare a dollar for Kids in Crisis — children who are down on their luck? I can give you a receipt, if you like."

"Here's a few bucks. Now, sod off."

The only kid in crisis was the one that I was talking to, and at the rate that he was raking in the greenbacks, he would be a millionaire by supper-time. Today's youngsters made Oliver Twist and Fagin look like amateurs. I had to accept the fact that I was a dinosaur and a proletarian peasant compared to Joel and his *enfants terrible*. I decided to go along with his plan, whatever it was.

"Paddy, welcome back. How was lunch? Did you try the yard of beer?"

"I thought they saw me coming. You must have anticipated which pub I would choose, and warned them. A good detective always thinks ahead. I like your style."

"It's a gift I have to live with, I'm afraid. I would rather be a sex object, but I suppose there is still time for that. Would you like to know what decisions we have made in your absence?"

"Yes, I would, especially as I am to be one of the conspirators in this crazy scheme."

"We are going to hit all the churches between ten pm and two am. It will probably take three nights to complete the job. As we're not old enough to have a car license, you will be the designated driver. James Shannon, here, will plant the bugs, and we have Jessica, from the kindergarten, on loan. She is four years of age, and very small. Jess will crawl through the ventilator outlets, and open the church doors from the inside. Once the listening devices have been planted, Kate and Genny will man the headphones in the girls' toilet."

It was a good plan, and I was glad that it didn't involve any social intercourse with the clergy. The young folks were very bright, but limited in life experience. They would be particularly vulnerable to an amiable exchange with one of the brethren. Of course, it is rare that any plan goes off without a hitch, and we all held our breath when Jessica fell asleep in one of the air-conditioning tunnels. We should never have asked her to work these hours.

Fortunately, we had brought along her favorite *Wiggles* album, and a few songs from Henry the Octopus got her going again. All in all, it was a successful night's work, and I staggered into bed at four am.

Over the next few days, the voice-activated tape-recorders in the girls' toilet were going non-stop, and there was a relay of female operators on call. It was like the Bletchley Park Cipher Center during the war years. The girls had to combine their lectures with their listening duties, but they didn't complain. Most of the confessions were of a sexual nature, and they had some promising names to investigate, once they had graduated.

On day three, they scored a hit. It was the day that I was finally able to eliminate Rita Green from my list of suspects. Evidently, the corporate jet was not owned by the Best for your Bowels Corporation, but a dog food company called Pal o' Mine. How ironic!

We all rushed to the girls' toilet. Sure enough, a squeaky voice was seeking forgiveness for an unforgiveable sin that had been committed four times. It could have been adultery, but the priest was shocked, and he was closer to the truth than we were. The sinner was now whispering.

"You have blood on your hands," said Fr Jacobi, who obviously had no previous experience with serial killers. We really wanted to stick around, and see what kind of penance the killer would get, but we didn't have the time. Everybody piled into my hire car, and we sped off to South Boston.

When we arrived, the confessional hour was over; there was no-one around except the parish priest. We couldn't tell him that we had bugged his beastly box, but Joel came up with some lame excuse that allowed us to fingerprint the whole area. We explained that it was a Harvard exercise, and we were keen to ascertain the sex and ethnic demographic of his flock, especially those who had been to church within the last hour.

Finally, we had a list, but it wasn't definitive. The cleric thought that there were about ten adults and three children that had come to confession. Most of these were female, but for one he couldn't tell. The majority were god-fearing Americans, although he thought he detected a Chinese, an Ethiopian, a Pole and a girl that could have been Irish.

"Could have been Irish; you have to be kidding, Father. Was her name Colleen?"

"Why, yes it was. And she was wearing the most captivating perfume."

I marked down *Irish* in my notes, and joined Joel and the fingerprint team outside the church. We now had some solid leads, and it would be down to the university computers to spit out some names. It was a morning well spent.

I dropped in on Rita at police headquarters, and brought her up to date with our investigation. Of course, I didn't go into details regarding the harvesting of this information, and she knew better than to ask. She couldn't make lunch, so I made do with some nachos and a beer at the Lolita Tequila Bar. A little worm was trying to tell me that I should try the house specialty, but it was early afternoon, and I did have an appointment with a couple of young Rechabites. Dr Haire met me at the door, once again displaying that cheesy grin of his.

There were three stand-out candidates for the third degree. One was a bus driver from Salem called Con McMahon. Certainly, he came into Boston with his tourist vehicle, but why wouldn't he go to confession in his own parish? He was a handsome devil, and I could understand how the ladies might think that he was a bit of all right.

The prissy hairdresser was something else again. I am not sure whether the photo did him justice, but it was hard to tell whether Pat Carey was male or female. The boys had already asked around, and most people thought that he was a horse's ass: not his clients, mind you. They loved him, and wouldn't let anyone else touch their hair.

Maureen O'Keefe was a regular at confession. At least, that's what everyone was saying. However, most people wondered what she was confessing. On the face of it, she maintained an unspectacular lifestyle, and was always around to help out the church, the school, and those in need. On her Facebook page, she had listed *Silence of the Lambs* as her favorite book, so the computer had thrown her up as a suspect.

The next job was to cross reference the suspects with the victims, and see whether anything came up. The results were so blatant, I couldn't believe it. All of the dead people were serviced by Pat Carey, when they were alive. He was their hairdresser.

Worse news was to come. He was also Rita Green's hairdresser, and you know how women like to talk under the blow dryer. If she provided him with classified information during the investigation, the lady could be in big trouble. She was up for election in a short while, and her opponent, the sleazy, slimy, salacious sycophant, Brian Brushfield, would milk every photo op and news bite to his advantage. I felt sorry for her. She could never have seen this coming.

"Rita, this case has taken a spectacular turn, and you may be severely compromised. I think that you should stand back, and let us investigate your stylist. Did he put that lick on your forehead? It is quite attractive."

"Gee, Paddy, I don't know what to say. He always gave me mate's rates. Where will I go, now?"

"Don't worry, Rita. I appreciate your predicament, and his. I will treat him with sympathy and respect. I am not an animal. I am an Australian citizen, both tolerant and compassionate. He couldn't be in better hands."

Sympathy and respect

Carey had been in the cells overnight. They dragged him into the interview room; he was bleeding from multiple wounds. His nose had been broken, his face was swollen, and he was totally disheveled. I gave him a moment to compose himself.

"You dirty scumbag poofta! Do you think we don't know what you did? Three beautiful young lives and an old fart that didn't deserve to die! Why did you do it? What possible motive could you have? Did they not like your blow wave? Did they reject your advances? Tell me ass-hole. I want to know."

This was my traditional opening salvo, and I wouldn't mind a few dollars for every time it worked. Unfortunately, Pat Carey was not easily swayed by invective and trash talk. He spat at me, and I gave him one in the chops. The attending policeman lowered his head over his Sudoku, and the recording technician suddenly slipped, and put his elbow on the pause button of the recorder. These were not moments for general consumption.

The think tank had reconvened in Cambridge, and Joel had added James and Jessica to the group, and for good reason. They had been real troupers during the bugging exercise, and they needed to be rewarded. Unfortunately, Jess kept falling asleep every few minutes, and I wondered where her mother was.

For the rest of us, it was a challenge to find a motive for this murder. None of us had any doubt that Carey had done the dirty deeds, but we had to prove it. Rita Green's career may be on the line, and Joel and I were now on an incentive payment. Don't you just love a job with a bonus attached?

As a member of the aforementioned Dinosaur's Club, and a technological buffoon, I am continually amazed at the information and statistical data that can be obtained from computer files. Of course, the machines are only as good as the people who operate them, and research is fine if you know where to look. The boy wonder knew where to look, and he promised me a result in two hours. I was in the act of obtaining a search warrant for Pat Carey's premises.

"Paddy, make sure that you call in here on the way to the house. I may have something for you."

When I returned to Cambridge, two hours later, he was true to his word. It was not what I expected to hear. It fact, his revelation was quite unbelievable. Nevertheless, I knew in my heart that we would be able to confirm the facts.

"Carey's victims were all long-standing clients, Paddy. Over the years, they were all as close and intimate as any hairdresser and customer can be. You know how it is. There's a lot of bending over, body-brushing, hot breath and aromatic smells of one sort or another. Eventually, these four people came to a unanimous conclusion: Pat Carey was a woman."

"Well, Joel, that is certainly some kind of revelation. However, I can't see why anybody would kill in order to protect such a silly secret, which may be patently obvious to anybody who meets him/her."

"This is true. However, there was a deeper secret that might be exposed if Pat's true identity were to be revealed. I am sure that Carey regrets the day that he/she supported *Burn your Bra Day*, an initiative of the local feminist group. It was the day that James Cahill and Kerrie Bartholomew had appointments. The clients usually like a bit of a gossip, so I am sure that the hair guru would have known that Kerrie would relay the information to the other girls at the Best for you Bowels Company."

"And Carey's real identity is?"

"Patricia Anne Wheeler of Woodstock, Connecticut, aka *Pat the Rat Wheeler*! The lady copped a life sentence for a series of brutal murders in the New England area, about five years ago. She is good with disguises, and escaped prison in a stretch limo, masquerading as the warden. When you turn over her house, do not be surprised if you find a midget's head, somebody's eyes in a bottle, and a Parson's nose. These were all missing from her various crime scenes, and they have never been recovered."

"I'll be looking for Annabel Carter's black knickers with Carey's fingerprints on them."

"That too," said Joel, as he wished me good luck. Homer Simpson was about to make his first appearance on the box that day, and the lad wanted to get back to it. I called Rita and asked her to meet me at Carey's house. I wanted her to take a back step, but if this was going to be the moment of denouement, she needed to be there, especially if there was a television crew in sight!

I will not go into the details of what we found, but there were no human remains in the house. However, we did find Annabel's knickers, some interesting perfume, and a closet full of shoes; they were exactly the size that we were looking for. It was a dog day afternoon for the Rat Wheeler, and she meekly surrendered when the police made their case.

Rita Green and the relatives of the deceased were all in court when Judge Griffin sent down his verdict, and it surprised no-one: another four life sentences.

I thought that it was a nice touch when they delivered her back to prison in a stretch limo.

PEST AND THE PIRATE QUEEN

I often spend time in the San Fernando Valley. It is a sprawling panorama of houses, factories, airports and shopping malls. The demographic householder ranges from Latino to suburban redneck to born-again Christian. The statistician will tell you that they have two point five children, one point seven dogs, a cat and a parakeet or budgie. In the driveway of the average home will be at least two pick-up trucks, and the Stars and Stripes will be flapping in the breeze on the lawn flagpole. Very special people will have a sign hanging in the front portal that reads "God bless this house."

I think that it is fair to say that God does bless America. Every day, a patriot somewhere intones this supplementation, and perhaps joins in a song of praise that drips with saccharin jingoism. That fella upstairs has blessed this nation with a social and financial lifestyle that, until recently, was the envy of many. Unfortunately, the big Kahuna's brother, Allah (or is he just a cousin) only wants to shit on the country. Can you believe that?

I don't usually like to get involved with fundamental extremists because they are an ugly lot and quite unfriendly. Of course, I say this in the nicest possible way. We don't want them to commission a fatwa or anything like that, do we?

Quite frankly, I don't know why they bother with all their rage. Leave us to our own devices, and we can cause more havoc on ourselves than they ever will. Or leave it to Mother Nature with her earthquakes, tsunamis and volcanoes. In the end, we will all muddle through, and this will be so, even after the Jihad brigade has done their worst.

All the same, we have to be seen to be proactive, and here I was in the north end of the San Fernando Valley, investigating a terror alert. I don't think that they would have called on me if I hadn't already been there: a bit of a catch-up with friends. I suspect that they also felt that if things went wrong, I was expendable. You can really feel the love, can't you?

There was credible evidence that there was going to be a suicide bomber let loose in the grounds of the John F Kennedy High School in Granada Hills. This is a campus of some five thousand students. It is a seat of learning that has produced many successful American achievers, including Major League baseball players, track athletes and professional footballers. I imagine that the terrorist was going to set the damn thing off by text. What action could be more incongruous in a sea of teenagers?

I have often felt that al Qaeda's strategic planning is the brainchild of Jubilation T. Cornpone. The more suicide bombers that they send out there, the more they deplete their own brigade of foot soldiers. Nevertheless, these fanatics persist with their hatred of all things American, and we had a suspect.

Peter Cox was a twenty-eight-year old former Marine. He had performed honorably in two overseas postings, but during his tour of duty in the Philippines, he had become influenced by a beautiful Filipino singer called Anna Ebreo. Anna was a bomb-maker, and a sleeper for al Qaeda. She was also a sleeper for a few of the lads over at the former US Marine base at Subic Bay. She radicalized Cox in no uncertain manner, and he was subsequently dishonorably discharged.

The Philippines is mainly a Catholic country, but more than five percent of the population are beholden to Islam, and mostly live in the southern islands. They are happy to harbor fellow travelers if they are designated as persona non gratia in other countries. However, for strategic purposes, it was decided that the fundamental fugitive from France, Abraham Ebreo, should raise his family near an American base. He chose a small village on the water near Subic Bay. Anna was the youngest of five, and spent most of her days as a toddler on the beach in her one piece bikini. She went into the sea, too. The C4 came later.

Being the youngest, she was daddy's favorite girl, and was always hanging from his arm when he entertained his friend from Saudi Arabia. Jelli Nitrate worked for a construction company, and was their explosives expert. His best friend was the owner's son, Ozzy bin Laden. You will all know who I am talking about, and you shouldn't confuse this person with Australia's Foreign Minister, who the media refer to as Aussie bin everywhere.

Boom Boom Nitrate made many visits to the Ebreo home over the years, and felt that he should repay their hospitality. When Anna became of age, he picked up the tab for her first visit to camp. Or should I say camps? They were in Syria, Pakistan and Afghanistan. She came back an experienced terrorist with diplomas in hand-to-hand combat, rocket-launching and bomb-making. I don't know whether Peter Cox was targeted, or she felt genuine affection for him. Nevertheless, they were married, and what can you say? Ain't love grand?

You will excuse me if I cut to the chase because the intervening years are not important. The fact is that Peter and Anna were now living in Mission Hills — just the two of them.

You may wonder why I choose to labor the latter point — only because it is unusual.

The Filipino credo of marriage is quite simple. If you live in a better house than the brother, sisters or parents, they will move in with you. Not that they would ever impose on your privacy; they don't all come on the honeymoon — only half of them.

So, it was relevant that they lived alone. It would be easier to plan their attack, and entertain their fellow conspirators without interference. Sometimes there were up to three pick-up trucks in the drive of their small bungalow. From my spy position down the street, I became aware of a pit bull terrier and a rabbit named José. How José survived I will never know.

The day that Peter Cox drove his dynamite-packed truck through the outer fence of the school on Gothic St, we were waiting for him. There were three helicopters hovering above, and I was standing directly in his path with an RPG-7 reloadable rocket launcher on my shoulder. The five thousand students were looking out of all available windows, and texting madly to their friends, relatives and favorite talk-show host.

I had to anticipate the cross wind and the relative safety distance before I pulled the trigger. My nerdy pal, Greg, was up in one of the helicopters with his lap-top, and I had a radio feed to his considered calculations. Unfortunately, he was a nervous person, and had a bad stutter. His affliction nearly killed me.

"N..n..n..n.. now, Paddy. For God's sake, now!

I pressed the trigger, and the rocket barreled towards the volatile vehicle. I could see that Cox was in a crazed state. His eyes were dilated, and he was brandishing a copy of the Koran as he drove at me. That was it. The truck disintegrated in an instant: the detonation of the explosives was incredible. I was lying flat on the ground when the after-burn swept over me, and petered out just short of the main school building. The things that I do for America!

I would have liked to think that this was the end of it but it wasn't. Anna and her other conspirators had been in the background in their respective pick-ups. When they saw what had happened, they did a runner. The authorities later discovered that the minor schemers were members of the Islam Isotopes, a bowling team in Woodland Hills. They were soon rounded up, but Anna Ebreo was nowhere to be found.

I decided to return to Australia. As I don't relish the long plane trip, I often decamp in Honolulu for a few days, and Chinatown is always worth a visit; it is a vibrant, bustling, seething mass of commercial endeavor and opportunity. I decided to eat Vietnamese, and was immediately impressed by the industrious nature of the restaurant owner and his female staff.

The waitress had my shrimp rolls in one hand and the fish noodle soup in the other. Resting on her inner forearm was the complimentary bean shoots, lettuce and Vietnamese mint. She cradled a cell phone between her glowing cheek and inverted shoulder, and the high-pitched voice coming from within was definitely not an urgent corporate booking. This was tittle-tattle, and she maintained the conversation for twenty minutes through at least another half-dozen customers. The beauty of it all was that she managed to revert to hold whenever a customer reached for their wallet.

I don't want you to think that I am hung-up on this multi-tasking thing with women, and I don't want to sound bitter or anything like that. It's just that I have bad memories. My girl-friend used to read *Who* magazine over my shoulder when we had sex. My shrink did her best to hose down the inadequacy complex that this kind of thing can evoke, but the lady was hardly convincing. I remain fragile.

A man who eats alone has a number of alternatives. You can stare into your soup; give the waitress the once-over; or look out the window at the passing parade. I had a window seat, and I nearly regurgitated my shrimp rolls when I saw an elegant Filipino lady walk by. It was Anna Ebreo: bomb-maker and vixen.

I slipped the waitress a tip and got out of there, quickly, leaving behind an unfinished meal and a bemused owner. Anna was half a block ahead of me, but I had little difficulty in slipstreaming in behind her. Hers was the kind of tail that I liked.

She led me on a merry chase: a bit of shopping; an early afternoon dip in the ocean; and a final surprise destination — the Hawaii Maritime

Center. Hawaii has a grand maritime history, and it is all here, including an original pirate ship, tethered up at the wharf. Built in Scotland in 1878, the *Falls of Clyde* is the only remaining four-masted, fully-rigged ship on God's earth. With all the popularity of Captain Jack Sparrow and the *Pirates of the Caribbean*, you can imagine that they are milking it for all it is worth. However, I couldn't imagine why Allah's favorite god-child was walking up the gang-plank. I gave her time to disappear into the bowels of the vessel, and followed her on board.

Putting a tail on Anna

The deck was deserted, but this would be a temporary situation. An A-frame and sandwich board were advertising a full-scale pirate attack at four pm, and twice on weekends. Adults were half-price. I wondered how my Beretta might fare against a musket and produced it, just in case.

The ladder down to the lower deck was tight. They must have been small people in those days. I could hear noises coming from a cabin at the end of the companion way, and I moved in that direction. I didn't hear the door open behind me, but I did see the darkness. It enveloped me in the aftermath of a strong blow from a hard object.

I don't know how long I was in black city, but a splash of water brought me back to the real world. Well, not really! I awoke to see Blackbeard the

Pirate staring at me, with musket in hand. He had a patch over one eye, and his visible pupil was bloodshot. His mouth smelled of garlic and dried camel dung. He must have been suffering from scurvy.

The female voice came from behind him. Anna was also decked-out in pirate gear. She must have been the all-singing, all-cussing Captain Blood that I saw advertised on the sandwich board. The kids would be in for a treat, but right now, she was only cussing.

"Who the fuck are you, sunshine? Don't you know that it is illegal to carry a weapon on a Matson Line vessel?"

"Well, you seem to be carrying them, or don't those peashooters work."

"The guy is a wiseass, Amir. Why don't we terminate his tattle? What do you think, Khalid?"

"Can we disembowel him, first? It will be fun."

I have to say that Khalid didn't look like he laughed a lot, and so I was glad that I could be instrumental in bringing a little joy into his world. However, it must have been close to four o'clock because there was a knock on the door, and the stage manager intervened.

"Five minutes, folks; everybody to their places."

Everybody bustled around for a bit, and then Amir put a gag on me, and checked my bonds. They would attend to me later. Meanwhile, they had a performance to provide, and the whole five of them skulked out into the passageway. Allah was on the side of the pirates. I was hoping that they would be up against Britain's best, and have their pants shot off.

It's not easy being bound, and having no-one to talk with. Naturally, I thought about escape, but thinking about it is a lot easier than actually doing it. If I was in Australia, I could rely on my pal Stormy Weathers to arrive with the cavalry, but I was on my own, and none of my buddies knew of my stop-over plans. Suddenly, I shifted my position, and sat on something sharp. It was a toothpick from the Vietnamese restaurant.

This was of no use whatsoever, but I was glad that I had it. Dental hygiene is very important and I wanted to look good in my coffin. In the end, it was the earthquake that saved me. Many of the earthquakes in the Hawaiian Islands are offshore, although the Big Island is particularly prone to seismic activity. In either case, both Oahu and Maui usually feel the effects. On this occasion, it was vibrant enough to throw all the pirates into the water and, as the ship lurched sideways, I slid over to the side of the cabin, as did everything else that wasn't bolted down. This included an armory of knives and cutlasses that were available for the use of the entertainment troop. I was sure that they wouldn't mind me using the sharp edges to secure my release.

There are certain field agents throughout the intelligence world that have a license to kill. Others have a license to communicate; I was one of those. We have a small transmitter sown into the waistband of our underpants, and when we are in trouble with terrorist groups, we activate it. The satellite configuration will provide instant navigation for those in the rescue party. Normally, I would have been able to activate the device with my hands tied behind my back, but for some reason, I had put my underpants on backwards that morning. I was now able to push the button.

When I made it to the deck, I came upon confusion and mayhem. Children were crying everywhere, and efforts were being made to rescue the pirates, who had fallen from the rigging — a big drop to the water below. I could see Anna in the swell and she saw me. She immediately duck-dived under the ship, and I lost her.

The chief CIA operative in Oahu, Tony Dow, had arrived in response to my underpants call. He introduced himself. I liked his easy-going smile and affable nature, and I could tell that he was a man who was prepared for anything. He was wearing a rain-coat, and it was a beautiful sunny day. The only time that he removed his hat was when he introduced himself to some of the mothers. There were only a few strands of hair left on his head, and there was a gigantic scar that reached around the front of his skull. He probably wasn't the first CIA officer to have received a lobotomy.

Tony's boys had rounded up most of the Arabs, but they had failed to find America's most wanted. Yes, Anna Ebreo had succeeded the late Osama bin Laden, and was just as elusive. At least she was still in Hawaii, and we would make it difficult for her to flee.

Kalakaua Ave is the main drag through Waikiki, and the tourists descend on it like lemmings at a cliff-top luau. On both sides of the street, the designer stores share the neighborhood with fast food outlets, gift shops and ice-cream parlors. Closer to the curb, the independents are at work. In the space of two hundred yards, I counted two portrait painters, three tarot readers and a gold and silver daubed mime artist. A little further along was someone dressed as a newspaper. There was also a Bob Marley impersonator, people with parrots and, the most desolate of them all, a man reading the Bible out loud. I guess everyone had heard it all before.

It would not be easy to locate Anna in this cosmopolitan environment of listless extravagance. People were here for a good time, and the locals were prepared to give it to them. Those who had an ulterior agenda could move amongst the shadows, and we would never be the wiser. There were a lot of dark haired vixens in Honolulu. How would I catch up with the one that I wanted?

I didn't know whether Anna had made any connection with my pursuit of her, and that ghastly occurrence in California. She had escaped my clutches at the Maritime Center, and I could only think that she might feel safer if she continued with her usual daily grind; that is, except for the pirate show. Given that she was a professional singer, I thought that a tour of the bars and night clubs might be a good way to track her down — all expenses paid, of course.

Tony Dow had given me his telephone number, and he was prepared to make himself available at any time. I managed to get hold of him, and we arranged a bar crawl that would start with drinks at my hotel.

The house band was local, and they churned out a mix of standard classics and traditional ballads that were totally acceptable if you were drinking your alcohol out of a coconut. The leader of the band was the biggest man that I had ever seen. Resplendent in a Hawaiian shirt and a pair of very large shorts, his angelic voice was testimony to the fact that you don't always get what you expect. Best of all, his sunny personality and clever sense of humor was everything that his adoring audience wanted.

"Does my butt look big in this?"

He loved to tease the customers, and the girls at a nearby table were prepared to laugh at all his jokes.

"Now, here's a special request for a very special young lady, who is here for her hen's night."

He then slipped into balladeer mode, and produced a half decent version of *Too Young to Get Married*. Tony and I looked at each other, smiled and quaffed our drinks. There were a lot of bars on our list, and we would also have to eat somewhere.

The eating is easy if you can dispense with the lei that they throw around your neck. The major hotels all offer a smorgasbord, and usually throw in a floor show with a big band and lots of girls. The palms always sway in Hawaii, and so do the hula dancers. I never realized how mesmerizing this particular performance art could be. These people are lyrical of both voice and action, and their hand movements make conversation seem irrelevant. For someone who was brought up with the two-fingered salute, I could empathize with what they were trying to do.

I don't know how many drinking establishments we covered before we arrived at *Loretta's Late Nite Laxative*. This was a funny name for a night club, and I wondered if they put something in the drinks. If they did, it wasn't alcohol because my fifteen dollar Daiquiri had definitely been watered down. However, you could never catch them in the act; the lights were so dim, we could have been in the bat cave. By the time that the entertainment sparked up, I was pretty tanked, and was starting to nod off. The CIA spook nudged me in the ribs.

"Hey Paddy, I think that's her. She has a great body, and she certainly looks Filipino."

I immediately became interested, and confirmed that Mr Dow was on the mark. Anna was wearing a strapless gown of light fabric that had a long way to go before it would reach her knees. Her jet-black hair was perfectly groomed, and she was wearing sapphire and ruby drop earrings that sparkled under the bandstand lights. The girl beside her was dressed identically.

"There's no girl beside her, Paddy. You're wasted."

"S…s…s…sure I am, but we have to arrest her anyway. My God, she looks horny."

"We can't arrest her. Not here, not tonight. We'll have to come back tomorrow. The public will not accept an inebriated member of their security service behaving badly. Anyway, she might get the better of us."

"Bloody hell, are you sure that you're not with the FBI?"

We managed to slip away without Anna setting eyes on us, and that would mean that she would return on the 'morrow to complete her weekly engagement. At least, we hoped so.

The 'morrow was not a happy morning for me. It all started with happy people at breakfast. I hate happy people at breakfast. Why would you rejoice just because it is a bright, sunny day? It is always bright and sunny in paradise. To make matters worse, I needed some kind of silencer on my toast. It was making a horrendous noise every time I bit into it. Then there was my table companion: Danielle, the health nut. She was impressed that I was eating my papaya. Little did she know that I was eating it because it was silent food?

I often feel that the best way to overcome a hangover is to have a complete makeover, so I put myself in the hands of Danielle, who took me to her therapist. After a steam, sauna, massage and haircut, I was a new man. I spent the afternoon oiling my Beretta.

That night at Loretta's, it was a full house, mainly due to the two dozen operatives that we had spread around the club. Everybody was dressed in Aloha shirts because you can carry so many weapons underneath. I was wearing a bullet-proof vest with my pistol tucked into my pants. Tony was carrying the only pair of handcuffs, and you know who they were for. The only mistake was the directive that members should not drink on the job. That is how we blew our cover.

I think that it was the waiter who complained to the barman that no-one was drinking booze, and this bit of information somehow filtered backstage. It gave Anna the incentive to check out her audience. She moved the curtain that separated the Green Room from the Blue Room (the entertainment was usually smutty adult comedy) and received one heck of a surprise.

Everybody in the audience looked like a cop. Then she saw me, and I just looked like me. It was her cue to run. Naturally, I followed.

As I spilled onto the pavement, with the rest of the law enforcers behind me, I could see her speed off in her SUV. A bullet whistled past my head as a deterrent. Where was Tony Dow and his wheels? As if in answer, I smelt burning rubber; a big Dodge appeared out of an underground car park. The side door flew open, and I scrambled in. There was hardly any traffic at this time of night, so we would be able to keep her in sight, if not overtake the elusive butterfly.

Kalakaua Ave was like Conrod Straight, and she was making good time. However, once we left the tourist precinct, there would be limited overhead lighting, and we would lose our vision. Tony put in a call to naval headquarters, and soon we had a chopper for company — one with a great big searchlight.

"It's Showtime, baby, and you're in the spotlight."

Having left the high-rise area, options were few. She chose the coast road to Diamond Head, and we were with her all the way. Once into the hills, the neighborhood becomes distinctly affluent. After all, who wouldn't pay big money for a plush house with a nice view? I suspected that one of these people was a sympathetic Middle Eastern merchant or politician, and that there was a safe house hidden amidst all this respectability. Otherwise, where could she be heading?

The good news was that we were joined by a SWAT team in two jeeps. They saluted as they drove past us in hot pursuit. The bad news was that she put the spotlight out of action. The horrendous hellcat must have had an armory in the back of that SUV because there were more shots, and we heard the helicopter cough and splutter. It wheeled off, mortally wounded. We could only hope that it would make it to Waikiki Beach.

"Tony, what if she drives past the safe house, and they pull out of the drive and settle behind us. We would be trapped."

"Good thinking, Australia. Hey, Captain, can you drop one of those jeeps behind us? We're expecting some rearguard action. Thank you."

No sooner had the vehicle taken up a position behind us when it exploded. It looked very much like the Jihad Jerries had an RPG unit similar to that which I had used in Granada Hills. I was very much hoping that their weapon wasn't a reloadable model. If you thought that Tony Dow was perturbed, you would be right. He was on the phone again, ordering some F-18 Hornet fighters from a nearby aircraft carrier. This guy had contacts everywhere.

While this was all going on, we were actually gaining on the spiteful spitfire in front of us. She seemed to be heading straight for the rim of Diamond Head. I wondered why.

This dormant volcano is off-limits to most of us, but the crater has been used at various times for military and weather installations. If this were an Ian Fleming novel, there would be a whole laboratory down there, with full nuclear capability. The place would be run by a mad scientist with an unlimited budget and ambitions of world domination. I live in the real world. I could see no more than a few bitter terrorists with computers, cell phones, a satellite dish and some bomb-making equipment. Of course, they would also have a year's supply of frozen kebabs.

Anna went as far as she could go. When the road finished, the lady abandoned her vehicle, and continued on foot up the mountain towards the edge of the volcano. I advised the SWAT guys to keep away from the SUV in case it had been booby-trapped. In fact, it was. When the iridescent orange and yellow flames spread out into the night sky, there was raucous applause from the maniacal Mujahideen, who were now following us in a clapped-out Volkswagen Kombi bus. They burst into song, which was obviously patriotic, but in no way lyrical. However, it must have been one of Allah's favorites.

We left behind our elite force to deal with this riff-raff, while Tony and I commenced the arduous climb in pursuit of the malicious miscreant. Anna made it to the top before we did, and turned around with a malevolent smile on her face. We were almost on her, and she had nowhere to go. All of a sudden, the Filipino fireball put two fingers to her lips, and produced the longest and loudest wolf whistle that I have ever heard. What happened next was staggering.

From behind her came the sound of trudging feet, and countless foot soldiers appeared over the rim of the volcano. There must have been a thousand of them: Arab, Indonesian, Pakistani and Filipino. The Taliban were also represented, and I even recognized one of the Muslims from that *World Wide Wrestling* show. It was a terrifying sight, as they waved their weapons of choice, which were glinting under the light of the moon. It was Tony and I against an army of fanatical freedom fighters, armed with AK-47's and grenade launchers.

It takes a lot for me to lose my cool, but I had to admit that I was nervous. I patted my Beretta as if to reassure myself that I would go down fighting. Tony had turned distinctly pale, and was already on his cell phone, tapping in amended co-ordinates for the Hornet strike force. Where on earth were they? They seemed to be taking forever.

I did have a moment for reflection, and it was then that I realized that the bomb affair in California had just been a diversion. This was the real deal. They had probably been preparing their troops for months, and the deserted crater had been an ideal training ground. An attack on Pearl Harbor wasn't a novel idea, but you can understand why these particular Americans would be a target. The place was still an American naval base, but a distance from the mainland. Because of their proximity to the International Date Line, their attack would receive immediate coverage on all news bulletins.

They say that before you die, you hear the sounds of silence. Thankfully, all I could hear was the ear-piercing scream of somebody breaking the sound barrier above my head. The three Hornets came in low, and strafed the terrorist army. The troops scattered but hardly far enough. The second wave of F-18's dropped their bombs with remarkable accuracy, dipped their wings and headed home. What was left of the reactionary force was negligible, but they had gathered in a group and raised their flag. It looked like a replay of the Battle of Little Big Horn, but their leader didn't have flowing blonde locks — she was a dark brunette.

"Come and get us, slime ball. You know you want to. My last bullet will have your name on it. God is great. Long live the LA Lakers."

She was certainly an impassioned person, and it was good to know that the brazen bomb-maker might well be down to her last bullet. Obviously, Tony Dow was relieved to know that his name wasn't on anyone's bullet.

"I would stand behind the attack team, if I was you, Paddy. It sounds like she means business. Captain, we want this woman taken, dead or alive. Is that understood?"

"Ten-four, Mr Dow."

I didn't know what it would take to kill this demented disciple of doom, but we tried our best. In the end, she threw up her hands in surrender, and we escorted the feisty firebrand and the remnants of her force to the lock-up. It was explained that rendition was a probability, and that she should prepare her farewells to her buddies on the island entertainment circuit. She gave us her rendition of the Edith Piaf classic *Non, je ne regrette rien* — no regrets.

You had to admit that this terrorist was a pretty ballsy kind of a lady, and she must have been good at her job. Even though they often live in tents, there are a lot of glass ceilings for women in the Muslim world, and to rise above all that is impressive. I wonder if Osama had been giving her one. From my experience, this kind of thing can assist with promotion and work satisfaction.

This is just about the end of the story. America's most wanted is no longer wanted. She rots in a jail cell, somewhere on the planet, while the judicial system mulls over the right way to penalize those who would separate us from our hard-fought freedoms. I am back on my usual bar stool at Sam's Fly by Night Club, and it will probably be some time before I return to America; perhaps when there are no more pirates in Hawaii, or the Lakers win another championship.

Tony Dow: CIA operative

PEST AND THE LITTLE PEOPLE

The Kentucky Derby is a time-honored event that is a magnet to bluebloods of the highest order; especially if you are a three-year-old racehorse. It is the most exciting two minutes in sport, according to legend. The patrons flock to the Churchill Downs racecourse in order to suck up the traditional Mint Juleps, and flutter away their hard-earned at the betting windows — not that there is anything wrong with that.

With so much going on, you would think that the last thing on anybody's mind would be murder. Yet, this is exactly what had happened. The body was found in the stabling area of the course precinct, and it was just a matter of co-incidence that I was in attendance. It is true that I like to attend the track at every opportunity, but in this case, I was a guest of the chief sponsor, the Yum Company; best known for their KFC, Pizza Hut and Taco Bell brands. I had been noticed at an Elvis look-alike contest in Memphis, and invited to perform Kentucky Rain before the big race. This was a great honor because no one can remember when the University of Louisville Marching Band didn't get this gig.

Pest in Memphis

I was one of the first at the murder scene, and I was fortunate that my reputation had preceded me. My guest ticket had *International Crime Fighter* stamped on it. The police sergeant in charge introduced himself, and was impressed that I had arrived with his chief, who was also a guest in the Committee Room.

Chief Jack Sullivan was a thirty-year veteran, who had a lot of confidence in himself, but had become disinterested in hands-on police work. He was counting the days until he retired, and received his big fat superannuation check. In the early days, I expect that he might have terrorized the younger members of his precinct, but he seemed quite docile in his current social mode. The red nose and telltale blotches on his skin gave away the fact that there had probably been many social occasions in recent years. However, he was still inquisitive, and keen to get to the bottom of this interruption to his day out.

"Is that the imprint of a horse's hoof that I see on the fellow's head?"

"Yes, sir," replied the capable sergeant, who was delighted to be in the presence of Louisville's number one law enforcer.

"Well, that's it then. This is obviously an accident. You don't need me, anymore, do you?"

I felt obliged to interrupt. My basic training in Australia had taught me to be observant and objective, and the golden rule of positive detective work was to never rule out the obvious.

"You don't think that the knife that is sticking out of his back may have contributed to his unfortunate situation?"

The lawman noted my sarcasm, and grunted disapprovingly. Nevertheless, I couldn't be overly critical as he had been on the sauce for two hours, and he did want to get back to the Committee Room. I believe that he had a hot tip in the next race.

"Don't worry, Chief, Sergeant Brady and I will take things from here. I'll report back to you later."

He was happy with these arrangements, and waddled off for another Mint Julep. I bent down to inspect the body. He was a small man, and a pretty natty dresser, although that knife had seriously damaged his stylish jacket.

"Is there anyone here who might know who he is?"

"Why Mr Pest, everyone knows who he is. This is Spyder Price, the leading jockey. He was down to ride the favorite in the Derby."

Well, suck my spit and call me messy. I couldn't believe it. I had spent the previous evening boning up on the current form, and all the experts said that the favorite was an unruly animal, and it was thought that this jock was the only one that could handle him. I excused myself and immediately went to the tote window.

"Do you think that I could have a refund? I have decided not to have a bet in the main race." The operator looked at me over her glasses, sighed, and then returned my money. When news of this incident was made public, there would be reimbursement mania. I walked back to the scene of the crime with a satisfied smile on my face.

"I suppose that we should find out if there is any next of kin. Do you know if he was married?"

"He had a wife and three kids: Huey, Dewey and Louie."

"Sergeant, you are very well-informed. I am impressed."

"Yes, well, he was my brother-in-law."

I stared at him for a full minute. I didn't know what to say. For a bereaved relative, he was taking it rather well, and I wondered whether I should include him in the list of suspects. Given that I didn't have any other suspects, I put him on the list. He could be removed later. In the meantime, the policeman's sister would be in the crowd somewhere. I dispatched him to find her, and console the widow. I would also need to talk to Spyder's woman. The wife is always a suspect.

As Sergeant Brady moved out, the coroner moved in. It was pretty tight in the horse box, so I gave him plenty of room. I could smell whisky, and I determined that he was also an on-course guest; the Live-longer Liver Company had a marquee near the winning post. One wondered whether he was a donor, recipient or a procurer. In any case, his predilection for a tipple didn't interfere with his analysis.

"The knife did it. No question! I can tell you that the head wound was sustained before death, but it wasn't fatal. There will be a tox report, but that's about it."

I didn't need to wait for a toxicology report or any other report. This was murder, and the culprit was probably still on the racecourse. I decided to seek out the obvious suspect: the rider of the second favorite.

Willy Breadmaker was in the jockey room with all the other little people. I was not totally *au fait* with the hoops that etched out an existence on America's dirt, synthetic and grass tracks, but I knew that I was in exalted company. Angel Gomez, Johnny Goose, Chick Winterbottom, Jerez Valencia and Jesus Caravaggio all had important rides in the big race, and they were in a state of shock, having heard the news of Spyder Price's bereavement.

"Willy, do you think we can have a few words? My name is Paddy Pest, and I'm investigating the murder."

"Sure, I'm heading for the steam room. Why don't you join me?"

I had never conducted an interrogation in a steam room before. I was glad that I was able to take off my coat jacket before we went in. The temperature was beyond hot. It occurred to me that the wily old jock was intent on making me feel uncomfortable, but I was unperturbed. Where I came from, it was as hot as a dingo's droppings. I loosened my tie in a show of relaxed confidence.

"So, Willy, were you good friends with the deceased? Did you ever invite him home for egg nog?"

"We knew each other professionally. We didn't mix socially. He was a good jock, but he did have an attitude problem. He thought that he was better than everyone else."

"I have heard that you once threatened him. Is this true?"

"I might have. Once or twice, but who's counting?"

"I'm counting, Willy, and so might the jury if they think that you were responsible for his unfortunate death. Where were you when Price got it in the back? Don't lie to me, Willy. I can tell when someone is lying."

I don't often bully a smaller person, but I could tell that Breadmaker had something to hide. He was sweating profusely. I went in for the kill.

"Give it up, little man. You did it, didn't you? You knew that you had no chance in the big race while Spyder was riding *Accelerator*. You were also having an affair with his wife, and you're in hock to half a dozen bookies. Tell me it isn't true, dirt bag."

"It isn't true. I have every chance on the second favorite. I am also gay, and a multi-millionaire, besides. Can I go, now?"

The prime suspect stormed out of the hot box, and now I was the one who was sweating. Damn! I may have to re-evaluate my interrogation technique.

As I was taking my leave from the changing room, Jesus Caravaggio caught my eye. Christ Almighty! Where do they get these names? He nodded his head ever so slightly, and indicated that he wanted to speak to me alone. I waited outside until he caught up.

"Signor, the Spyder was having women trouble. You should talk to his wife. Also the almost unbearably beautiful senorita, Jennifer Youngblood! Around the track, they call her *Sporting Jenny*."

Of course they do, and so did all those Irish balladeers; they had another name for it. However, it appears that Jennifer Youngblood's credentials were impeccable. She was an on-air personality for one of the networks' sporting affiliates, and there was nothing that she didn't know about football, golf, baseball and horse racing. I wondered what she knew about Spyder Price's murder.

The lady was on air when I caught up with her. The rumors concerning Spyder's demise had made it to the OB van, and the network people were trying to confirm with race officials. So far, there had been no announcement of a jockey change for the big race. I could tell that she had been crying. The make-up people had done what they could, but she was not at her effervescent best when she threw to the host commentator, and accepted a cup of coffee from her personal assistant. I had never had a mint coffee before, so I also accepted what was offered.

"This must be a shock to you, Miss Youngblood. I believe that you knew the deceased."

"So, it is true, Mr Pest. Poor Spyder really has been murdered."

"I'm afraid so, but I can't divulge any details right now. By the way, please call me Paddy."

She put her coffee down, and immediately burst into tears. I could see the make-up lady throw up her hands in disgust. Her tears seemed pretty real to me, but I made a mental note to check whether she had been an actress before she moved into television. One thing was certain. She was a fine looking woman. Jesus had certainly got that right.

My investigation had to be delayed a little as there was a race in progress. Both Willy and Jesus had given me tips, but there was some doubt as to the veracity of Willy's information. Sure enough, the nag came last, and I therefore retained him at the head of my suspect's list. I needed to catch up with the widow, but decided that this encounter could wait a little. I returned to the Committee Room and my sponsors. I had forgotten all about my vocal responsibility, and I would need some Dutch courage. I settled for French Champagne. The leader of the marching band was also in the room, and he was looking daggers at me.

While I was in the rest room, having a gargle, the announcement came through that Spyder Price was indisposed, and that replacement riders for the rest of the program would be systematically advised. However, Digger del Santo would have the mount on *Accelerator* in the Kentucky Derby. Digger was very much an Australian name, and I decided to re-invest my original bet. Prevarication is an insidious habit amongst gamblers. It is always best to follow your instincts, and hope that the object of your desire is not a follower.

It is easy to be impressed by the preliminary entertainment at Churchill Downs. The crowd tends to get tired and emotional very early, and they just love a good sing-along. As a performer, it is difficult to muck things up. My version of Kentucky Rain with an Aussie accent was a novel experience for them, and Mr Upstairs did his bit. It actually started to rain when I got to the second verse. The water shorted the microphone, and the amplification system gave up the ghost. To tell you the truth, I thought I saw a couple of university students hovering around the podium, but they needn't have worried. They will be back with their marching band next year.

The Run for the Roses is always an exciting event. It is the first race in the Triple Crown series, and the ten-furlong trip is usually a challenge for these young horses that are often attempting this distance for the first time. They will carry with them the hopes of their connections and supporters, alike. The rewards are fantastic, and a winning performance can often set up the owner, breeder or jockey for life. I wouldn't say that this is a race to die for, but some people might see it that way. Certainly, Digger del Santo would be nervous. This was his best opportunity yet to make his mark.

I won't drag this out. Jesus Caravaggio won the race on *Some Day Soon*. It was the tip that he had given me earlier in the day, and I had forgotten all about it. The odds were over 50/1. I was left absolutely spitless.

Nevertheless, with the race run and won, I had to get back to my investigation. While in the Committee Room, I had bonded with the police chief, and before he hit the wall with yet another Mint Julep, I had obtained the necessary financial commitment to continue with my consultancy role. I looked for his sergeant, and found him with the widow. They were sitting very close, and had their heads bowed. I didn't know whether they were praying or conspiring. Brady introduced me to his sister.

"I am sorry for your loss, Mrs Price. Are you up for a few questions?"

She was a pretty little thing, although quite a bit older than Jennifer Youngblood. I wondered if there was any bad blood between them, and pondered on how I might bring up this subject with delicacy.

"Somebody has suggested that the horny-looking TV girl was screwing your husband. Was this true?"

Sergeant Brady's mouth dropped open at the insensitivity of my question, and his sister started bawling her eyes out. The policeman tried to placate her.

"Calm down, sis. He is Australian, and he means well." He turned to me, and tried to diffuse the situation.

"I'm afraid that Caroline is not taking this well. Your assertions might best be addressed at another time. Are there any other avenues of interest that we could investigate?"

Bloody marvelous! In one foul swoop he had diverted attention away from his kin, and, at the same time, jumped on to the Paddy Pest bandwagon. I had the impression that with every move that I made, he would be by my side. I hoped that he was just ambitious. If there was a nefarious aspect to his motivation, he would stay on my suspect list.

Derby Day always winds down slowly, and the socializing continues well after the last race has been won. As I was making my way to the gate, a voice rang out across the concourse.

"Hey, Mr Pest, over here."

Jesus Caravaggio, the winning jockey, was entertaining a large group of well-wishers around a large ice-bucket full of champagne. He was no longer in his racing silks, but looked a picture of sartorial elegance. The lad was wearing a colorful check blazer, pink shirt, flared slacks, white shoes and a fedora hat. It was the kind of gear that you would wear on a date with Stevie Wonder. Quite frankly, I thought that he was too young to be smoking a cigar, but it was his day, so why not?

"Mr Pest, I would like you to meet my folks, Mary and Joseph Caravaggio. They have never met an Australian before."

We exchanged greetings and, I have to say, they looked like nice, honest people. Mrs C had a problem with the English language, and her attire was more conservative than her son's. That black lace mantilla that she was wearing was never going to be a fashion statement north of the border. Mary and Joseph, eh! I wondered if he was a carpenter.

As Jesus filled my glass, I couldn't help but notice an attractive lass, who looked like the boy's twin, in the group behind us. Five would get you ten that her name was Magdalene.

"Hey Maggie, come and meet an international crime fighter. Mr Pest, this is my sister, Maggie. She just loves older men. Don't you, sis?

"Hello Maggie. Please call me Paddy. Are you going to be a jockey, too?"

Magdalene Caravaggio didn't say a word. She just stared at me with her goo-goo googly eyes, and I knew that I had won another heart. In my mind, I couldn't see her becoming a jockey. She was too top heavy, and would probably fall off any horse that she mounted. I wondered if they still employed go-go dancers. This would be a natural for her. Jesus interrupted my train of thought.

"Paddy, we are having a celebration tonight. I hope that you can come."

It looked like I was his new best friend, so I said that I would be delighted to attend. I bade an interim goodbye to the folks, who were now tucking into the sponsor's Mexican product, which had been delivered, gratis, via one of the fast food outlets.

The address that Jesus had given me was a Chinese restaurant in downtown Louisville. For some reason, horseracing people believe that it is essential to celebrate a big win at a Chinese restaurant. The whole place had been booked out, and the owner of the winning steed would pick up the tab. Everyone was there except the horse (Chinese food affects his stomach) and champagne was being quaffed from one of the trophies. Most of the guests were drunk, except for Mary and Joseph. I found it surprising that one of the beaten jockeys had been invited: Willy Breadmaker.

Willy had his life partner with him, and they didn't appear to be in the best of moods. There was certainly a lot of sniping and bickering, and the other guests were not impressed that they had brought their personal war into the celebration room.

Cal Kleinmeister was another natty dresser, who was perfectly coordinated, in more ways than one. He was a taller man than the stocky hoop, and considerably younger. With that permanent suntan and irrepressible smile, he would be a target for passing trade, and it would be my guess that he had recently been rolling with someone other than the Breadmaker.

I would not normally subject you to this kind of innuendo, but Calvin Kleinmeister might well have been an important player in this tale of fast horses and Chop Suey. You see, at approximately eleven pm, Willy Breadmaker was found dead in the restaurant rest room. He had been stabbed in the back.

When they heard the news, Jesus, Mary and Joseph crossed themselves and reached for their rosary beads. Jesus had to borrow some because he had misplaced his about five years earlier. Calvin went weak at the knees, and had to be assisted to a seat. I sealed off the bathroom and called the police.

To my surprise, the first policeman to arrive was Sergeant Brady. He was wearing a silk smoking jacket and a cravat. He was accompanied by a delicate Chinese woman.

"Brady, what are you doing here? You are supposed to be off-duty."

"I live here, Paddy. This is my wife: Chin Chang Choy."

Well, there you go. The sign above the restaurant door read *Choy's for Dim Sum*. Brady was married to the owner's daughter, and that must have been one of the Choy boys who had served me my banana fritter. You should never let the ice cream melt, so I ordered three green teas, and sat down with Brady and his wife. He was the first to speak.

"Is the weapon the same type that killed Price? We could have a serial killer here, Paddy."

"I'm not sure about that. There has been a bit of friction with his partner. It may have been a gay blade that killed him. We will have to wait for forensics"

The CSI people from the Jefferson County Coroner's office arrived in due course, and started asking questions. One of these questions was particularly pertinent. Why hadn't he seen the killer if he was in front of the mirror? Michael Brady thought that he had the answer.

"The murderer may have been a very small person who came in low. It might have been an apprentice jockey."

I could understand why this particular policeman had never made it to the Homicide Squad. There wasn't even an apprentice jock in the building, so my suspicious mind went into overdrive. This man was trying to divert attention away from the real motive.

"No way, Brady. Willy was snorting cocaine when he was killed. And he wasn't invited to this bash; he was here by co-incidence, to collect his regular supply of cat's pee (cocaine) from his regular supplier — you. Like Spyder, he didn't appreciate the fact that you had upped the price, and they were both prepared to shop you to the drug squad. This would have meant the end of your career, and a decent holiday at Club Fed. You killed your own brother-in-law."

"You're a lot smarter than you look, Pest. Sure, I killed them both, but you'll never be able to do anything about it. We've put a little something in your green tea, so your days on this earth are numbered. In fact, I would start counting in seconds."

"Gee, Mike, you don't mean that cup of tea that I just swapped with your wife, do you?"

Chin Chang Choy went blue in the face, then black, and one of her eyes popped out. She clutched at her throat as she slumped to the ground. An observant diner made his own assumption.

"I told you, darling. They put too much MSG in the food, here."

Like all conniving criminals who had access to a Triad group, Brady had a back-up plan, and he was thinking a little faster than me. To tell you the truth, I was astounded at what had transpired. All my conjecture was just another fanciful rant, and I was gobsmacked that it was all true.

The police sergeant took one look at his dead wife, and bolted for the kitchen. However, not before he had alerted the house ruffians by sounding the giant nipple gong outside the kitchen door. It was a gong for the Tong. They suddenly appeared in the room, and surrounded the assembled group of diners. Jesus could see that there was something happening and beckoned to his sister.

"Trouble, Maggie; we might need the young senoritas."

I had noticed Maggie's friends earlier in the evening. Some of them were downright attractive, and I was told that they were all from her club. What I should have noticed was that they were all wearing black belts. Now, what kind of club requires you to wear a black belt?

The Kick-Ass Kung Fu Club was the most decorated of all the fighting groups in Kentucky, and the fact that the members were all female was of little consequence. They attacked the nasty oriental thugs with relish, and while confusion reigned, I gave chase to the escaping executioner. Brady had made it through the kitchen and out into the back lane. I heard a motor-bike start up, and I recognized the throaty throttle of Milwaukee's most famous two-wheeler. He had gunned his Harley Davidson Softail, and the *Hog* was roaring off up the deserted laneway.

It is always hard to know what accessories to take on a job. I sometimes travel light when I am at a social occasion. Nevertheless, I did have a small boomerang in my inside jacket pocket, and I would have to say that this wooden wonder has become a most effective deterrent in my fight against the evil and malevolent forces that surrounds us.

Most people would be aware that a returning boomerang is often used for sport and ceremonial activities, but it is also a weapon. Throwing sticks are used with great success by Aboriginal tribes to immobilize animals and recalcitrant wives. I have adapted the returning model to suit my purposes, and am confident in my ability up to a thousand feet (the world record is 1400 ft).

Michael Brady was nowhere near that distance. I aimed carefully, and flicked the boomerang at him. It whizzed past his ear, and gracefully soared high into the night air. At its zenith, the wooden wonder-stick reversed, and deftly caught Brady on the left temple. He fell off his bike, and the Harley continued on its way, alone and friendless. The man tried to get to his feet, but he was as stunned as a mullet: also bewildered. I collected two tin lids from the restaurant's garbage cans, and gave him the coup de grace. I had wanted to do that ever since I had seen that cymbal scene in *The Man Who Knew Too Much*.

The commotion at Choy's Restaurant was enough to alert an armed response, and even Chief Sullivan arrived at the scene; he was still a bit tipsy. I was able to separate the bad guys and the good girls, and my relationship with Jack Sullivan helped my credibility. There was nothing left for me to do other than find out whether any of these good girls were prepared to be bad. I was beginning to like the way that Maggie Caravaggio was looking at me.

In the wash-up, they couldn't pin the jockey murders on Brady, but they did convict him for Chin Chang's demise. Life's a bitch, isn't it? It was sad that we had to lose two of racings' perennial postilions, but they should never have turned to drugs in order to give themselves an edge. I never did get to find out who hit Spyder with that horse's hoof, but my guess is that it was Jennifer Youngblood. I think that she discovered that he was sleeping with his wife.

Jesus, the jockey

THE TRIBUTE TOUR

I had seen the musical *My Fair Lady,* and had therefore conditioned my mind to accept the fact that the Hungarian people were enchanting; oozing charm from every pore, he oiled his way around the floor. The Gellert Hotel in Budapest is a magnificent Baroque monster that fights to maintain grace and elegance in an era that is beset by contemporary pillage in the name of a fast buck. Wide stairs and passageways are shaded by stained glass windows, and marble accoutrements provide an old world charm that is magnetic to an old world charmer like me. The thermal spa, which is attached to the hotel, is the biggest in town, and breathtakingly ornate. The mosaics and sculptures that adorn the plunge and swimming pools would even give Nero gas.

On reflection, I probably shouldn't have opted for a massage because this is where the enchanting Hungarian tried to strangle me.

At this stage, I should mention that I am not a large person. I may be taller than the average night-club bouncer, but not nearly as thick (a debatable point). I am less than twelve stone in my wet socks. The masseur was a monster, and he sure looked as if he worked out. His biceps were enormous, and his stomach muscles were like human cobblestones.

With his arm around my neck, and his knee in my back, I knew that this wasn't the soft option massage that I had paid for. The bad guys were onto me, and I had no idea who the bad guys were. I managed a weak squeak through my rapidly closing windpipe.

"Could you go a little lower, please? I have a bit of an itch in my back."

The brute not only ignored me, but pressed on my windpipe even harder. There was only one thing to do.

The Paddy Pest cross-over crotch kick is a technique that I had mastered when locking horns with that masterful KGB assassin, Nadia Nickoff, the minx from Minsk. It has rarely failed me, and is mostly successful because of the spontaneity of the damn thing. You feign death, and then immediately elbow your assailant in the bread-basket, do a full body rotation, and then kick out strongly into his or her groin. A follow-up knee jerk is always a satisfactory conclusion to the action.

The menacing Magyar from Budapest was certainly taken back, but not completely down for the count. I was hardly off the massage table, and he was after me. We raced over the slippery marble floors of the pool room, and through the main swimming area. I was completely naked, and he was completely incensed. The other bathers were totally aghast.

I wonder if you are familiar with the design of the Hotel Gellert and the adjoining Gellert Thermal Spa. The latter is a tourist attraction in its own right; sightseers come to set eyes on the gothic architecture of the grand entrance. The hotel can be accessed by crossing the hall, and moving on to another floor. It is not unusual to see people in white bath-robes mixing with tour groups in the foyer. However, a naked man being chased by another is a rarity. It was a shame that I had to dart in front of a group of nuns, and their primary school class excursion — perhaps, this was an appropriate time to explain human biology!

No, he didn't catch me. I am fleet of foot, and can turn on a silver dollar, if required. However, I was apprehended by the local constabulary in the middle of a busy shopping precinct.

"Can we see your papers, please? You are not allowed to be naked in a public place in Budapest."

"Well, I actually don't have them on me, at the moment. Can I get back to you on that one, officer?"

"What is your name? Are you a citizen of the glorious Republic of Hungary? If not, where are your clothes? You are not allowed to be naked in a public place in Budapest."

I will not bore you with the rest of the conversation. They took me down to the police station, and then confirmed my identity with people at the Gellert Hotel. I watered down the explanation, and got out of there with my modesty intact. I also obtained the desk sergeant's telephone number. She had taken a liking to me while I was shivering in the foyer, and said that she could recommend a much better massage parlor. She had a lot of addresses in one of her folders.

I didn't complain to the hotel management. I was sure that the would-be assassin was a blow-in who took advantage of a slack security system. He would be gone, and nobody would be much the wiser. What was bothering me was the motive for such an unprecedented attack. Who would want to exterminate little old me? I'm one of the good guys.

Another of the good guys was Zoltán Varga. We had crossed paths when he was doing piece work for MI6, and he was instrumental in flushing out one of their bad apples. Nevertheless, they had not thanked him for it. They actually reduced his freelance opportunities. This was a man who knew where all the bodies were buried, and there were a lot of bodies buried in Budapest. I was hoping that mine would not be next.

"You old sod, Paddy Pest! What are you doing in Buda, Paddy?"

"Hi, Zoltán, it's great to see you again."

We were in the small bar at my hotel, and the place was packed. I think that's the way he liked it. With the constant hum of conversation, listening devices would be useless. I came straight to the point.

"Zoltán, why would somebody want to kill me?"

"We have been pals for a long time, so I would rather not answer that. How many ex-girl friends do you have?"

I thought about this for a moment, but I couldn't see it.

"No, I don't think so; although, it could have been something that I said."

"Paddy, this is a divided city: Buda and Pest. You have breezed into town as the fabulous Mr Pest. There is bound to be animosity by those in high places. They probably wanted to take you down a peg or two."

"Sure, but it wasn't my peg that was the problem. They tried to throttle me."

"I understand. If you want another massage therapist, I have a list."

"Thanks, Zoltán. It appears everyone has a list."

The next morning, I received a call from the manager of a city restaurant. They had discovered the body of a man in their kitchen when they opened their doors that morning. His name was Zoltán Varga. In his pocket, they found a piece of paper with my number on it. I rushed over there. When I arrived, I couldn't believe it; however, the manager confirmed that they were doing soup, goulash and a glass of beer for less than three thousand Forints — but only on Monday and Tuesdays.

Poor Zoltán! Who could have done this to him and why? You often hear about people being split open with a meat cleaver, but you rarely see it. The man's head was as separated as Buda and Pest, and a river of blood had cascaded down the center of his hairless skull. He was lying in a pool of O positive.

Although I was first to the scene of the crime, the law wasn't far behind, and you're not going to believe this. It was the constable that had apprehended me in the city square. However, I don't think that he recognized me with my clothes on.

"Can I see your papers, please? What is your interest here? Are you a waiter?"

So many questions and so few answers! I didn't want to get involved in a drawn-out investigation, so I offered to lock the front door, and subsequently made a dash for it. Knowing that the manager would have my telephone number, if not my address, I checked out of the Gellert, and moved into less salubrious accommodation.

Sergeant Edith Szabo was a ten-year veteran of the police force, but she was still behind a desk. At least, she was when they brought in the naked Australian for interrogation. The piece of paper with her telephone number was still behind my right ear, and I thought that this was a good time to test the hospitality of the locals. She picked up on the third ring and didn't seem surprised to receive my call. She was very sympathetic to the fact that I was now homeless.

I promptly moved in to her small apartment, and was delighted to discover that there was only one bed on the premises. It was very generous of her to put me up because we didn't know each other that well, although there was an implied promise to alleviate that situation. I had also held back on some of the details concerning my predicament. One would have to avoid any social contact with her co-workers: one constable in particular. There would also be no more massages. I was sure about that.

We had three glorious days and nights together. She took me to the *Cotton Club,* and I squired her to *Fat Mo's Speakeasy.* They were all contrived versions of their American counterparts, but the booze was cold and the jazz was hot. Edith was such a wicked lady; it was hard to believe that she was a cop. Eventually, she asked me why I was in Hungary. This is something that I have yet to tell you — how remiss of me.

The truth of the matter is that I had asked my travel agent out to lunch, and when she asked why, I said that I was hungry. So, she booked me to Budapest. I might mention that I have a very uppity travel agent who has silently seethed, over the years, because I have never included this great city in any of my itineraries. Yes, she just happens to be Hungarian, and you know how people feel obliged to promote the city of their birth. However, her list of massage parlors was restricted, compared to some that I know.

I accepted this diversion because it was on the way to Vienna, more or less. The City of Dreams was preparing to acknowledge their most famous canine crime-fighter, Inspector Rex: the wonder dog. He had been twelve years on the force, which equated to over eighty years in human terms. I couldn't let him retire without attending the function, and paying tribute. I was one of his greatest fans.

None of this explains the attempt on my life, and the death of my good friend Varga. I am never prepared to let sleeping dogs lie, and I decided that I needed to play hard ball with these culinary cowards. A meat cleaver, indeed! Didn't they know that Zoltán was a vegetarian?

After a few days, I felt that I could no longer afford to be aligned with a member of the police force, so I regrettably vacated Edith's apartment, and moved into the Hotel Pest in the Terezvaros neighborhood. It was a modest three star kip-joint that was only a few blocks from Heroes' Square. I hoped that I wouldn't get mobbed when I went for my morning constitutional.

The booking clerk was just a kid, and when I gave him my business card, he must have assumed that I owned the place or the city. He gave me the honeymoon suite, and I never received a bill. Thank God I didn't complain about the service.

I was only one block from Andrássy Avenue, one of the main boulevards in the city, and a chic address if you were shopping for merchandise with names like Vuitton, Gucci or Armani. Parallel to my street, in the other direction, was Király utca, a refurbished promenade that was now a haven for smart restaurants and cafés. The *Trofea Grill* was such a restaurant, and I don't know what Zoltán was doing there. He was a vegetarian. There must have been an assignation of sorts, and I don't know what he could have contributed. He was pretty ripped when he left me.

You have heard about the masterful disguises that I sometimes produce. It was necessary for me to dine at the said restaurant, and I didn't want anyone to recognize me. I was shocked to find that their prices were a lot higher than their tourist specials, which they had advertised earlier in the week, but I couldn't complain. I was masquerading as a rich American from southern parts.

"Howdy, fella, I'm from Gaylord, Texas, and we like big steaks. Some rump with a bit of hickory in it, and don't bother cookin' it too much. Just wipe its ass and serve it up."

"Yes, sir; will you want fries with that?"

"Of course I want fries with that. Asshole!"

I have recently learned that my stateside accent is not as authentic as I might have believed; but in downtown Pest, everyone who is not local sounds like an American.

The *Trofea Grill* is not an à la carte restaurant. You pay a set fee, and you can eat as much as you want. However, they put a time limit on your dining experience: three hours. I couldn't believe what I was hearing from my table near the reception desk.

"Mr Varga arrived at nine pm. He was taken to the morgue at eleven am. Should we send the extended account to the police or his lawyers?"

"Leave it with me, Anatoly. I will take up the matter with his sponsors."

Holy Guacamole, its Anatoly! That sounds Russian to me; and what sponsors are we talking about? I was beginning to think that Zoltán's clandestine days might not have been behind him, although they were now. I wondered if I should give Nadia Nickoff a call. Although the minx from Minsk is supposedly retired, we were on good terms when I last saw her at a spy's conference in India last year (Pest Takes a Chance — still a great buy for birthdays and Bar Mitzvahs).

The steak arrived and it was great. I particularly enjoyed the asshole. I was prepared to give the waiter a big tip, but I needed to have a look at their kitchen. When the lad saw the currency being bandied about, he started to salivate, and I knew that he would jump to my tune.

"Do you know, young man, I have never seen a commercial kitchen? You wouldn't like to give an old cowboy a short tour, would you?"

He furtively looked around, and saw that the manager was tied up with some customers.

"Certainly, sir, just follow me."

The kitchen was operating in overdrive. Anatoly and a young girl were running around like scalded cats. Hot dishes were laid out in a row on a long table, and the spike with the orders was overflowing. Pots of steaming soup and other delicacies were bubbling on the stove, and the chef was manipulating half a dozen meat dishes on the grill. I have to say; he was the biggest chef that I have ever seen. His biceps were enormous, and his stomach muscles were like human cobblestones. My God! It was the masseur from the Gellert Hotel.

If my face went red, nobody noticed. The whole kitchen was a steam room, and I was glad to get out of there. We made it back to the main part of the restaurant, and the *maître d* was none the wiser. I paid the lad for my meal, and he was delighted to receive the generous tip that I left him.

"Regards to all the folks in Gaylord," he stammered, as he pushed the notes into his back pocket. I figured that he was probably the only innocent Hungarian in the restaurant. In fact, it was possible that he was the only Hungarian there. The others all looked like rejects from a Siberian labor camp. I wondered if they were doing what they were doing for love or money. Or fear!

The rest of it is just spy's text-book stuff. You wait for the big geezer to finish work, and follow him home. You get his address, the registration of his car, and then his name spits out of a computer data-base somewhere. Before long, you know all his known associates, and most of his social diseases. If you need help, you call in British Intelligence, Mossad, or the CIA. I sometimes wonder why they pay me as much as they do.

Still, it is a different world, these days. Gumshoe dinosaurs, like me, can grapple with some of the basic principles of technology, but the latest stuff is hard to combat. I certainly have limited access to sophisticated data gathering, satellite spying, coronial imagery and space-age weaponry. This is how they cottoned on to me in Budapest. I had nothing to do with Zoltán and his personal vendetta against the Russians. I didn't even know that they had slaughtered his family.

I was listed as a known associate, and my arrival in the Hungarian capitol set off alarms. They decided to treat me with extreme prejudice. I wonder what my travel agent would have said if they had been successful.

In the real world, motive and opportunity need to be proven in order to obtain a conviction under accepted legal guidelines. The Paddy Pest world is not like that. I didn't want a conviction. I wanted retribution. Boris, the Magyar of misery, who was really Russian, wanted to kill me. This was proof enough that he was probably the bod who buried the hatchet in the humble Hungarian's head. His days were numbered, and time was on the wing. I needed to be in Vienna for my day with the dog.

One of the most endearing aspects of Inspector Rex's tenure with the Homicide Squad was his penchant for ham rolls. It so happens that amongst my arsenal of deadly gadgetry is the exploding ham roll. I have used it on a number of occasions, and this would be most appropriate if one is planning to eradicate a chef. Of course, the other alternative was to strangle him with his own spaghetti.

In the end, I discovered the perfect location to do away with this desperado, and dump him in the Danube. The man had received an invitation to be guest chef at the celebration of Franz Liszt Day. The function was to be held on the upper deck of one of the cruise boats that continually plied the river: from Budapest to Nuremberg and beyond. They had flown in André Rieu and the Johann Strauss Orchestra for the occasion, and there were celebrities and other luminaries everywhere. I was disguised as a waiter.

By mid-afternoon, pretty well everybody was Franz Liszt. Even Boris had retired from the kitchen, and was having a quiet ale with the guests. In my pocket, I was carrying a small vial of liquid that contained a beer-colored piranha fish. These critters are very rare, and not often found this side of South America. The Ustasi had used them with some success in Croatia, but there are very few fatal fish tanks still around in Eastern Europe, today. I believe that my baby had a hammer and sickle tattoo on its tail. This would be sweet justice.

I slipped the slimy creature into Boris' fresh beer, and he gulped it down immediately. He even had the bad manners to burp.

Not many people would have seen a man disintegrate before their eyes. What happens is that the fish eats you from the inside out. When he has broken through your stomach cavity, he then has access to all your other organs, and you get very thirsty. In fact, Boris just screamed out, and then jumped overboard. I didn't even have to push him.

The Danube is a fast flowing river, and it took a while to recover his body. By then, the police had arrived, and all the questions started. I even recognized one of the voices.

"Can I see your papers, please? Are you a citizen of the glorious Republic of Hungary? Did you know the deceased?"

I answered no to all his questions, and he didn't seem perturbed. He didn't recognize me, and sent me on my way. As I was leaving, I enquired after Edith. My lasting image was a man with a severe frown on his face.

The function for Inspector Rex in Vienna was all that we could have wished. The organizers had persuaded the Bonzo Dog Doo-Dah Band to reunite for one last performance, and they had hired out the State Opera Theater. The finger food and dog biscuits were excellent, and most of the intelligence community was there, including Nadia Nickoff and a few guys from MI6. They were shocked to hear what had happened to poor Zoltán.

"I know this comrade Boris," said Nadia. "This is bad man, and he is getting his Apple Strudel."

"You mean *his just desserts*."

"That is what I said, Paddy. Would you like to slip away for some vodka, no?"

"Why, yes, that sounds like a great idea. Your hotel or mine?"

It's hard to believe that we used to be sworn enemies, but that's Perestroika for you. I was glad that Nadia wasn't involved in that Hungarian mess because she is basically a good person with distorted values, but that's communism. What more can I say? By the way, don't think that we slipped away without saying goodbye to Rex because we didn't. He was a bit of an old dog himself, and his bark of approval said it all.

Good night, Paddy — Good night, Nadia

Good night, readers

ABOUT THE AUTHOR

This is Gerry Burke's fourth book, the second featuring his irreverent hero, Paddy Pest. A few years ago, the prospect of Gerry writing crime stories would have been rather fanciful in itself. He had taken early retirement as a Creative Director in his own advertising agency, and was starting to wax lyrical about all matters pertaining to politics, entertainment, sport and travel. Then Paddy came along.

While Mr Pest is gallivanting around the globe, the author sits at home in Melbourne, and contributes with his own wealth of life experience. He has been an accountant, copywriter, producer and commercial film director. Sadly, he has never been a detective, secret agent or crime buster, although it doesn't show. Gerry's writing talents may well be hereditary. His father came to Australia from Ireland with a degree in blarney.

Other books by Gerry Burke:

From Beer to Paternity – one man's journey through life as we know it

Down-Under Shorts – stories to read while they're fumigating your pants

Pest Takes a Chance – and other humorous stories from the Paddy Pest Chronicles

Gerry Burke's books are available on-line through iuniverse.com, amazon.com, barnesandnoble.com and other reputable outlets

Keep up to date with Gerry on his website — www.gerryburke.net

He would be delighted to receive your comments — gerry@gerryburke.net

18653051R00121

Printed in Great Britain
by Amazon